HOTEL LUCKY SEVEN

ALSO BY KOTARO ISAKA

Bullet Train
Three Assassins
The Mantis

HOTEL LUCKY SEVEN

A NOVEL

KOTARO ISAKA

*Translated from the Japanese
by Brian Bergstrom*

THE OVERLOOK PRESS, NEW YORK

This edition first published in hardcover in 2024 by
The Overlook Press, an imprint of ABRAMS
195 Broadway, 9th floor
New York, NY 10007

Abrams books are available at special discounts when purchased in quantity for premiums and
promotions as well as fundraising or educational use. Special editions can also be created to
specification. For details, contact specialsales@abramsbooks.com or the address above.

Copyright © Kotaro Isaka / CTB Inc.
Translation from the Japanese language by Brian Bergstrom
English translation rights arranged through CTB Inc.
Originally published by Kadokawa in Japan as 777 in 2023
First published by Harvill Secker in 2024
Jacket © 2024 Abrams

Library of Congress Control Number: 2024937348

Printed and bound in the United States

1 3 5 7 9 10 8 6 4 2

ISBN: 978-1-4197-7703-5

eISBN: 979-8-88707-416-0

ABRAMS The Art of Books
195 Broadway, New York, NY 10007
abramsbooks.com

HOTEL LUCKY SEVEN

BLANKET

Two days ago, in a different hotel

'IT'S ROOM 415, RIGHT?'

Blanket is talking to Pillow, who's walking ahead of her. They're both wearing the beige tops and brown bottoms that constitute the uniforms worn by the cleaning staff at the Hotel Vivaldi, Tokyo.

'Exactly. 415. Rhymes with *For One Life*.'

Blanket met Pillow ten years ago, while they were both on the girls' basketball team at her high school. She'd seen her face before, of course, but despite being on the same team, they'd never exchanged words. Though neither girl was the kind to talk much with classmates in the first place.

'What bullshit. Everything's decided at birth,' murmured Pillow, looking off in the distance after another game spent without even being allowed to fill out the bench. She wasn't actually trying to start a conversation – rather, her innermost thoughts had simply spilled from her lips, and Blanket had been there downstream to catch them. But Blanket knew what Pillow meant.

1

Both of them were conspicuously small-framed, even among the other girls. The taller girls were obviously prized even if they were less athletic, and the smaller girls knew that no matter how hard they trained, they'd hardly ever be allowed to play.

'You're right,' said Blanket. 'It's so unfair, isn't it? The advantages some people are born with.'

'You have a pretty face and a good sense of style, and bang: you're on Easy Street. Even school will be fun. Your whole life will be smooth as silk. Makes me sick.'

'Well, that's not true for *everyone*...'

'It is! It's a truth determined at birth. Like, by your genes. So unfair. It's not as if they worked hard for it or anything. It's just always been like that, their whole life. Look at me: my face is only okay, I'm short, I have no style. Makes me want to go, *What did I do to deserve this?*'

From the outside, Blanket was in exactly the same boat as Pillow, but it had never occurred to her to ask, *What did I do to deserve this?* She felt a certain relief to hear Pillow say it. As if to reassure her: *It's okay, you're allowed to respond this way to the world.*

'Don't you think even privileged people have their problems?' Blanket said this just to hear Pillow's response.

'Absolutely not.' Pillow waved her hand dismissively. 'I mean, yes of course, everyone has problems. But if you ever asked them to switch places with you, you know they'd refuse! Deep down, they know Easy Street problems aren't really problems at all.'

All Pillow had done since opening her mouth was vent personal grievances, but Blanket didn't find herself put off. Perhaps because Pillow's tone was resigned, even philosophical, rather than spiteful. *It's not like there's anything we can do to fix it, anyway.*

'You know, I noticed something else about them.'

'What?'

'These Easy Streeters, they always drag other people into their lives.'

'You make it sound like Easy Street is an actual place,' said Blanket, giggling.

'*You can only be happy if you have a boyfriend*, they say. *Let's all go have fun!* Everything they want to do you can't do alone. I have plenty of fun staying by myself at home, but from where they sit, I have a sad, pitiful life.'

Where they sit? Blanket didn't know where that would be, exactly, and it seemed like a rather arbitrary way of speaking, but she nonetheless answered, 'You're so right.'

And this was the first real conversation she ever had in high school.

They reach the elevator. The one for the cleaning staff. Pillow walks in first, then Blanket. She pushes the button for the fourth floor.

'By the way, Inui seems to be looking for someone,' says Pillow.

'He does?'

'Someone who used to work for him. A woman in her thirties. He's really going after her.'

'Did she walk off with his money or something?'

'Worse than that, I think. Though I admit it's kind of fun seeing him all upset.' Pillow laughs.

'He's still our savior, though.'

'Or, put another way, he's a manipulator who saw we were in trouble and used that as a way to mix us up in this world.'

'He might be our age, but you just know he's had a completely opposite life from ours. He's so the type to spend every day in high school singing its praises, you know? Boys and girls both hanging on his every word, making him feel good. An Easy Streeter, 100 percent.'

'Singing praises, huh? Like Fujiwara no Michinaga? "I feel as if the world belongs to me."'

'If he'd been in a band, he'd have been the lead singer for sure.

3

He'd never have even spoken to the likes of us if we'd been in the same school.'

Inui may not be quite as handsome as a pop idol, but he's clean-cut and fresh-faced, with a tall, lean frame and a charismatic way with words – a born communicator.

'I really thought he was a nice guy when we first met him.'

'Pure calculation. Knowing everyone, kissing up to VIPs – everything. He's the type who gets everything handed to him. Making moves behind the scenes and then stealing the credit. He never does anything himself.'

'It's true! He leaves all the dirty work to his underlings. I remember calling him out on it once, and he all he said was, "That's not true, I flush my own toilet."'

'He does a lot for politicians. Oppo research, covering up scandals.'

'But it's everyone else who's breaking a sweat! Inui just rides high, soaking up praise for other people's work. I bet finding this woman is a job for some politician, too.'

'He's been sending her picture around. "If you see this woman, let me know." Showing taxi drivers and delivery people, or low-level employees like us. Her name is Kamino-san, I think, the woman he's searching for. Something-something Kamino.'

'It's only a matter of time before he finds her. Inui's reach is amazing.'

'And once they find her, it's going to be horrible for her.'

'You think he'll paralyze her and dissect her alive?'

The girls exclaim in unison: 'Gross!'

'You think it's really true? That stuff about him liking to cut people up?'

'It's awful. We're right to try to get away from him.'

'But when will that be?'

The elevator reaches its destination.

4

They pass through the employees-only passage into where the rooms are. The halls are dim, the indirect lighting lending everything a sense of unreality.

After checking the room number – four-one-five: *for one life* – Pillow passes the keycard through the reader and listens as the door unlocks. She opens the door carefully, making as little sound as possible, and slips into the room.

Blanket, pushing the cleaning cart, follows after.

A man is sitting on the sofa, facing the television. It's always easier when they're standing, but what can you do? No big deal, all things considered.

'Excuse us,' says Blanket, nodding respectfully. She recalls how she would address the senior players back when she was on the basketball team.

The man startles, then rises from his seat. He's obviously thrown by Blanket and Pillow appearing like this. He can see they're cleaning staff, but he's confused as to why they'd enter his room without knocking.

Blanket pulls a white sheet out of the cart.

'Hey, I think you got the wrong room!'

The man is wearing beige slacks and a navy blue shirt. He's very tall, and conspicuously well-built.

'Oh my gosh,' says Pillow, her voice rising in surprise. 'Though I think I see a chink in your armor.'

Animals confronted with things larger than themselves naturally become wary, but when confronted with the opposite – anything smaller than themselves – they feel no fear. Humans share this trait. They prostrate themselves before anyone who seems bigger and stronger and look down on anyone smaller. Blanket and Pillow shared their thoughts about this long ago: if women were ten inches taller than men on average, the whole world would be different.

Watching the man turn toward her, Pillow can't help but

wonder at his stupidity. The moment he looked at them and decided they weren't a threat, his fate was sealed.

Will he try to grab their clothes? Or kick them? Those are the choices. Blanket imagines scenarios as she throws one end of the white sheet to Pillow.

After that, things go like they always do. The two girls approach the man, each holding one edge of the sheet. Unfurling it as they advance, they engulf his entire upper body, including his head. He's immobilized at once. Blanket throws Pillow her edge of the sheet. Pillow almost immediately releases the edge she's been holding, and Blanket grabs it. Repeating this exchange again and again, Blanket and Pillow wind the sheet around and around the man as if he were a mummy.

Wrapped in the sheet, the man loses his balance and falls to the floor.

He kicks up a fuss, moaning, but it makes little difference to the girls. Over the sheet, they wrap a towel around the man's neck and then, after pulling with only a slight bit of combined effort, they hear it snap.

'Thank you, leverage,' whispers Blanket. The principle of leverage is the magic wand that wipes away advantages like height and strength.

They make the dead man hug his own knees, folding him up so they can haul him into the cleaning cart. The bottom is reinforced, so it doesn't give under his weight. They stack folded linens on top of him to hide him.

Now, to remove any evidence, they start actually cleaning the room. Partway through, though, Pillow stops and points at the wall. 'Oh! It's Yomo-pi!'

The flatscreen TV mounted on the wall is showing the news.

A reporter holding a microphone listens as a man in a suit talks. The interviewee has sharp, manly features and holds himself proudly, so that despite being in his late fifties, he seems much younger.

'Saneatsu Yomogi! Isn't he a politician?'

'He's part of the Information Bureau now, our version of the CIA. He's the head honcho there. He quit politics after the accident.'

The accident. Blanket recalls it immediately. Three years ago, someone in an imported electric car driving down a wide boulevard downtown suddenly swerved onto the sidewalk, running over a mother and child. Apparently the fault of a drunk driver, it ended up causing quite a stir in the media, as the victims were the wife and child of Yomogi, then a sitting member of Parliament.

Now he's on TV, a microphone thrust in his face. 'Director Yomogi, is it true your life was threatened back when you were in politics?'

'I can't really comment on that,' says Yomogi, a rueful smile on his face. 'But if you were the one coming after me, this would be it for me – I've let you get too close!'

'You know, I've always liked Yomo-pi. He says whatever's on his mind, but I usually find myself agreeing with him,' says Pillow. 'Like how he always said there should be fewer members of Parliament.'

'Well, that I agree with. Private industry has had to restructure and fire so many people, we should do the same with politicians! As a cost-cutting measure.'

Yomogi called for the reduction in the number of members of Parliament from the moment he was elected to the moment he left politics. His statement, 'It would be better if older politicians retired,' caused a firestorm of debate at the time.

'And he's also right about old politicians! As you age, you naturally lose your physical strength and your memory, even your judgment. It doesn't matter how great you are, that's what happens. You even lose your ability to drive! Younger is better, absolutely.'

'Too young is scary, though.'

'Well, think about it. Who would you want running your country, Oda Nobunaga when he was fifty, or when he was eighty? Fifty, right?'

Blanket finds herself stumped by the question. Pillow pushes on.

'Come to think of it, though, Oda's a pretty scary guy, maybe I wouldn't like that. He'd probably be easier to get along with as a grandpa.'

Blanket finds herself feeling bad about Oda – who lived hundreds of years ago and would never meet either of them – being called 'a pretty scary guy.'

'Sounds like some people really hated Yomo-pi, huh? I guess, though, if you ask for politicians to be sacked then you make yourself their enemy.'

'I bet that's true. People with power make it their life's work to hold on to that power. Maybe that's why he quit being a politician and became a bigwig at the Information Bureau – he decided to change things another way.'

'Change things? Like, the system?'

'He seems pretty tough. Remember the story about when he was first elected and he tackled that guy on the train who was stabbing everyone?'

It was fifteen years ago, when a passenger on an express bound for Shinjuku started stabbing the other passengers around him. Over ten people ended up killed or injured, but the person who put a stop to things was Yomogi. He was forty at the time, and he ended up sustaining injuries that put him in the hospital, but not before grabbing the guy and neutralizing him.

'You know, I heard that the accident three years ago, with the

8

drunk driver, was no accident. And that the real target was Yomo-pi, not his family,' says Pillow, still staring at the TV screen.

'No accident?' Blanket is shocked.

'It wouldn't surprise me.'

Blanket recalls a certain senior member of the basketball team. She hadn't agreed with the coach's methods, especially his erratic leadership style, and she tried to change things to make the team better and healthier for everyone. But the other senior members of the team resisted her efforts, ganging up on her until they drove her out entirely.

'People who try to change things are seen as troublemakers.'

'That's so true,' Blanket agrees, looking again at Yomogi's image on the screen.

'Don't give up, Yomo-pi!'

Their clean-up complete, Blanket and Pillow leave the room.

NANAO

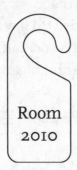

Room
2010

'I'M HAPPY SHE REMEMBERED MY BIRTHDAY!'

There's something about this guy that makes him seem like a good boss. A certain good-natured magnanimity, a trustworthiness, as if he'd say to an underling who failed, *Don't worry about it, these things happen.*

'So it's been a while since you've seen your daughter?' Nanao doesn't really care, but he can't stand being silent any longer, so he says the first thing that pops into his head. 'She's overseas now, somewhere in Europe?' He doesn't know the exact country, so he's forced to be vague.

'Yes, that's right. Europe.'

'Studying to be an artist, is that it? On exchange?'

'Art, yeah. She's an exchange student.'

Nanao's on the top floor of the Winton Palace Hotel, in Room 2010. It's business as usual, being the feet on the ground for a job Maria got from somewhere.

'Go to the room and hand over the package. That's it. Easy.

Shockingly so.' She gave him the same song-and-dance she always did when she asked him to do a job, then followed it with a description of the hotel's layout. 'Twenty stories high, with an underground parking lot. A lounge in the first-floor lobby, and three restaurants on the second floor – Japanese, Chinese, Western. Four elevator shafts run through the center of the building. Banquet rooms are on the third floor. Hallways run east–west, with about ten rooms in each direction. Two emergency stairwells per floor, located at the end of each hallway.'

'What's in the package?'

'A girl wants to send a birthday present to her father. Your job is to deliver that present to him. It's almost unsettling, isn't it, how safe and easy it is?'

'What's unsettling is you using the words "safe" and "easy."'

'All you're doing is delivering a present!'

'Why can't she do it herself?'

'She's overseas. An exchange student. What choice does she have? Seems they didn't get along in the past, but now that she's away, she realizes how grateful she is for all he's done for her. So she wants to give him a present on his birthday. Isn't that nice?'

'Why does it have to be delivered while he's on a business trip? Couldn't she send it to his house?'

'He's a busy guy, always away on business. Hardly ever at home. Besides, what good's a birthday present that's not delivered on his birthday? In any case, the job is to take this present and hand it over. Aren't you the one who asked for no more dangerous assignments? So here you go, it doesn't get easier than this. I don't see how you could refuse.'

'That's what you said about the E2 job, too, remember?' Nanao's tone was forceful. Everyone in the trade refers to that incident by the make of the Shinkansen bullet train on which it took place: E2. An incident that produced a mountain of bodies; he'd been a hair's breadth from being one of them. Despite it

being a simple matter of bringing a suitcase onto a train and getting off at the next station – what could be easier?

'This time will be different. An actual easy job. You'll hand over
the present, and that's it. Though it might be nice if you could
take a picture of the father as you do. As proof the job is done.'

Maria's not one to prattle on; rather, her tendency is to speak
coolly, matter-of-factly. It's the secret to her persuasiveness –
whenever she catches your ear, you can't help but think, *Yes, of
course, you're absolutely right.* Nanao ended the call to evade further brainwashing.

But now here he is, in Room 2010 in the Winton Palace Hotel,
facing a guy wearing khaki chinos and a white shirt, the type of
guy who you want to stick a badge on saying *World's Best Boss.*

He seems like a guy with a high-level job at a company that's
doing well, at least judging from the expensive watch peeking
out from beneath his sleeve and the luxury brand logos on the
bags scattered around the room.

The man seemed extremely surprised by Nanao's sudden visit
to his room. Which means the sender must not have warned
him beforehand. Which makes it Nanao's problem. The man
peered at Nanao through the barely cracked door, only open as
far as the bar lock would allow, his face filled with undisguised
suspicion.

Nanao tried to sound as non-shady as possible as he explained
what he was there to do. 'Your daughter wants to give you a
birthday present, that's all, once I hand it to you I'll leave.' The
man's face lit up. 'Aaah, I see!' And then he invited Nanao in,
saying the package looked heavy, so should he help bring it
inside for him?

Nanao looks now at the parcel they'd brought in and set on the
ground. It isn't very thick, but too big to carry in one hand.

'I wonder what she got me!' The man reaches out to touch it,
his eyes glittering. Or, at least, that's how it seems.

'I wonder,' says Nanao, and then, thinking he sounded a bit dismissive, he hastily adds, 'Maybe it's a painting!' It seems like a safe enough guess, since she's supposedly overseas 'studying to be an artist.'

'True, yeah. Maybe it is,' says the man as he begins unwrapping it.

It's not part of the job to know what's in it, so Nanao starts to leave, but as soon as he turns, a postcard slips out from somewhere and lands on the floor at his feet. He picks it up and sees what's written on it.

I painted this based on how you looked when we were video-chatting, Papa! Looks just like you, right?

The present is indeed a framed painting. Oils, from the looks of it. A superbly rendered portrait of a man facing forward, smiling, with a kindly gaze. It looks quite realistic. Nanao lacks the ability to assess its artistic quality, but it's clear it was painted with a great deal of care, making Nanao feel a certain affinity for the sender, despite having never met her.

Great. It's done. Nothing happened. This is what Nanao decides to tell himself. *This should be the beginning and end of it. Perfectly safe, perfectly easy. No problem at all.*

All he has to do is leave – and ignore his growing anxiety.

'Wait a second. What's going on?' says Maria on the other end of the phone. 'Did something happen? Even on a job this safe and easy?'

'Safe. Easy.' Nanao hasn't forgotten her favorite buzzwords.

'Where are you?'

'Still at the hotel. The Winton Palace. What a hotel, right? The rooms are so chic and classy, they'd satisfy even the most discerning aristocrat.' The dark wood-grain wallpaper on the accent wall sets off the beige flooring nicely, he notes.

'I'm not familiar with what discerning aristocrats like or dislike.' He hears her sigh. 'It wasn't an easy job? Just handing over a gift?'

'It was a really nice painting! Of her father, it seems.'

'So what's the problem?' Nanao gets the clear sense she doesn't want to hear him go off on any more tangents.

'The face was different.'

'The face?'

'The face in the painting wasn't the face of the man in the hotel room. Different body, too.' The man in the painting is hearty and round-faced, while the man in Room 2010 is slim. Too few points in common to be explained away by perspective or weight loss.

'Is that so? Well, that's art, isn't it? It doesn't have to reflect its subject exactly. Look at Ryūsei Kishida, or Modigliani.'

'That's what I thought, too. It looked to me like realism, but who's to say it's not intentionally avant-garde in some way? Not something I'm qualified to judge. I don't know anything about art.'

'That's for sure.'

'So I decided to call you and ask what you thought. About the discrepancy. What's going on? Is it just an art thing? I wanted your sage advice.'

'And this is that call?'

'No. This is the call *after* that.'

'What do you mean?'

'So there I was – I'd decided to give you a call . . .'

Nanao looked at the man in Room 2010 and asked, 'Would it be all right if I made a phone call?'

'A phone call?' The man cocked his head.

'It's really nothing. Just a matter of paperwork.' Nanao kept it vague. He'd never had to do any 'paperwork' since he'd started working with Maria, but he figured that what he did do with her was close enough to qualify.

'Can I ask you to step outside, then? Otherwise I'll end up overhearing.'

'Of course.'

It made Nanao nervous to leave the room. Would the door lock automatically behind him? Would he have to ring the bell to get back in? Though he'd already done what he had to do; maybe he should just leave. Who cared if the painting didn't match the subject? Wasn't art supposed to reveal reality's true nature? Maybe it was something like that.

Nanao was busy telling himself this as he turned again toward the door, but as he did, he encountered a sofa in an unexpected place and nearly stumbled into it. He twisted his body at the last minute to avoid a collision.

'That was a mistake,' Nanao says now to Maria. He's a little worried she's no longer listening, but then she says, 'What was?'

'It startled him. He rushed me from behind, trying to put his hands on my throat. I think because I made an unexpected sudden move, and it scared him.'

'Wait a minute. What do you mean, he tried to *put his hands on your throat?*'

'Judging from how it all ended up, he must have been an imposter. The man in the room was counterfeit, and the man in the painting was real. The man in the room wasn't the father of the girl who painted the picture.'

Maria presses him: 'I don't understand what you're telling me. Try to explain more clearly; tell me again what you think happened now that it's over.'

Speaking quickly, Nanao does his best to explain.

'The man may have been suspicious from the moment I

showed up out of the blue with that painting to give him. I don't know if he'd already made the decision to kill me when he let me into the room or if he decided to do it after seeing my reactions while we were talking, but whatever the case, as soon as I turned my back on him to leave the room, he tried to strangle me from behind.'

'Why would a normal person do that?'

'Because he wasn't a normal person! He's like us, a professional who does his business outside the law.'

'I wonder if he was on a job he felt uneasy about.'

'Maybe. Unfortunately, he's no longer in a position to tell us.'

Maria falls silent at that. And then, another sigh.

Nanao glances up at the sofa in front of him, where the man is sitting but no longer breathing.

'So he's dead?'

'That's a rather heartless way to put it.'

'Who cares how I *put it*! Okay, fine: did you *usher him into the next world*? Better?'

'Better. But it wasn't me. As I said before, he rushed me from behind, going for my throat – but then he fell. Maybe he slipped on the paper on the floor. He went ass over teakettle all on his own.'

The man's forehead connected with the corner of the marble-topped table in the center of the room as he went down. As Nanao watched, eyes wide, he collapsed, convulsed a few times, then grew still.

Some time passes, and then Maria finally responds, saying, 'I see . . .' in a dull, distant voice. It's unclear whether she's mulling things over or simply upset at this unexpected turn of events, but eventually she says, 'Okay, you can't get mixed up any further in this. There's nothing else to do but just leave. The door will lock automatically behind you, right?'

'But we'll be exposed the moment housekeeping comes by.

They have a master key that allows them to enter any room, right? Or, I guess, a master keycard in this case?'

'Of course they do. Otherwise they wouldn't be able to get into a room during an emergency. But normally, the cleaning staff won't go into a room until after checkout, right? I don't think they're going to bust their way in there anytime soon. You can hit a Do Not Disturb switch to keep them out as well, I think.'

'How many days was he scheduled to stay here?'

'How should I know?'

'Well, it *is* you, after all.' Nanao doesn't bother to hide his irritation.

'It's 5 p.m. right now. So, worst-case scenario, his checkout time will be sometime past noon tomorrow. Housekeeping shouldn't come until after that. I'll ask around, see if there isn't someone who can do something about the body before then. Could you hide it in the bathroom or the tub for safekeeping till then?'

'Absolutely,' replies Nanao, despite not being all that sure about any of this. 'But just to confirm: do you know for sure that the person who hired you is who they say they are?' He's beginning to wonder if the doting daughter even exists. 'If they're coming to *you* for this, it's unlikely to be just some regular person off the street, right?'

'They have ties to the trade, yes.'

'I knew it!'

'But they're not the type to do anything crazy. Simple requests to move goods for them as they go back and forth overseas, or to pass information through discreet channels, things like that. I ask them to do things for me from time to time, even.'

'I wonder why he went for me, then,' muses Nanao, and then he remembers. 'Oh, right!' The man in the room and the man in the painting are two different people.

'Can you take a photo of the man in the painting and send it to me? I might know who it is. I'll get back to you later.'

'Later? You can't do it now?'

'I can't right now. I didn't say, but I'm driving at the moment. I'm on the freeway, using the "hands-free" system to talk to you. So I can't look at a photo right now.'

'You're on a trip?' Without adding: *Even as you make me work?*

'Don't be disagreeable. I'm *returning* from a trip. People need a breather from time to time if they're going to do their best work, right?'

'What should I do, then?'

'Do some general clean-up, then go home. I'm going out after this anyway.'

'Going out?' *Aren't you already out?*

'I have plans to go see a show after I get home. Doors open at six thirty, show at seven.' And then she tells him the name of the troupe putting on the show. She goes on to name the theater and the dates of the show's run, chatting about how popular the show has been and how lucky she feels having gotten her hands on the tickets, despite Nanao asking for none of these details. After she's gone on like this for a while, he cuts in.

'So you're moving directly from taking a break to taking another break?'

'Okay, so, I just want to remind you,' says Maria, her voice hardening noticeably, 'go straight home. And be careful.'

'Be careful? I'm going to leave the room, take the elevator, and get off on the ground floor. Then I'll leave the hotel and head to the subway station. That's it.' Nanao is saying this less to reassure Maria than as a kind of prayer to whatever entity controls fate (or luck) who might be looking down at him right now. 'Nothing tricky about it.'

Right?

'You know better than anyone, surely. It's exactly when there's

18

'nothing tricky about it" that you somehow end up getting mixed up in something you shouldn't.'

'You're right, I do know better. Of course I do.' Nanao's in no position to deny it. He sighs. 'It's you who seems to forget. First, you tell me how "safe" and "easy" this job is, and now you're telling me "be careful." Which is it?'

'This wasn't a job that should have produced a dead body. So yes, now I'm scared. Of your sheer unluckiness.'

Nanao looks again at the white-shirted corpse before him. 'I do try my hardest not to get involved in people's deaths.'

'There's something else I'd like you to remember.'

'What?'

'I know you don't like to take people's lives. I respect that. But it's a separate issue if someone's trying to take *your* life.'

'Separate from what?'

'If someone tries to kill you, you can't just let it go. If that's their aim, you have to make it your aim, too. It's like a penalty kick in soccer – both the kicker and the goalie have to engage to make it work.'

'That doesn't seem like the best analogy I've ever heard, but I get it. Once I leave the hotel and things seem settled, I'll send you a message.'

'I won't be able to check my messages during the show, though . . .'

'Check it afterward, then, it's fine.'

Nanao hangs up and then moves the body, dragging it into the bathroom and putting it in the tub. He does his best to scrub away the bloodstains from the carpet with a wet towel. Then he throws the towel in the tub, too.

After checking to make sure there are no traces left, he's left wondering what to do with the framed painting that started all this. And why the wrong man was in the room in the first place. Then it comes to him.

Nanao picks up the paper the painting had been wrapped in and flips it over. A label showing the intended recipient's name and room number is still stuck to it. The handwritten label reads 2010 – but, looking again, couldn't it also be read as 2016? Was that what happened? In the blink of an eye, doubts begin to bubble up in Nanao's mind. Did he misread 2016 as 2010?

It's possible he went to the wrong room. A mistake.

Whose mistake?

His.

And if that's the case, then this man in Room 2010 let Nanao in with very little hesitation despite the name on the package not being his own.

A normal person would have said something like, 'Are you sure you have the right room?' But someone engaged in something shady might decide to see where it was going and invite him in, thinking, *Is there some hidden meaning to this?* It's a definite possibility.

Is this a case where expecting the unexpected has ended up backfiring? The world is filled with such ironic incidents.

But the question remains: should he take the package to its intended destination, Room 2016?

KAMINO

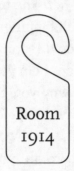

Room
1914

'THE WINTON PALACE is a grand hotel, isn't it? The building itself isn't so big, but the interior is truly magnificent. Even just walking around in one of the rooms can give you a little thrill.'

Yuka Kamino, watching Koko talk, is reminded of her long-departed mother. Affable, friendly, yet not overly so – the type of person who makes you feel instantly close to her. Kamino supposes she's in her sixties, but she wouldn't be shocked to learn she's in her fifties, either.

Kamino has been staying here since yesterday, and Koko has just arrived.

'I made my reservation with the idea that I'd run through my entire life's savings here.'

Wha-at? Koko's voice is a mixture of admiration and horror. 'You know what they say about this place? That it's a hotel where you can't die even if you want to.'

'Eh?' It's Kamino's turn to be brought up short.

'Oh, people don't mean it in a scary way. They mean that

staying here, you become so happy that even if you came here wanting to die you'll end up wanting to live, that's all. So if you feel like you hate your life, you should try staying here for a bit.'

'I see.'

Koko reaches into her bag and brings out a tablet, placing it on the round table in front of her. She unfolds a small keyboard as well, and then busies herself tapping away on it.

'So, um. Can you really do this for me?'

'Really do this? You mean, help you escape? Of course! Why else am I here? Isn't that why you called me? Oh, I know ... when I arrived and you saw how old I am, you began having second thoughts? Is that it?'

Kamino shook her head in an emphatic *No*. 'Inui was very clear – if you want to do a total reset on your life, call Koko. She's the best.'

Inui never said this to Kamino directly, of course. It was something she overheard him say on the phone to someone else.

'If you want to drop out of your own life, leave it to me!' Koko says the line with a practiced flourish. 'So you got my contact info from Inui?'

'I have all of Inui's business contacts in my head.'

'In your head? You have that kind of memory?'

The more questions Koko asks, the more she reminds Kamino of her mother.

'Yes.'

'Wow. You sound sure of yourself. Despite seeming so modest.'

'There's no denying my memory. It's why all this is happening, after all.'

Her stomach twists as she speaks. She brings her right hand to her head as if to grab it. Grab it, then pull her own brain out.

'All this? What do you mean, all this?'

'It's why my life has become what it's become. Why I started working at Inui's office. And now, why I have to get away.'

And, perhaps, it's also why she's had to live her whole life without ever having a friend.

'Isn't having a great memory a good thing? Like when you're playing cards, for example?'

'I've always been good at cards, it's true.' Kamino's tone is forceful due to the immediacy of the memory. As a child, she remembers blithely flipping over cards during a matching game, filled with pride at her own abilities. *Here it is! Here, too! Why does everyone guess wrong all the time?* Gradually, she began to realize that other people didn't share her ability to remember each and every little thing, and, at the same time, that there might be utility in the ability to forget.

Isn't it best to just forget the bad stuff?

People say this to her, and Kamino always answers the same way.

Forget? How?

'I remember everything, for all time. Whatever it might be – if I see it or hear it, I remember it. Sometimes it's okay if I zone out while I'm watching something, but the moment I become conscious of myself doing so, it's too late.'

'So everything ends up inscribed in your memory?'

Kamino nods emphatically. '*Inscribed.* That's exactly it – the perfect metaphor. It never leaves my head again, no matter how much I try to scrub or wash it away.'

'Really?' Koko's eyes grow wide. Koko gets up and walks across the room, her purpose becoming clear as she picks up a folder from next to the bed and brings it over to Kamino. 'So, what you're telling me is that you could read this and remember everything it says?'

Kamino opens the folder and sees that it's the terms and conditions of her hotel reservation. She nods her head and looks the document over. Less than thirty seconds pass before she says, 'Okay, I've got it.'

And then, looking the half-disbelieving Koko straight in the eye, she recites every sentence on the page from memory.

'Oh my gosh, that's amazing!' says Koko, and then, after looking off into the middle distance for a bit, adds, 'I admit, I can't help being a bit jealous. I feel like I can't remember anything.'

'When I was a kid, I remember wondering why my friends and family kept forgetting things all the time.'

'You must have been good at taking tests, right? Most schoolwork ends up being a matter of memorization anyway.'

Kamino is compelled to nod her assent again. From elementary school on, she never had to work for her grades much at all. At some point, she noticed that people were saying, 'Oh Yuka-chan, she's such a good student!'

'But everything else ended up in my head, too – a little thing a friend might say, or if I didn't like someone's attitude. It was all there.' Kamino taps her head with her finger. She remembers ruminating over things people said to her – even minor, throwaway remarks, or things said with no ill will behind them – and, unable to forget, she'd begin having unbidden thoughts like, *I think she said that because she doesn't like me,* or, *Maybe I wasn't being nice enough then,* her head filling with increasingly terrible, yet imaginary, slights and regrets.

Getting close to someone always means painful memories. Not just of what the other person says or does, but one's own personal failures and misjudged words, and to be unable to forget them is even more painful. Kamino, remembering everything so well, found herself besieged with feelings of guilt and regret that never lessened over time, only intensified.

So, when she became a teenager, Kamino began to avoid contact with others as much as possible.

'I never had friends, not even one. I made the minimum conversation at school to get by, but I never met anyone outside school, not for fun or for anything.'

She doesn't remember feeling lonely, though. But sometimes, she'll look at social media and see a lovely couple having fun together, or meet a handsome man and his beautiful wife who proudly show her pictures of their cute children, and she finds her mood growing dark, thinking to herself, *What am I doing with my life?*

Kamino tells all this to Koko, who responds by waving her hand dismissively. 'Those people aren't really happy. They only feel good when they show off like that. Having a lot of friends doesn't bring happiness – they only suck you into a vortex of jealousy and dissatisfaction.'

'A vortex?' Kamino knows Koko's only saying this to cheer her up, but she nonetheless finds herself smiling at her words. 'But having no friends is lonely too. When I entered college, I thought a lot about it. How should I live? What sort of job would be right for me?'

'How about becoming a lawyer or something like that? With a memory like yours, you'd be able to memorize the various laws and regulations with no trouble at all.'

'I did think of that.' She remembers regretting not entering the Law Department. She also remembers thinking that qualification exams of any sort would be easy work for her, so she should perhaps become something specialized in that way. 'But then, well, it may sound strange to say it this way, but doctors and lawyers are people who help people in trouble, right?'

'I mean, sure, they rescue people from their problems.'

'If I end up having to remember the stories of all the people in trouble I meet, I don't think I'd be able to stand it.'

'I think I see what you mean.'

'So, after thinking it over for a long time, I came to a conclusion: I should make sweets.'

'Really? Just like that?'

25

'I could easily memorize the recipes – all the various amounts, all the various steps – and while I didn't really know if I had the knack for it, I knew I could do as I was told and do it well. And besides—'

'Besides, people would eat what you made and be happy.'

Kamino nodded emphatically: *Yes.* 'So, I dropped out of college and went to a trade school.'

She wanted to make others happy. She wanted others to make her happy. She'd given up on having friends, but if she had the opportunity to exchange happiness in this way, she felt she had to take it.

She was so excited then, thinking she'd finally found the right path for her life. And in fact, going to trade school was the period in her life when she felt the most at peace.

'After graduation, I started working at a European-style pastry shop in the city.'

'How was it?'

'Not great.' Kamino is forced to tell the truth.

'Oh no!'

'The work itself was fine, but . . .'

'But no matter where you work, you have to deal with others, don't you?'

Koko seems to understand what had happened even without Kamino telling her. The *pâtissier* who owned the shop controlled the whole atmosphere there with his moods, and Kamino found herself saddled with unreasonable demands from her senior coworkers, followed by scolding and criticism. It was a shop where all anyone ever thought about was the owner's state of mind – not the quality of the pastries, not the happiness of the clients – and all she found there was sadness and pain.

'After all, though, it's a common enough story.'

'No! Don't say that! Who cares if it's a *common enough story*? It was an important event for you! It's like saying that death is a *common enough story*, so who cares if you live or die. Never say that. Who cares if it's common? This story is yours.'

'In the end, I left that shop. But the pain from that time remained within me.'

'It wouldn't work, in your case, to say that time will heal these wounds by allowing you to forget them.' Koko seems truly sympathetic, as if to say, *It must be so rough for you.*

'I had a bit of a mental breakdown and ended up in the hospital, and they gave me some medication that made me able to manage somehow. But most of my money was gone.'

Broken body and soul, she got by using as little as possible from her savings, but eventually, wanting some sort of link with society, she began volunteering, only to end up mixed up in a complicated scam and losing almost all the rest of her money in about six months.

'Oh dear,' says Koko, frowning.

'That's when I met Inui.'

She'd gotten a gig that involved standing all day under the blazing sun, and as she was returning home, exhausted, she noticed that a brand-new pastry shop had opened up near her. Several beautiful fruit-festooned tarts were displayed in the front window, drawing Kamino to peer through the glass to see how they were decorated. Catching sight of her staring so intently at the pastries, Inui had called out to her, 'Hey, looks like you want those real bad. Why don't you let me buy you one?' Flustered, Kamino explained that she was just looking, but it sounded like a flimsy excuse even to her. 'Don't worry about it. I'll get us both one, we'll eat them together.'

'That's so like him. I don't know how to put it exactly – that he's light on his feet, or that he's good at seeming up for anything . . . But, in any case, it's the secret to his success, how he gets people to do what he wants.'

Kamino doesn't quite know how to respond to Koko's remark,

so she forces a smile. Then she decides to put what's troubling her into words.

'He was never a bad guy to me.'

'That's the way the really bad guys always are.' Koko's tone is sympathetic. 'How many years did you end up working for him?'

'Two. Paperwork, mostly. Some accounting.'

'Did you know what kind of work he really did?'

'Of course not. Or at least, not at first.' This isn't a lie. It's true that she'd been finding it hard to find a job then, so she was grateful to be able to work at Inui's office, but she doesn't think she'd have accepted the offer if she'd known his real business involved doing such shady, violent things.

'I assume Inui knows about your ability to memorize things, Kamino-chan?'

Kamino nods. She'd told him when she first started working for him. She'd figured it would be best to explain herself and her situation as clearly as possible to any new boss to avoid trouble.

'I bet he was happy to hear it.'

'Yeah . . .'

'Inui loves having everyone else do his work for him, while he does as little as possible himself. There's no way he didn't have a plan for how to use your gift. I heard him say once, "You know, when no one's around, I don't call other people 'people,' I call them 'tools.'" It was such a bald-faced confession I couldn't help but laugh.'

Kamino nods again: *It's true.* If Inui has someone around to rely on, he'll do so without the least compunction; the majority of his work is 'outsourced' in precisely this way.

Thinking back, Kamino remembers accompanying Inui outside the office and him not only having her memorize the contact information for any client they had to meet, but also reciting his schedule aloud and ending with a blithe, 'So, remember that for me, okay?' He would sometimes take her along to meals with politicians and then say to her afterward, 'What did that guy say to me again?' as if pushing a button on a tape recorder to play the conversation back. In this sense, it did seem as though Inui thought of her primarily as a voice-activated recording device.

'What's so funny?' Koko asks, making Kamino realize she must be smiling.

'I was just thinking about when Inui would ask me, "Did I eat lunch today? Do you remember?"'

Koko laughs. 'As if you need a superhuman memory to remember that! What a thing, to rely on others that much.'

'I wonder how serious he was being.'

'I heard a rumor about him – a pretty unsettling one, to be honest.' Koko's expression changes suddenly, as if she bit into something bitter.

Kamino finds herself getting nervous. 'What is it?'

'Did you ever hear anyone talk about how Inui has a dissection fetish?'

'Dissection?'

Seeing Kamino's reaction, Koko's expression changes again, this time as if to say, *Oh shit!* – as if this were something she'd have preferred not to mention if Kamino didn't already know about it. 'Well, according to the rumor, he finds young people who have nowhere to go, knocks them out with a drug, and then . . . cleans them.'

'Cleans them?'

'Like you'd clean a fish.'

Kamino brings her hand to her mouth, momentarily speechless. This is the first she's heard of such a thing. The image of a person laid out on a cutting board appears unbidden in her mind. As she begins to imagine the unimaginable, she shakes her head to ward it off.

'Of course, it's only a rumor . . .'

'Of course . . .'

But even as she says it, Kamino's memory is jogged.

She remembers seeing books lying around Inui's office – anatomy books, showing the bones and muscles of the human body in detail. She remembers Inui looking at them hungrily, running his fingers over them.

Kamino understands the pained expression on Koko's face, evidence of her worry: *That may well be you, too, if he catches you.* The hair stands up all over her body and coldness spreads within her, as if a hole has opened up in the pit of her stomach. Imagining her own skin being peeled painlessly from her body, a shaky breath escapes her lips.

THE SIX

On the road

THE SIX ARE PILED INTO AN SUV heading for the Winton Palace Hotel.

'How long till we get there, Asuka?'

'If we can believe the GPS, about fifteen minutes.'

'So, this is where the woman Inui's looking for is staying?'

'What was her name again?'

'Kamino. Yuka Kamino. Try to remember at least that much, Kamakura.'

'Hang tight, Kamino-san! We're almost there!'

'This is fun, isn't it?'

'What is, Heian?'

'It's fun to find someone who's trying as hard as they can to not be found, to ferret 'em out and nab 'em.'

The SUV holds all six of the Six. Asuka's driving, with Nara in the passenger seat beside her. Both are twenty-three, the two youngest of the team. They're both the third daughters of rich families, both went to international schools and grew up as outcasts from their families – they have much in common, but there are also differences. Asuka is slim and pretty, for example, and once punctured a guy's eyeball with a toothpick when he sidled up to her saying, 'Hey beautiful, are you a model?' Nara, on the other hand, is unusually tall for a woman, nearly 175 centimeters, and once plunged a ballpoint pen into the ear of a guy who made fun of her by saying, 'Look at you, taller than the Great Buddha!'

Sitting directly behind them is Kamakura, a twenty-six-year-old who, like Asuka, possesses an appearance so 'conventionally attractive' that he was once scouted by a men's fashion magazine to be a model.

Next to Kamakura is Heian, twenty-eight years old and small of stature, with droopy eyelids and a drawling way of talking that, by her own admission, makes people assume she's sweet and gentle, though also slow-witted and scatterbrained. But this couldn't be further from the truth, as her mind is always whirring, helping her ascertain the most efficient ways of doing things and pushing for the shortest possible path to accomplish any task.

Back in the third row, on the left, is Sengoku, a hulking thirty-one-year-old possessing the air of a former football player with his thick chest and bulging arms. A man of few words, he keeps his emotions to himself. But one thing he does enjoy is dealing out violence to those smaller than himself.

Beside Sengoku, though careful to leave a bit of space between them, sits Edo, the oldest of the crew at thirty-five. It was Edo who gathered the other five together and started them all out doing jobs as a team. He acts even now as their leader.

Kamakura turns around to speak to Edo in the third row. 'Edo, I heard recently that there was once an assassin-killer out there.'

'Oh, I heard that, too! Though it was quite a while ago, right?'

'You're always so surprisingly well-informed, Heian. I haven't heard any of this, what are you talking about?'

'Nara, I'm not well-informed, you just don't pay attention. There was apparently someone out there who took out other professionals – a pretty strong bastard, it seems. In less than a year, this one professional apparently liquidated twenty to thirty colleagues.'

Asuka speaks up from the driver's seat. '*How* many? Twenty to thirty? That seems unlikely. And not even regular people, but people in the trade?'

'This was about fifteen years ago, just before I got in the business myself,' explains Edo.

'I was in elementary school!'

'Me too!'

'Where are they now? Was it a man? A woman?'

'Sounds like you're a little too interested, Heian.'

'Listen, I heard five other professionals ganged up on them once, and all five ended up unable to use their arms! How could I not be interested?'

'Their arms were broken?'

Edo cuts in. 'I heard that all five had their arms *dislocated*.'

'Wha—*really?*' Heian's reaction is like that of a sports fan hearing about an athlete setting a new world record, a mix of joy and curiosity.

'There's some sort of trick to it, I guess – before they knew it, all their shoulders were popped out of joint and then, unable to use their arms, they ended up beaten to death.'

Nara and Kamakura whistled loudly in appreciation. 'How frustrating, to be unable to move your arms! And how fun, to have a target you could do whatever you wanted to and they couldn't fight back!'

'Yeah, I'd love to have a go at that myself!'

'But these are all just stories. Legends. You've heard of the Pusher, right?'

'The professional who pushes people in front of cars and trains?'

'The Pusher might well be nothing more than an urban legend. People saying a professional did it when it was just a simple accident. In the same way, this might be nothing more than a case of people at the time chalking up any professional's death to a legendary assassin-killer.'

'Maybe it was some rich guy with a special homemade weapon, taking out bad guys on his own! Like in a movie,' says Asuka.

'A bringer of justice who dislocates people's arms before killing them – not a bad concept. The Darkest of Dark Knights. Though maybe such a hero wouldn't appeal to anyone but us.'

'The thing is, though, they were active for a year and then just stopped.'

'Is that the right way to put it? "Active"?' Sengoku's tone is low, as if musing over an idle thought.

'There was a woodblock print artist like that, right? Only *active* for a year, then he disappeared? A "mystery artist." '

'That was Sharaku. There are all these theories as to who he really was. It's true, this assassin-killer might be a similar case. Why were they only active for a year before disappearing?'

'Don't you suppose they just died? Wouldn't that explain it?'

'Maybe they faked their death and ran off to Mongolia!' says Heian. 'I've always liked that theory about Yoshitsune.'

'The thing is, the assassin-killer seems to have reappeared recently,' says Kamakura. After all, that's the reason he's brought the subject up in the first place.

'Reappeared? What do you mean?'

'I mean, a professional was killed recently.'

'Who? Where?'

'Well . . .'

'If nobody's really talking about it, maybe it wasn't so formidable a guy. And besides, it's not so rare for a professional to end up dead. The job comes with risks.'

'I heard both shoulders were popped out of their joints though.'

'Oh!'

'So people are wondering if the assassin-killer isn't swinging into action again.'

'There's no way to tell at this point, though,' says Edo. 'Might be a copycat.'

The SUV brakes suddenly. Kamakura, sitting in the second row, flies forward and hits the back of the driver's seat in front of him. 'What was that, Asuka? Learn how to drive already!'

'It's this guy in front of me!'

Nara, in the passenger seat, folds her arms, her sullen expression unchanged by the sudden stop.

The SUV starts moving again.

Kamakura leans over so he can peer through the windshield. He sees the back end of a black sedan in front of them. Its brake lights go on, and it stops again. Asuka stomps on the brakes, slamming the SUV to a stop as well, throwing everyone inside forward once more.

She tries to swerve out of the line of cars to go around, but the car turns slantwise to block her way.

'Edo-san, if this keeps up, we won't make it in time! Can I hit him?'

'You're right. Okay – but gently.'

From that point on, things go as if according to plan, despite no one having actually made one.

The car ahead of them stops again. This time, though, Asuka refrains from stepping on the brake. With the predictable result that the SUV bumps the black sedan from behind.

Bamph! The sedan lurches forward as it's hit. A momentary stillness ensues, followed by the black sedan's driver's and passenger's doors both opening at once, disgorging two young men.

Dressed in T-shirts and shorts, they look like they just came from a summery seaside. Their pumped-up arms bulge from their short sleeves.

35

'I'll be right back,' says Kamakura, hitting the button to slide open the right-hand door and then hopping out. Heian jumps out of the left-hand side.

'Hey there, you rear-ended us! I think you owe us an apology.'

The man's tone is flippant. After all, Kamakura looks no more threatening than the handsome lead in a romantic comedy, while Heian looks for all the world like a cute young girl. No wonder the men are so relaxed, as if facing down a couple of children.

'Sorry about that. You stopped so fast we ended up running into you . . .'

'But if you think about it, it's more like *you* ran into *us*, right?'

Kamakura and Heian seem completely unbothered, and the two men's faces darken.

They're interrupted by a loud noise. It's the back window of the black sedan shattering. Shards of glass rain down on the pavement.

The young men's jaws drop, as if to say, *What on earth is going on?*

'Cars these days, right? They're designed so if you start driving erratically, their rear windows blow apart,' observes Kamakura.

'What did you just say?' Hopped up on their anger at the window breaking, the two men advance on Kamakura and Heian.

Kamakura remains perfectly calm. He pulls a small tube from his back pocket, then slides a finger into his shirt's chest pocket and fishes out a cartridge with a tiny dart in it, loading it into one end of the tube.

He brings the tube to his lips.

It was a dart fired by Heian that broke the rear window. She'd readied one made for the express purpose of breaking glass, then blown.

Kamakura fills his chest with breath, then releases it through his puckered lips. His target's so close there's no reason to think he'll miss. And indeed, just as he intended, the dart strikes one of the men in the throat.

Ouch!

But before the man can even quite say it, he stops in his tracks. The young man next to him cries out like an animal, then grows still. A dart from Heian has embedded itself in his left eye.

Heian looks proud, raising a finger in victory. *Got 'em!*

The two men manage one or two more steps, but their movements are sluggish, and they collapse to the ground. Kamakura squats down where they've fallen, leaning over toward their faces to explain what's happening.

'These darts are smeared with poison. It'll paralyze you as it circulates through your system. But you can still hear me, right? You'll remain conscious, able to see and hear even if you can't move.'

Kamakura begins dragging one of the men. Seeing this, Heian turns and hops back in the SUV, as if to say, *I'll leave this part to you – I didn't sign up for manual labor.*

'Ugh, so heavy! What a pain,' grunts Kamakura, huffing and puffing as he drags the man back into the sedan, sitting him up in the passenger seat. He drags the other man to the car as well, sitting him up the same way in the driver's seat, and then reaches under the steering wheel to pull a lever. The gas tank pops open.

'I'm going to light this car up, you see? You'll get nice and toasty. It's a known fact that reckless driving can lead to these kinds of accidents.'

The two men's eyes roll desperately in their heads. Seeing tears well up in them, Kamakura feels happiness well up within himself. He closes the driver's side door and walks back to the gas tank, unscrewing the cap so he can begin preparations for setting the car alight.

NANAO

The twentieth floor

AS SOON AS NANAO REACHES Room 2016, he encounters a round-faced man coming out of it. The man in the portrait! He recognizes him immediately.

Despite not really knowing what he was doing, Nanao has done his best to rewrap the package, and as soon as the man sees it, he breaks into a wide smile. 'Oh! You brought it!'

So he was right – this was always the intended destination for the painting, and he simply misread the number. Now that he's in the right place, things go smoothly.

'I was just stepping out for a bit,' says the man, but he nonetheless invites Nanao into Room 2016. 'I'd heard my daughter had sent me something, so I was looking forward to this!' The man nods as Nanao hands over the painting, and then his eyes crinkle at their edges, as if he were warmed from the bottom of his heart. It's a situation that couldn't be more different than what occurred in Room 2010. Why couldn't he have read the room number right from the beginning?

Nonetheless, as Nanao receives the man's thanks and takes the requisite picture of him with the painting, he finds himself filled with the satisfaction of a job well done (eventually).

The round-faced man and Nanao leave the room together.

'Oh, that's right! I meant to tell you,' says the man as they reach the elevators. 'I heard something from a fellow professional.'

'What is it?'

'There's someone out there who's resentful of their handler, and tonight's the night they're going to finally do something about it.'

'Resentful? You mean, they're planning on harming their handler?' *Is that—?*

'In this case, it seems like the handler in question might be your Maria.'

'I guess she *is* my handler . . .' Not just Maria, but anyone who does middle management work in the trade can end up having conflicts with the professionals who actually do the dirty work. 'But there are plenty of them out there, right?'

'Tonight, this particular handler is going to a show. The plan seems to be that the professional will sit next to her and, when the opportunity presents itself, do the deed.'

'Maria did say she recently got her hands on some hard-to-get tickets . . .'

'Well, there you go. Bet it's a trap.' The man sighs sympathetically; Nanao finds no reason to think he's lying. 'When I heard that Maria was handling the delivery of my daughter's gift, I thought it would be a good opportunity to let her know. I can't believe I almost forgot just now! I don't know Maria's contact information to tell her directly, and when I tried to get ahold of my daughter to pass the message along through her, she didn't pick up her phone. Can you tell her? All she has to do is avoid the show and she'll be fine.'

'I see,' says Nanao. 'I'll tell her before anything happens.'

Then that would be the end of it.

A downward-bound elevator finally arrives. Nanao decides to stay behind and call Maria, so the man gets in by himself.

'Thanks for the delivery!' says the round-faced man, and Nanao raises a hand in reply.

Maria doesn't answer her phone. *At a time like this!* Nanao clucks his tongue in annoyance. He's just about to leave a message when the next elevator arrives.

A couple who seem to be staying for the night emerge, and Nanao, even though he's not really doing anything suspicious, reflexively puts away his phone. Once the job's done, get away as quick as you can. Nanao remembers a fellow professional passing along words of wisdom to this effect long ago: *Do it and get out.* Even though there wasn't anything particularly noteworthy about the words themselves, something about their import made them stick in his mind, and he's never forgotten them. As soon as your work is done, go home. Words to live by.

Thinking it would be a waste to let this elevator go, too, Nanao gets in at the last minute, prying open the doors as they begin to close. He can send the message once he reaches the ground floor. As long as nothing stops the elevator, he'll be home free.

KAMINO

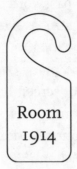

Room
1914

'INUI HAD ME COMMIT ALL sorts of things to memory – data regarding his clients, accounting information, contacts, you name it.'

'Wow,' says Koko. Then, sincerely impressed, she adds, 'He's no fool, that Inui. Digital data is vulnerable to clickety-clackers like me, but info that's in someone's head is pretty hard to steal.'

'Clickety-clackers?'

'Like on the keyboard. You know, accessing information and passing it around on the internet.'

'So you're a hacker?'

Kamino hasn't even finished saying the word when Koko stops her. 'Don't call me that, it's embarrassing. Too hip for an old lady like me! In any case, digital data is easy to steal or secretly alter. We've gone back to a time when writing things down on paper is the most secure way to store it. Especially if the handwriting is messy and hard to read. So, my question for you, Kamino-chan, is: do you have passwords in that head of yours?'

'I do.'

'If they're important, then Inui will be after you. Did we go over this already?'

'Yes. Maybe.'

'Maybe?'

'It's hard to say what's a password and what isn't.'

'Hard to say? How is that possible? You mean the strings of numbers and letters are too long?'

'No, it's that there are too many choices.' The fact is, Kamino never actually saw the input screen herself, so she has to rely on her imagination. 'The prompt was in the form of a series of questions, like, "What's your favorite color?" or, "What was the name of your elementary school?"'

'Oh yeah, there are formats like that. Basically asking, "What's your favorite password?"'

'I remember there was a handwritten chart. A huge number of answers were listed on it.'

'Handwritten, huh?' Koko accepts this with a nod.

'A random set of questions would be generated with answers that could be found somewhere on that chart.'

'Random how?'

'Well, it's impossible to answer however many hundreds of questions, so what the system does is pick four or five at random from the list each time. That's how Inui explained it.'

'So, you never knew which questions would come up, and therefore had to memorize them all?'

'At first I thought it wouldn't be necessary to memorize them, as we could store the information as photos or on video.'

'But that's way too dangerous! The whole point would be lost.'

'You think so too?'

'Of course. If you store the passwords like that, then wherever you're storing them becomes a new target. If you take a picture, for example, it could leak. You just end up adding endless opportunities for information to be stolen or passed around – that's what it means to create records like that. Inui was smart to have you memorize them instead.'

'He showed me the paper and said, "Memorize this." Then he burnt it.'

'Pretty thorough.'

'If you asked me to write them all out right now, it would take some time, but I think I could do it.' Kamino looked at Koko as if to say, *Shall I start?* But the other woman waved away the suggestion.

'No, no need. Again, if we create such a document, we'd be creating something worth stealing. Just like now, how everyone wants to get ahold of your brain, Kamino-chan. Which reminds me – why did you run away, anyway?'

'What do you mean?'

'It might have been safer for you to keep working at his office. That way, they would know their password archive would be kaput if something happened to you.'

'Inui is involved in something related to handing over the data in question right now. I overheard him assure someone that once the job was done, all passwords would be liquidated.'

'Liquidated? Does that mean . . .' Koko points at Kamino's head.

'From the way he was talking, yeah, it seemed like he meant he'd erase my memory.'

'But that's not possible.'

Kamino's brow furrows. 'Not while I'm still alive, no.'

'Can't the passwords you memorized be changed, though, once they're used? If they just did that, there would be no need to *erase* your memory.'

'It doesn't seem like it's possible to change them.'

She'd even heard Inui say, *The only solution is erasure.* He seemed sure there was no other way.

'And so that's why you decided to run.'

'Inui made sure to act like he always did with me, but still, something was clearly off.'

'Off?'

'I'd hear him stomping around, being really moody.'

'Sounds like you were right to get away. I'm repeating myself, but the fact remains that you never know what Inui might be capable of.'

Kamino couldn't help but recall the 'unsettling rumor' she'd just heard.

Unbidden, the image of Inui holding a scalpel appears in her head. He's using it to peel the skin off a woman's body as if scraping the scales from a fish. The woman is her. She shivers, hair standing up all over her body once more.

'You didn't go to the police?'

'Inui is tight with the police at all levels. He does a lot of work for politicians, after all.'

'I see. It's true that I know a number of people who've hired Inui to do things for them. Including higher-ups in the police. It's possible that there aren't any members of Parliament left who haven't had Inui do a job for them – something small, something major – at one point or another.'

'I truly have nowhere to go. I spent the last week staying for a night or two at various places, but I never felt safe, as I couldn't help but imagine someone he hired popping up and taking care of me. So I ended up contacting you. Can you really help me?'

'Of course I can!' Koko's reply was firm. 'Who do you take me for? I'm the old lady who showed up to get you to safety! I promise you'll be able to live your life without fear again once I'm done.'

Koko walks up to Kamino and pats her on the shoulder. Her touch banishes the goosebumps that have been spreading across Kamino's body as she imagines Inui's horrible hobby.

Koko returns to her tablet and begins tapping away again. 'I asked you over the phone yesterday, but to confirm: there's no

GPS tracker or anything in your luggage? Here, I'll check myself, just to be sure – can you bring your things over to me?'

'Yes, of course,' says Kamino as she heads over to where she'd set her suitcase down.

'Oh, that's right – say, Kamino?' Koko's voice follows her as she walks away.

'What is it?'

'Before I came to your room, I killed some time wandering around the hotel.'

Kamino picks up her suitcase and sets it down in front of Koko. 'You could have come up right away,' she says, as if apologizing for inconveniencing the other woman.

'No, no, I wanted to get a sense of the place before I met you: how the front-desk staff operate, who else might be staying here, things like that. The second floor is where the restaurants are, and the third has banquet rooms. I walked around gawking at everything, looking for all the world like your typical Nosy Old Woman.'

'Did you see anything interesting?'

'Nothing much out of the ordinary, except for one thing: a celebrity sighting. He was heading into a restaurant.'

'A celebrity sighting?'

'Director Yomogi. That guy who was a member of Parliament, but now he's the head of the Information Bureau?'

'Oh, I remember him,' says Kamino, nodding. *Of course I do*, she almost adds – after all, how could she forget? 'Why do you suppose he's here?'

'Sampling the cuisine? Now that he's Information Director, maybe it's a matter of national security to gather intel on where all the good food is.'

'I can't believe he's here! Yomogi!' Kamino hears the tone of her voice rising.

'You're a fan?'

'Not exactly . . .' Kamino says, contradicting Koko but also refraining from elaborating further. Koko looks at her as if to say, *Now, don't hold out on me*, prompting Kamino to open her mouth again. 'It was fifteen years ago, but maybe you remember that incident on the train he was involved in, with that guy stabbing all those people?'

'Of course I remember! Everyone does. That's what anyone seeing his face will think of even now, surely.'

'I guess that's true.'

'I remember thinking at the time that this incident would make schoolchildren want to become politicians again! Definitely good for their image, at any rate.'

'Would it be so bad if that really happened?' Kamino couldn't help but laugh. 'But Yomogi truly was heroic in the moment. Everyone running in every direction trying to get away, except he and his assistant putting themselves in the way of danger.'

'You talk like you saw it yourself.'

'I did.'

'Really?'

'Yes, I was on that train that day.'

'You were?' Koko's eyes are round.

'On that very train car, in fact. I was in middle school.'

'What a thing!'

The attacker's shouting and the victims' cries; the blood spreading across the floor of the train like paint; a salaryman slipping in the blood and falling on his face; the woman with her hands in the air, screaming, 'Please don't kill me!'; the father protecting his children with his body; and above all, the attacker's face as he wielded the knife, his expression determined, as if to say, *My life will amount to nothing if I don't do this* – all of it, every image, returns to Kamino's head in all its original vividness. Nothing forgotten, or even dimmed in the slightest by the passage of time.

Forget? How?

She shivers, chilled by a cold wind passing down her spine.

'How horrible it must have been for you, Kamino-chan! And how horrible even now, surely – it has to have had an impact on your life.'

'Perhaps, but it affected Yomogi at least as much,' says Kamino, feeling compelled to add this caveat. She remembers being surprised when Yomogi went on to become a member of Parliament, though she also felt happy to support him. 'When his wife and child were killed three years ago, I was shocked to my core, even though it really had nothing to do with me.'

'They say it was a drunk driver. So tragic. Yomogi's life has been filled with tragedy and hardship, it seems – I hear there's even more bad stuff than most people know.'

'More bad stuff?' Kamino can't think of anything Koko might be referring to.

'There are quite a few people out there who don't exactly think well of our Yomogi. I hear he's being targeted again – that there might be someone hired to do it.'

'Really?'

'Maybe Yomogi's here like you are, visiting this hotel to regain the strength to go on living. The fabulous Winton Palace, where you go to stop wanting to die!'

'That might very well be true,' says Kamino, meaning it from the bottom of her heart.

'But enough of that – we need to focus on you, Kamino-chan.'

'Oh – yes! Of course.' Kamino returns to herself. This isn't the time to worry about others.

Images are coming into her head again: of herself, laid out on a cold surface like a surgical table, looking up at Inui looking down at her. He's smiling, filled with joy, a scalpel in his hand. Kamino shakes her head as if to shake off her own imagination.

'You know,' says Koko, intentionally upbeat, as if sensing Kamino's growing terror. 'I hired some protection, just in case.'

'Protection?' Kamino looks around the room, searching for a previously unnoticed bodyguard.

'I'm just one old lady, so I wanted backup. I reached out to someone I know in the trade. As soon as your call came in, Kamino-chan, I knew I needed to get help yesterday – I had almost no time at all.'

'Sorry for that.'

'Anyway, I put out some feelers, and luckily a couple of trustworthy souls raised their hands. *Yes!*' Koko punches the air cutely.

The idea of two bodyguards heartens Kamino considerably, though she knew they must cost a pretty penny. Worried that what she's paying Koko won't be enough to also pay them, Kamino can't help but voice her concerns.

'Don't worry about that. I'm not trying to squeeze blood from a stone. These two aren't that concerned about money anyway.'

Kamino cocks her head in puzzlement. Professionals who aren't concerned about money?

'But there is something that's beginning to bother me.'

'What is it?'

'I hired the two of them as protection, but so far today, I haven't heard from them at all – not a peep.'

THE SIX

On the road

ASUKA HAS THE SUV ROLLING again when Edo speaks up from the back.

'I'm getting a call. It's from Inui.'

'He's mad we're late?' laughs Heian.

'I'm going to connect him on the car speaker,' says Edo, and then they hear Inui's voice, casual as you please.

'Where are you guys?'

'We're on our way to the hotel. How long now, Asuka?'

'Ten minutes.'

'Ten minutes and we'll be at the Winton Palace. What room is Yuka Kamino in?'

'Don't know yet. Find out yourselves once you get there.'

'Brusque as usual, I see.'

'Japanese gets so cumbersome when you try to be polite. So long and complicated, trying to guess how humble you need to be to whoever you're talking to. It's inefficient.'

'Anyway, the hotel is twenty stories tall, with about twenty rooms on each floor.'

'There's six of you, maybe it would be quicker to split up.'

'How many exits?'

'Well, there's the front entrance into the lobby. Then there are back exits to the east and west on the ground floor. There's an underground parking garage as well. You can't get there directly from the guest rooms, though – you need to get in an elevator to the ground floor, then transfer to a separate elevator to get to the garage. Sound good to you?'

Easy for him to say – he's the one asking, not the one doing, thinks Kamakura, sighing with irritation. 'How would we know if that sounds good or not?'

'Having to go over each floor with a fine-tooth comb is hardly *efficient* as a strategy, you know.'

Nara cuts in, asking, 'Is it a hotel where guests can only push the elevator button for the floor they're staying on?'

'No, the Winton Palace isn't like that. You can get to any floor you want,' Inui assures them.

'Seems like a good way to have people secretly sneak in and stay there for free!'

'Maybe they'd rather have people think they're generous and want to come stay there again, rather than seem cheap and controlling.'

'Well whatever the case, how did you find out Kamino's staying there?'

'I sent around a notice, something like a wanted poster. It's just as I thought – it's these old-fashioned methods that work best. Send a notice around saying, "Contact me if you see this woman," and sure enough, people do! Taxi drivers, pizza deliverymen, I got tips from all over. A lot of people saw her enter that hotel.'

'Luck's not with her, it seems.'

'I found a worker who regularly goes in and out of the place who's willing to cooperate with me as well.'

'Cooperate?'

'A guy whose job is maintaining the computer systems in the hotels downtown. He's buried in loans, so I ask him to do things for me in exchange for a little spending money from time to time. We had a brief negotiation and he agreed to help us here – he's giving us access to the security cameras.'

'Classic Inui – using people as tools again.' Asuka mutters this under her breath.

'You know how hard I've worked to create that reputation?' Inui responds, laughing. 'Anyway, as soon as you secure Kamino-chan, contact me. You can call me or send a message, I don't care. Even if I can't get back to you right away, I'll loop back as soon as I can. And one more thing—'

'What is it?'

'Deliver Yuka Kamino to me unharmed.'

'What?' It's Asuka's turn to laugh. 'That's no fun!'

'This isn't like you,' agrees Kamakura.

'What you mean is, you want her able to use her head and her mouth, right?' Edo surmises. *Sounds like she has important info you want to get out of her.*

'Yeah, something like that,' agrees Inui, vaguely. 'And I want you to make sure not to involve any guests. It'll queer the deal if you attract too much attention. It's in none of our interests if the police show up.'

'What "deal"? As long as she can think and speak, that should be enough.' But Inui doesn't respond to Edo's question.

'A head and mouth alone won't work. I need the rest of her body too.'

Listening to Inui, Asuka recalls something Edo once told her.

That guy has a fetish, it seems – he likes to skin and dissect people, like cleaning a fish. He told me about it once, all excited. I think he thought I'd understand, that I'd be excited too. But why would I be? We're people who enjoy seeing others suffer. What's fun about knocking someone out with anesthetic and peeling their skin off while they're unconscious?

Asuka had agreed, disgusted. What a gross hobby.

NANAO

The twentieth floor

ONCE IN THE ELEVATOR, Nanao pushes the button for the ground floor.

Keep going, keep going. Nanao stares at the numbers counting down on the screen above him, internally egging them on. Perhaps externally, too, under his breath. Once on the ground floor, he'll send a message to Maria warning her, then slip out the front entrance through the revolving doors and head to the subway station. That's it. No part of this plan should present the slightest technical difficulty. A series of tasks that could be completed with ease by the vast majority of people on Earth.

The elevator's descent is so slow.

'Be careful – bad follows good.' Nanao recalls being told this once. It was a time when a job called for the gathering of many professionals together in one place.

'Bad follows good? For me, things don't have to be good – I get into trouble anyway, even when things don't go well at all! What then?'

It was a job that forced them down a long, dark tunnel – not a metaphorical one, either, but one bored straight into the side of a mountain. The man who'd gathered the team together and was now leading them, a professional called Kabuto, continued his speech.

'If you leave everything up to luck, you'll always have to be on guard. But what if you act like you have everything under control, as if to say, "Oh, this is how I thought things would turn out!"? Then they'll be disappointed, and might even rethink their plans for you.'

'*They'll* be disappointed? Who are you talking about?'

'Whoever's in charge of distributing good luck and bad, I guess.' Kabuto got a look on his face like he'd said too much. 'You know what they say, the moon invites clouds, a flower invites wind.'

'They say what now?'

'As soon as you look at the moon and think, *Oh how beautiful!* a cloud is sure to come and obscure it; as soon as you enjoy some cherry blossoms in full bloom, a strong wind is sure to come and blow them to the ground. I guess it boils down to the same thing as "bad follows good." So you're telling me, Ladybug, that for you, the clouds and wind are there all the time?'

'Indeed.'

'There are two ways to think about it, then. Either you cling to the hope that however bad things are now, one day the beautiful moon will re-emerge from behind the clouds and the beautiful flowers will bloom again, or you think, well, how bad are clouds and wind anyway?'

'They both sound like shit options,' Nanao said. 'I'd prefer to go right to the source and see how this guy handing out the luck is doing things.' He remembers that making Kabuto laugh.

Thinking about it now, Nanao recalls him as an extremely talented professional, but he hasn't heard his name in quite a while.

He did hear he got married, though. Nanao finds himself wanting to know what kind of husband he'd be, what kind of father.

The elevator dings, halting its descent. Praying that the screen will tell him he's reached the ground floor, Nanao looks up and sees he's on the eleventh.

Still?

Nanao sighs. This hotel's so fancy, and this elevator's so new, that it can't be that it's actually moving unusually slowly. His emotions must be clouding his sense of time's passage.

The doors open in front of him, allowing a slim man to slip into the elevator.

Ah! thinks Nanao, and before he's even completed the thought, he walks out as if switching places with the man. The moment he saw him, he knew he'd seen him somewhere before. Tall and slender, with hair so curly it makes one wonder if it's natural or a perm, he looks like an artist or a musician. He's wearing a blue suit, no tie.

Who is he?

Nanao searches his memory. Someone he's encountered while working, an acquaintance of Maria or another client, someone in his neighborhood – he rifles through his inner catalog. Soon enough, he remembers: a guy named Soda. They worked on a job together once.

A professional, with expertise in explosives.

'They're a duo – Cola and Soda. Nice, right?' he remembers Maria saying at the time.

'A carbonated twosome. 'Cause they work with things that explode, right?' asked Nanao, to which Maria responded with an absent, 'Yeah, I guess . . .' Then she went on, 'There are some rumors about their strange history in the trade, though.'

'Like what?' Wouldn't anyone in the trade have a strange history? It seemed to Nanao that it would be stranger if they didn't.

'They originally ran a business overseas, a company dealing in explosives. Supported by venture capital. Its valuation went through the roof at one point, and it seems it was acquired by a major IT company.'

'I don't get it – what do explosives and IT have to do with each other?'

'They made millions off the deal, it seems.'

'Really?'

'Surprising, right? Makes me jealous just thinking about it. Cola was in his forties at the time, Soda just thirty. They got all this money and went a bit crazy with it, buying expensive watches and luxury cars and so on. Nouveau riche to the extreme. But I guess people like feeling useful, so they started taking jobs here and there in the trade.'

'Huh.'

'Takes all kinds, right?'

'So, are these bubbly guys any good?'

'It seems Cola's the brains of the operation, keeping it all together like a CEO. But Soda, he's another story. How should I put it? It's like he's too pure for this world – naïve, susceptible to swallowing whole anything anyone tells him. People assume he's a deep thinker because he dresses like an artist, but the reality is, there's nothing deep about him. Competent Cola and Simple Soda.'

'Simple Soda.'

'I only know what I've been told, but it seems he's quick to give people money when they're in a bind, or to try to save animals in trouble, to help kids with rare diseases, things like that.'

'That doesn't sound so bad.'

'He's easily taken in by scammers, is the problem. *This beetle has hay fever, we have to do something!* Things like that.'

'I see. You have to distinguish the real from the fake.'

And so it was that Nanao ended up working with Soda three years ago.

'Cola's busy with another job, so it'll be just him,' said Maria.

'I don't know how I feel about working with someone so gullible.'

'Don't worry. It's a safe and easy job.'

Maria was giving him the same old song-and-dance as always, but, shockingly, this particular job really did turn out to be safe and easy.

It was after the job that things became unsafe and difficult. Nanao had needed to kill some time while Soda was busy setting up some explosives, so he went over to where a local festival was taking place and bought some yakitori from a food stand. He brought it back to the car to eat, and when Soda returned, he'd looked over at Nanao and, eyes shining, said, 'Man, nothing hits the spot after a job better than some yakitori!' Begrudgingly, Nanao ended up handing over a few sticks to share.

The problem was, the yakitori was undercooked. The food stand's grill wasn't hot enough, maybe, or the vendor inadvertently put the meat on a cold spot. Needless to say, raw chicken is bad news. It can host campylobacter. The incubation period of that particular bacteria is long, so five days passed before Nanao got sick.

He ended up spending days in bed, plagued by classic food poisoning symptoms.

Later, as Maria was passing along some 'trade rumors,' he learned that Soda had suffered a similar fate.

'He had food poisoning, but it seems he felt he needed to do the job anyway. Things went south fast. You need total precision when you work with something as delicate as a bomb, after all.'

Thinking back to when he spent half of every day on the toilet, Nanao had to admit that Soda deciding to do a job in that condition was a bit heroic.

'It was a disaster – an unexpected explosion occurred, and Soda ended up in critical condition. The client's upset, of course, and Cola's going out of his mind. Everyone's talking about it.'

'I can't help but feel responsible,' said Nanao, shocked that his yakitori had resulted in such bad fortune. 'I hope he doesn't hate me for it.'

'All you can do is pray.'

And now here's the man himself, getting on the same elevator as him!

What are the chances? Nanao feels like crying out to the heavens, but on the other hand, shouldn't he be used to this kind of bad luck by now? Moreover, he managed to slip out of the elevator and evade him – that, at least, was a nice move.

All he has to do is wait for the elevator to descend, carrying Soda away with it. He can kill a little time, then press the button to call another one. Or he could take the emergency stairs.

Nanao turns, intending to walk down the hall to the west. Looking back one last time, though, he sees that the elevator doors are still open.

Soda's standing there, his eyes fixed on Nanao. His finger's pressing a button in the elevator to keep the doors from closing.

His expression is that of a man looking up at an unidentified object flying through the sky, thinking, *Could it be? A UFO?* The moment Soda's eyes meet Nanao's, though, he springs into action, leaping out of the elevator as if to say, *I knew it!*

Nanao considers turning tail and running away, but he knows it would do neither of them any good to raise a ruckus. Instead, he raises a hand in an attempt to stop the other man from drawing any closer, saying, 'Wait a second—'

But to no avail.

'Wait a second – we need to be quiet!' Nanao's voice is purposely hushed. 'No violence! Let me explain!'

A significantly taller man than Nanao, Soda extends his long arms, going for Nanao's neck. Exactly the same plan of attack as the man in Room 2010. Is this the day he's meant to get his just deserts for all the necks he's snapped in the past?

Nanao leaps past Soda, kicking against the wall and pushing off so he ends up behind the other man. Did he drop his glasses? But there's no time to worry about that. He presses up against Soda's back and wraps his arm around his neck. But he refrains from breaking it – after all, another corpse would represent nothing more than yet another problem to solve.

It takes almost no time at all. A guest could emerge from a room at any time. He compresses the other man's neck with just enough force that, after a few beats, he loses consciousness.

Then, the elevator sounds. Nanao hurriedly stands Soda up, wrapping an arm around his shoulders. A group of five pour out of the elevator, guys in their twenties it looks like, walking and talking companionably down the hall as they make their farewells – 'All right, this is me! I'll see you at dinner!' – before splitting into two groups and disappearing into the two rooms in front of them.

Lucky bastards! Nanao finds himself thinking. *Able to stay all together in a fancy hotel like this downtown.*

Then he sighs and steps forward. His foot comes down unpleasantly on something. There's a crunching sound, like a phone breaking under his heel. And in fact, that's what it is – he's stepped on his own phone. And broken it. He can see the shattered screen even before he bends down to pick it up.

KAMINO

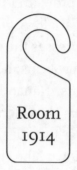

Room
1914

'WHAT NOW?' ASKS YUKA KAMINO. 'What can I do?'

Koko's at her tablet, playing it like an instrument. 'For now, you can have some tea.'

She sounds so carefree that Kamino first assumes she's joking, but she's serious. 'Look in my bag, there should be some instant herbal tea in there. Heat up some water and have a cup. There's lavender and chamomile, take your pick.' She looks up at Kamino and adds, 'Right now, your most pressing task is to get ahold of yourself.'

As if anticipating Kamino objecting that a cup of tea will hardly do anyone any good at this point, Koko continues. 'There's a little aromatherapy bottle in there too. Give it a sniff if you want. I know it might seem impossible to relax, but it won't do any good to run around like your head's cut off either. It's difficult to banish worries and upset from your head, but you can trick your body with a cup of something warm or a nice soak in a hot bath. If nothing else, try taking some deep breaths.'

'Deep breaths?'

'Deep breathing and stretching can be surprisingly effective!'

Kamino gets up and reaches into Koko's luggage, pulling out a teabag. The water in the kettle is already hot.

Kamino remains standing as she brings the cup, now full of hot herbal tea, to her lips.

'The first thing I'm going to do is connect to the security camera system and check for any images of you. We want to erase as many traces of you as possible. Inui surely has contacts all over. Your cover might be blown at any moment.'

Koko sits at the table, 'clickety-clacking' away on the tablet's keyboard. Not even ten minutes pass before she softly says, 'We're in. The security system here is as new and top-of-the-line as you might expect, but I managed to – well, here you go. This is the control screen.'

Koko turns the tablet toward Kamino. The screen is split into multiple images, each showing a different view. It looks to Kamino like the kind people in convenience stores use to foil hold-ups. The views in each section of the screen change every few minutes.

'There are cameras in the hallways on each floor, on the ceiling above the elevators, on the ceiling *in* the elevators, in the lobby, and over the front desk. You can easily see the areas where people go in and out, as well as the underground parking garage.' Koko guides Kamino through the camera views as if introducing a tourist to the famous sites in a city. 'Press this to flip between the views. You can also set a view so it *doesn't* change, if you want to keep a steady eye there.' Koko deftly demonstrates the various functions.

'So this is showing what's there right now?'

'These are real-time feeds, yes. But they simultaneously record what they show. I want to look through those files and see where you show up, Kamino-chan.' Koko takes back the tablet and starts clacking away again. 'Remind me – what time did you check in yesterday?'

'Just past 3 p.m.'

She'd started the process right after check-in time had begun. By using the self-service terminal at the edge of the front desk, she didn't have to interact with the staff at all.

'So, we should be safe if I check the data from the camera system from just before three until just after. It looks like the feed is split up into hour-long files as it's saved. I'll have to play them back to find you, so sit tight – it might take a while. I also think it would be best for you to stay in this hotel for a few more days, Kamino-chan. I'll use that time to set up a new place for you to live and a way to get you enough money to cover living expenses. I'll make sure there are plenty of places you can use to make cashless transactions, so you should be able to get by.'

'You can do all that?'

'One can do almost anything playing around with data. Say you wanted to go work at a famous *pâtisserie* – I could provide you with the appropriate CV and background to get you the job.'

'Background?'

'I can use the internet to give you a work history so rich and varied, they'd be fools not to hire you. When they conduct their own research to authenticate your claims, they'll land on sites and info I've put there.'

Kamino has her doubts that all this would really go so smoothly, but on the other hand, it may very well be that this is how the world works. 'So I don't have to change my face?'

'Your face? You mean plastic surgery?'

'I thought a full life-reset might involve that, too . . .'

She finds herself on the verge of imagining Inui peeling the skin from her face. She hastily shakes the image off. She mustn't let herself think things like that. Once the picture's painted in her head, it'll remain there always, never to be banished.

'We can change your look quite a bit with makeup and wigs; security cameras are easily fooled. So there's no need to do anything drastic right away. Of course, if there's a real danger you'll be recognized – if you're very likely to come in contact with people who know your face well – then we'd have to look into getting you under the knife quick. It's a case-by-case thing. If we decide to do it, I can introduce you to some clinics I know. Though they aren't necessarily the best, I admit.'

The sight of Koko sitting before her tablet, tapping away at the keyboard, is so peaceful and comforting that Kamino finds herself reminded of how she would feel watching her mother fold laundry. The tension of the past two weeks slowly loosens its grip on her body. Her shoulders relax, allowing her to feel for the first time how clenched she's been. She reaches up to massage her shoulder with one hand.

Are your shoulders stiff, Kamino-chan?

She remembers Inui coming up to her once, quick to massage her. She'd recoiled slightly at his touch, but he was so casual about it that she soon relaxed, and eventually had to admit that he was, in fact, quite skillful.

After she thanked him, he said, 'I've studied both massage and *seitai* acupressure, it comes in handy dealing with older politicians and businesspeople. Getting a little skin-on-skin access with a quick massage!' She couldn't tell if he was joking or not as he said this, laughing.

Is that—? She's imagining again. *If the rumors about Inui are true, then he'd be well-versed in the inner workings of people's bodies, right?*

A little time passes, and then Koko speaks up. 'There you are, Kamino-chan. You're on camera. This is from yesterday, at precisely 3:18 p.m. The camera's the one in the hall in front of the elevators on this floor. It shows you going to your room right after check-in.'

Kamino gets up and walks over to stand beside Koko. Peering at the screen of the tablet on the table, she sees a view from what appears to be the ceiling. She imagined the images would be black-and-white, like the ones she's seen on the news, but they're full-color and quite sharp.

So, there she is. She's used to seeing herself straight-on, as she appears in her mirror, and so she finds this view of herself from above and to the side defamiliarizing, even discomfiting.

What's happened to her? Why is she in this situation?

She feels like she's watching herself from afar, a third party to her own predicament.

She should have been able to lead a normal, upstanding life, but instead, imprisoned by her ability to remember (or rather, her inability to forget), she'd ended up in crisis, her health damaged, unable to do things straightforwardly, with little choice but to work for Inui and lead a life she'd be hard-pressed to call 'upstanding' – and now, just look what's become of her.

Despite wanting to live a life free of wrongdoing, despite never trying to take a shortcut or get off easy.

She's never had even one true friend, not then, not now. But she can accept a life in which good things are few and far between. Her only wish is to avoid being subjected to horror.

Looking at herself onscreen, she can't help but feel sympathetic, even wanting to cheer herself on – *you can do it, girl!*

Koko taps at the keys, and the image begins to move. Yuka Kamino walks into the hallway, then disappears.

'After that, you went straight to your room, right? You didn't leave it again?'

'That's right.'

'Great. We'll just take care of this file, then.' *Clickety-clack* go her fingers, and then Koko draws up short: 'Ah!'

'What is it?'

'This,' she replies, pointing at the security camera footage as it plays. It shows a uniformed man in the hall in front of the elevators.

'This worker seems to have come out of the hallway you just went down. Do you remember passing him?'

Of course I do, thinks Kamino, nodding.

'I got off the elevator, and as I headed toward my room, I passed by this man, a porter. He must have tripped or something, because he cried out and fell down. I remember calling out to him, saying, 'Are you okay?' He had a name tag, too. It said Tanabe.'

Koko rewinds the footage and plays it again. It naturally doesn't include their interaction in the hallway, but Koko scrutinizes it anyway, as if watching events unfold invisibly somewhere within it. The porter is rubbing one hip as he walks up to the elevators, perhaps due to having just fallen.

'Do you remember talking about anything else with him?'

Of course I do. 'I asked him, "Which way is Room 1914?" I forgot to check the little floor map on the wall when I got out of the elevator, so I wasn't sure.'

'Oh my . . .' breathes Koko.

'Is that bad?'

Kamino feels dizzy, her vison darkening. It's terror, of course, but also a sense of profound injustice – why must misfortune keep piling up around her, no matter what she does? No matter how much she wants to never bother anyone, to simply live her life in the best, most respectable way she knows how?

Koko is silent for a moment. Then she pats Kamino on the shoulder, saying, 'Oh, I think it'll be okay.'

She continues, 'Look at your face! So worried. Be careful, or you might call down a plague god – he'll pop through the door like, "You rang?" Try smiling instead.'

Kamino tries her best to manufacture a happy face. It doesn't go well.

65

YOMOGI

The restaurant on the second floor

'YOUR *SAUMON MI-CUIT*, SIR, with French caviar. Please enjoy with the *endives braisées*.'

The waiter, in his white shirt and black bow tie and waistcoat, places the plate before Mitsuru Ikeo.

He's in the Winton Palace Hotel's French restaurant. The restaurant's mission statement goes on at length: *A careful attention to ingredients. An encounter between Japanese spirit and French technique.* As a reporter, he's used to sharing meals with interview subjects, but being in a restaurant so fancy nonetheless induces a certain nervousness. As does facing who he's facing across the table.

'So, Ikeo-san, you've only been at the Politics desk for three months? I don't remember seeing you around.' Director Yomogi is saying this to him now.

'Uh, yes. That's true. I was messing around in Sports before that.'

'*Newsnet* has quite a reach. More people read it now than read nationwide newspapers back in the day.'

'Is that so?' Ikeo trails off, swallowing his words.

The fact is, he's well aware of the influence wielded by *Newsnet,* the site he writes for, and how it has grown with each passing year. The way former colleagues and old friends from his previous job respond to him now makes that clear enough.

'Regular newspaper circulation is down because people think internet news is enough, but information online always includes some fake news, doesn't it? It's frightening to think of a world without a source of well-reported stories, but it's also hard to imagine a regular paper that could fill the gap. The difference in speed between print and online is too great. So, to have a site emerge like the one you work for, a site that takes reporting seriously and presents real news online, is something the whole country should be thankful for. I think politicians should grant you all the access your heart desires.'

Hearing the Director talk freely, even using the informal 'I' to refer to himself, puts Ikeo so at ease that he has to remind himself that the person he's conducting this one-on-one with is the Information Director of Japan. A director who, from the look of him, seems to be keeping up with his training; even a former rugby player like Ikeo is impressed. As he talks, his mobile, expressive face is boyish, as if he were still a strapping young man.

'Well, thank you. You know, I voted for you back when you first went up for election.' Ikeo decides to steer the conversation back to the opening gambit he'd thought up beforehand. 'My family's home was in your district. It was the first election I ever voted in. I was sixteen.'

Ikeo had figured that this would be an effective way to get in Yomogi's good graces.

'Oh really, is that so?'

And indeed, it seems his quarry's taking the bait.

'You know, that whole thing was such a shock. The train where the incident happened was one my classmates used to take all the time.'

This was the incident on the downtown train, with the knife-wielding man. A housewife and a man who was there with his small child ended up dying, and many more were seriously injured. Also on the train was Yomogi, forty years old at the time, and his personal assistant, Satō, who was a year younger.

Yomogi and Satō successfully subdued the attacker, but not without sustaining serious injuries themselves.

'If you hadn't been there, Director, there surely would have been many more people hurt or killed that day.'

'With Satō in a coma after the incident, I seriously considered pulling out of the election.' Yomogi glances over at Satō, who's enjoying the same *prix fixe* meal at an adjacent table.

Ikeo had suggested that they could all sit together, but the bespectacled Satō, with his air of studious diligence, had demurred, saying in a half-joking way, 'With both of us at the table, it would be like we were ganging up on you. Besides, I have to see Yomogi day in and day out, I'm tired of his face. I thought I'd be allowed to retire after he left Parliament, but here we are!'

Fifteen years ago, Yomogi was seen bursting into relieved tears upon receiving the news that Satō, in critical condition since the incident, had regained consciousness. The duo's relationship became fodder for the popular imagination, giving rise to various stories and even memes, but this only created a greater sense of intimacy between Yomogi and the general public.

'Even after you were elected, you never betrayed your supporters' expectations. You made me really feel it was worth it to vote. Thanks to you, I never missed another election!'

The fact is, while he does occasionally vote, Ikeo misses most elections. He's been busy with work since becoming a reporter, after all, but he's also always felt a bit foolish going to the trouble of voting with so many non-voters around him.

'Are you doing this interview just to flatter me, Ikeo-san? Did Satō put you up to this?' Director Yomogi's eyes narrow with merriment, making him seem almost like a high schooler.

'No, no, of course not,' replies Ikeo, waving away Yomogi's question. He knows there are few people who don't respond well to flattery, and politicians, in particular, respond to it better than most. 'Look, one of the things you're most known for is trying to change a political world dominated by older people. It seems to have been one of your most cherished missions.'

'I proposed a system that would bar anyone over fifty from voting, it's true. You can imagine how angry that made everyone!'

'Indeed.'

The edges of Director Yomogi's eyes crinkle even more. 'All I did was ask them to imagine for a moment: What it would be like if you lost your right to vote at fifty? People got so mad! "Don't you understand the Constitution? Don't you understand the principle of one person, one vote? Do you want to drive a wedge between the generations?" But what really shocked me were the older people who said, "If we do that, the elderly will be cut out of society!" Wasn't it really *them* pitting the old and young against each other? Younger people have a natural interest in helping older people live happy lives. In any case, I just wanted politicians to imagine, as a thought experiment, what it would be like if only people fifty and younger could vote. What would society be like? What sort of policies would be pushed? I wanted them to remember why they ran for election in the first place. But all I received for my troubles was opposition and pushback.'

'What with how the birth rate's falling, even if every young person in the country turned out to vote now, they might still be outnumbered by old people.'

Director Yomogi lowers his voice. 'Talking about this sort of thing is what makes people call me a troublemaker. It's something all living things – not just us humans – have had in common since the beginning of time, isn't it? We fight back the hardest when we think something rightfully ours might be taken away from us.' He laughs ruefully. 'Good thing I left politics.'

'Do you mean you're still trying to change Japan, just from another direction?'

In lieu of a response, Director Yomogi spreads his hands palms-down on the table, as if to hide whatever he might have in them.

The waiter returns, deftly whisking Ikeo's empty plate from the table and carrying it away.

THE SIX

The ground floor

ONCE THE SIX PILE OUT of the SUV in the parking garage beneath the Winton Palace Hotel, it's Kamakura who heads to the front desk. He's wearing a deliveryman's uniform and an unbecoming pair of glasses, a cardboard box with a delivery note stuck to its side tucked beneath one arm. The sticker bears the name and address of a well-known online shopping site, the name and address of the Winton Palace, and the name of the intended recipient: Yuka Kamino.

The other five of the Six are scattered around the hotel, connected via earpieces so they can communicate freely. The earpieces have mics in them that can pick up sound, enabling them to speak to each other without hooking up to a cell phone or any other device.

'Kamakura, do you read me? Ka-ma-ku-ra?' Heian is standing against the wall in the lobby with Nara, amusing herself speaking nonsense into her device. They're wearing different-colored suits. Wearing a suit is the best way to fly under the radar and

71

avoid suspicion. Suit jackets also tend to have hidden pockets, all the better for stowing blowguns and darts.

The man at the front desk is wearing a suit of his own, and, seeing Kamakura approaching, puts on a perfect professional smile to greet him, elegantly inquiring, 'And how may I help you today?'

The moment he meets anyone, Kamakura makes an assessment. Are they more attractive than him? Do they have something he wants? His head whirring with calculations, he makes his initial decision: would it be more effective to be dominant, or submissive? And if they're a woman, he makes another assessment: how susceptible to seduction might she be?

We're so lucky to have our looks. Both Kamakura and Asuka say this a lot. They're half-joking, of course, but they know there's truth to the sentiment as well. Or rather, Kamakura feels that his well-balanced features, his tall, trim frame, and his natural athletic ability are less things that make him 'lucky' than things that confer power.

'I'm good at sports without having to practice, girls have always come easy to me . . . the fact is, I'll always be happier than people of average looks and abilities, even if they work their whole lives trying to better themselves. And knowing that, well – it's delicious.'

'Looking at them working their asses off to make it through life makes me feel like I'm more advanced than them – a truly higher being. I even feel a bit guilty.'

'You do? Really?'

'No, not really. I've been blessed, what can I do about it? A reward for all the good I did in a past life, maybe.'

These were the kinds of conversations Kamakura and Asuka would have with each other.

'I have a delivery for someone. Is she staying here?' Kamakura places the box on the front desk.

'Please wait a moment.' The front-desk employee looks to be in his mid-twenties, his professional smile fixed firmly to his face as he begins accessing the system behind the counter.

Kamakura already holds him contempt. This man would never constitute a threat. He's nothing special, has nothing to distinguish him from anyone else. He can't hold a candle to Kamakura in terms of his face or body, and will surely go to his grave having never tasted the kinds of experiences Kamakura does as a matter of course – so thinking, Kamakura's brain floods with happiness.

It takes only a moment before the hotel employee looks back up.

'I'm very sorry, but Kamino-san does not appear to be here.'

'She's not here? Do you mean she's not here now? Or that she's not staying here at all?'

'She does not appear to be a guest at our establishment.'

'Is that so . . .'

So she's staying under a false name?

Kamakura thanks the man behind the counter and, replacing the box beneath his arm, leaves the desk. He knows the rest of the team were listening to the exchange through their earpieces.

'Kamakura, return to the car and change.' This is Edo's voice. 'Roger that,' he replies, heading for the elevator to take him down to the parking garage.

'Guess it's my turn,' says Asuka, resplendent in a suit of her own. She doesn't want people to remember her face too clearly, so she's wearing a pair of glasses. She makes eye contact with a porter who's standing at one end of the front counter. He's just returned after taking a pile of suitcases into the back using a large luggage cart. She hurries over to him, saying, 'Oh, excuse me, I know you're busy, but . . .'

The porter straightens his back at her approach. 'How can I help you?'

'The thing is, I'm looking for my sister. She's a guest here.'

Like Kamakura, Asuka's first instinct is to assess. Is this person more attractive than me? Do they have anything to offer? How is my appearance impacting them? Should I be aggressive with them, or would it be better to be sweet and accommodating?

The lean-framed porter is wearing a short jacket and a pillbox hat. He's seemingly in his mid-twenties, with the face of an elementary school student eager to do everything his teacher tells him to.

'I'm sorry to be so personal, but my sister ran away from home. I heard from one of her friends that she's staying here. But I can't get ahold of her. I don't want her to end up getting into trouble or causing trouble for the hotel, so I thought I'd try to at least get her a little bit of money, if nothing else. Do you think you might be able to tell me which room she's in? Or at least give her a call from the desk?'

'This is her,' adds Asuka, showing the porter a photo on her phone. The photo is, of course, of Yuka Kamino.

'That sounds like quite a situation, ma'am. Please wait a moment, I'll see what we can do.'

Seemingly sympathetic, the porter nods his head and walks toward the desk.

'Seems like a serious fellow,' whispers Asuka into her earpiece's mic.

'Everyone seems "serious" compared to you, Asuka.' This is Sengoku. Asuka doesn't reply.

How would the porter respond to her request? *Show me what you got*, she thinks, and then he returns, accompanied by a woman in a necktie.

The woman's wearing a name tag as well: *Akané Hara, Manager*.

74

'Akané Hara, Manager.' Asuka reads it aloud for the benefit of the team.

'I hear you are looking for your sister. Can you tell me more about your situation?' The woman is smiling, obviously intending to reassure, but her manner is crisp and professional. *A proper manager who manages things properly*, thinks Asuka. And now the assessment: in terms of face and style – everything immediately visible – Asuka's the clear winner. This woman may have never been propositioned by anyone of the opposite sex her whole life. *Poor thing*, thinks Asuka, laughing inwardly.

She shows the photo on the phone to the manager. She invents a name for her on the spot. 'When I heard my sister's staying here, I came over right away! But I don't know what room she's in. I do know one thing, though: she doesn't have the money to stay in a hotel as nice as this. Do you think you could tell me if she's here, or what room she might be in?'

Ms. Hara's expression is filled with sympathetic worry, as is her professional obligation. 'That sounds like a very difficult situation.' Her expression arouses Asuka's hatred; she suppresses, barely, a sudden urge to punch her in the face.

Ms. Hara continues, her tone full of regret, 'But I'm afraid that divulging information about our guests is something I cannot do.'

'What if I give you my sister's name and my number? Then you can get in touch with me if anything comes up.'

'Of course,' says Ms. Hara, nodding deeply, and then she produces a pen and paper out of thin air and hands it to Asuka.

Asuka writes down the name she fabricated for her 'sister,' assigning characters to the syllables on the fly. She writes down a phone number. Then, she pulls out her phone and shows Kamino's photo to the manager one more time, so as to reinforce the image in the other woman's mind.

'Of course,' says Ms. Hara again. How sincere is this woman?

Did she really take the request to heart? Asuka has regrets – *I screwed up!* Now she wishes she'd gone with another story besides *My sister doesn't have much money*. Something like *My sister has a terrible disease* or *There's a chance my sister will cause trouble to your other guests*. Something with a heightened sense of danger might have made the management nervous enough to respond more urgently.

But it's too late now; adding more details would seem suspicious. She simply thanks Ms. Hara and leaves the scene.

'Excuse me.'

Asuka is heading back to the lounge to rendezvous with Edo and the others when she hears a voice behind her. She turns and sees the porter she first approached standing there.

Asuka braces herself, thinking she's been made, but the porter, back as straight as a Queen's Guard, lowers his voice and says, 'I think your sister's staying here.' He looks around, keeping an eye on his surroundings. His name tag reads *Tanabe*.

Asuka voicelessly prompts him to continue.

'I brought some luggage up to the nineteenth floor for a guest, and as I was returning, I tripped and fell.' The porter describes the incident as if describing a huge, unforgivable error. His ears are red with embarrassment. 'There was someone walking toward me from the elevators just then – it was your sister, I'm sure of it. She kindly asked if I was all right, so I remember her clearly.'

'Really?' Asuka brings her hand to her mouth, performing the surprise and excitement of someone witnessing a miracle.

Seeing her so excited, the porter blushes more. It's a common occurrence for people confronted with Asuka's beauty, especially men, to lose themselves in it, forgetting what they were doing or what they were going to say.

After a moment, the porter manages to return to himself. 'The hotel has a duty to protect guests' information, so it can be very inflexible,' he explains. 'But you don't strike me as a bad person. Please think of this as simply one concerned individual sharing information with another.'

'My savior!' Asuka exclaims. She doesn't know whether she'll be able to pull off seeming so happy that she can't help but jump up and down right then and there, but she decides to give it a try. She follows this up by pressing her hands together as if in prayer and bowing. *You're my guardian angel, my knight in shining armor, sent from heaven to save me!* Thinking these things to herself, Asuka manages to manufacture an expression of overwhelming gratitude.

Her over-the-top performance pays off. Seemingly craving further thanks, the porter offers more info. 'She's staying in Room 1914.' There's a twinkle in his eye. 'When we passed in the hall, she asked which way her room was. It's the year the First World War began, so it stuck in my head.'

Asuka works to open her eyes even wider. Is she laying it on too thick? Will he grow suspicious? But she has no need to worry.

'I'm just happy I could be of service.'

This porter! Going out of his way to tell her all this out of a sense of duty to help. Asuka suppresses the urge to laugh at his stupid honesty.

He walks away with his head held high, every inch the hero who just saved the day, leaving Asuka to whisper into her mic as she watches him go, 'Did you get all that?'

'Room 1914.'

'What a proper porter!'

'So, Edo, what's the plan? Who's doing what?'

'First World War, huh? Well, whatever works . . .'

BLANKET

Two days ago, in a different hotel

BLANKET AND PILLOW, their work done in Room 'For-One-Life,' take the employee elevator back down to the first basement level of the Tokyo Vivaldi Hotel and emerge into the underground parking garage. They push the cleaning cart all the way to the back of the garage where a large van awaits them, and then pull the corpse out of the cart and put it in the van. The side of the van is emblazoned with the name and logo of a cleaning company that doesn't exist.

Blanket and Pillow spent their high-school days seeing each other at every basketball practice. Just as they predicted as first-year students, they devoted themselves to attending every practice without fail, diligently polishing their skills at defense and making three-point shots, only to receive almost no chances to play in any actual games. Pillow would complain vociferously while Blanket would nod, saying, 'You're so right,' but neither quit the team, practicing and commiserating together until, before they knew it, graduation day arrived.

Blanket and Pillow both went to trade school, Pillow to become a hospitality worker, Blanket to become a systems engineer, and so their relationship necessarily became more distant, though after trade school was done and they both found employment, they'd occasionally run into each other on their way to their respective jobs and sit next to each other on the subway.

During one such chance meeting, they got so carried away seeing each other again after so long that they decided to leave the subway together and go to a nearby izakaya, only to realize after they sat down that neither of them drank. 'We should have gone to a coffee shop!' they said, while at the same time inwardly appreciating that they had discovered yet one more thing they had in common. This sense of connection only deepened as they realized that they both had lost their parents, though at different times, and that neither of them had any other family save for some distant relations.

'Listen to this. You won't believe it,' said Pillow. Her conversational habits hadn't changed at all, it seemed.

'I don't want to, but I will.'

'So, at the hotel where I work, one of the workers was making fun of a senior colleague for never having had a boyfriend.'

'That seems pretty believable, actually.'

'But why should that be a reason to make fun of someone? I've never had one either, but it's not because I've done anything wrong – I've just lived my life normally, like anyone! Why should I be made to feel like a criminal or something? It's no different than if someone's never eaten ice cream.'

'Maybe it's exactly like that – that people are like, *What, you've never tasted it? But it's so delicious!* I mean, I've never had a boyfriend either. What of it, right? Though perhaps it makes people think you lack something, like you aren't attractive enough for a member of the opposite sex to pay attention to you.'

'I don't know. Is that why people don't get into relationships?

Because they're not attractive enough? I think the question is more, is being attractive how people get in relationships? I have my doubts. I think they just like playing along. Some people are good at the whole love thing and some aren't, simple as that. But anyway, the other thing that puzzled me was how ashamed my coworker seemed to be about having no boyfriend experience! When I piped up and said that I'd never had a boyfriend either, the guy who'd made fun of her seemed to get interested in *me* all of a sudden.'

'I've had similar things happen to me.'

'There were girls like that at school, too, right? Strutting around because they had a college-age boyfriend.'

'Were they really strutting?'

'But why do people act like you need to be in a relationship to have a full life? Where does that image come from? You could be with a guy who hits you! Everyone acts like the most important thing in life is to be popular with the opposite sex, but why?'

'Why? How should I know?'

'Now that I think about it, this whole thing really works to the advantage of older guys.'

'How so?'

'If girls end up getting ridiculed if they aren't with someone, then there's pressure on them to try to fix the situation. So then these guys swoop in. *You should get some experience, I can help with that.* Lines like that. But I think I get it. There's instinct at play, too, the animal drive to fill the world with your offspring. So we set up this whole system to push you to fall in love as quickly as possible and have babies. A form of brainwashing.'

'Maybe it's capitalism.'

'Huh?' Pillow was at a loss.

'Humans are animals that always strive to attain higher status than others. Capitalism uses this tendency to its advantage, or maybe it's more like an extension of it. Nice clothes, a fancy home, how you look – your height, the size of your chest – the whole economy is filled with goods and services to make you feel superior by making others feel inferior! If you trace the impulse to make fun of someone by saying, *What, you don't have a boyfriend?!* back to its source, you'll find capitalism there, its eyes glittering. *Do it! Make fun of her! Get her to spend more money on herself!'*

'Capitalism has eyes?' Pillow asked this with a serious look on her face. Then she continued, 'I guess, though, if everyone was happy living their lives at the level they're at now, no one would ever buy anything beyond their most basic needs.'

'The fact is, I don't really want anything more than I have.'

'Me neither.'

'I wonder if this is something that also makes us different, though. People spend money on things for reasons besides wanting to attract a lover. Anime figurines, for example. Or video games.'

They left the izakaya soon after, and it was when they got to the subway station that it happened.

The two girls were walking along the platform when a man came up behind them and bumped hard into Pillow. She lost her balance and fell to the ground, but the man continued walking as if he hadn't noticed.

'Hey! Wait a minute!' After making sure Pillow wasn't hurt, Blanket angrily pursued the man. Pillow got up and followed.

It was hard to tell how old the man was, but he was clearly in shape as he plunged through the late evening crowd, bodychecking several more people along the way.

'It looks like he's deliberately targeting people smaller than him!' said Pillow, jogging slightly to catch up.

'Even if he's running into them by accident, he's being a real shit about it.'

People stared at him in shock after he ran into them, their

81

eyes like daggers, but the man paid them no mind at all, leaving them to stand vibrating with anger in his wake.

In the end, Blanket and Pillow were unable to keep up with the man, and lost sight of him in the crowd.

Several days later, Blanket was reading the news online when she came across an item that brought her up short. A woman had died on the stairs of a subway station. She'd been pregnant, and someone had run into her, making her lose her balance, and while a nearby woman noticed and tried to help her, she was too late, and the pregnant woman tumbled down the stairs.

She got a call from Pillow right away.

'It's that guy! From the other day! The surveillance footage was blurry, but I'm sure it's him. It's not far from where we were.'

'That's true . . .'

'I wonder what kind of crime that would be.'

'What do you mean?'

'If he ends up arrested, I mean. The woman he bumped into was pregnant. But even if it's clear that the domino effect he started resulted in two deaths, he could easily claim he wasn't the direct cause.'

'That's probably how it would go.'

'Right?'

'It's unlikely that guy will get arrested at all, actually.'

'It's so fucked up.'

It was several days later when the subject of the Bumping Man came up again. It was a day of destiny, when the course of both their lives ended up changing forever.

It all started when Blanket got a call from Pillow. It was nine o'clock at night, so Blanket was at home, but Pillow was working at the hotel.

'I found him. I couldn't forgive him. So I did it.'

Blanket didn't understand Pillow's words at first. All she could think of was the message Julius Caesar sent after victory in battle: *Veni, vidi, vici* – I came, I saw, I conquered.

Pillow explained: she had discovered that the Bumping Man was a guest at the hotel where she worked.

'Really? But he bumped you from behind; how could you be sure it was him?'

'He said so himself. He bragged about it!'

'He did?'

'I ran into him in the hallway, and before I knew it, I was confronting him about it.'

'What did you say? *Oh, hello, are you the Bumping Man?*'

'I thought he'd deny it, but he didn't! He even bragged about how someone died because of what he did. I told him I'd call the police, and he told me to go ahead and try, he didn't care.'

'How could he not care?'

'I'd heard enough. I couldn't forgive him.'

I couldn't forgive him. So I did it. Blanket recalled how the conversation had begun with those words. 'What did you do?'

'I used the master key to enter his room.'

'That's so dangerous!'

'I found him sleeping and put a pillow over his face. I pressed down as hard as I could.'

Blanket's breath caught in her throat. She felt a sudden tightness in her chest. Less out of horror at Pillow's actions than out of sympathy for her feeling that she had no choice but to do what she did.

Blanket wished Pillow hadn't had to do it. 'That's so dangerous,' she repeated softly.

'He woke up and leapt out of bed. Then he hit me.'

'Oh my god! Are you okay?'

'Sure. He had no idea how many times I'd evaded opponents ten times my size, dribbling a ball all the while. Never let your guard down around the little guys.'

'Where are you?'

'Still in his room.'

That's when Blanket understood. The reason why Pillow was able to talk so freely with her was because the man was no longer a threat; the possibility that he might come back and attack her had been reduced to zero.

'Stay there. I'm coming right now,' said Blanket. She flew from her home to the hotel.

And that was that. From then on, Blanket and Pillow were forced onto a path to the dark side, never to return to their normal lives again.

As Blanket gets in the van with the fake cleaning company's name on its side and starts the engine, Pillow's phone begins to ring.

'It's Inui. I bet it's because we mentioned those rumors about him.'

Blanket nods. It's true they'd been talking about them before they did the job in Room 415.

Pillow puts the phone on speaker, then answers. A carefree, lighthearted voice begins to speak. 'Hey guys, I have another little job I'd like you to do if you don't mind.'

'You know we're not your employees, right?'

'Of course! And you know I'm your benefactor, right?' Inui laughs.

'It seems like you should recognize that we've done more than enough by now to repay your charity.'

Blanket and Pillow have done plenty of jobs for Inui already, though nothing too dangerous or difficult. So they have little to complain about.

But the rumors persist, so they try to keep their distance.

Inui getting his hands on someone, anesthetizing them, and then, once they're unconscious, taking them apart. Not for any reason beyond finding it 'fun.'

'I'd never forgive myself if you ended up taken apart like that!'

'The wisest man keeps himself the furthest from danger.'

'You'll never be punished by a god you never pray to.'

'We must braid the rope before we try to catch the thief.'

Blanket and Pillow had exchanged aphorisms as they came to the conclusion that they should try to get away from Inui as soon as they could.

'I'm not telling you to do this as my employees! I'm just making a friendly request. I have a job that needs to get done ASAP.'

Blanket cuts to the chase. 'You want us to find that woman?'

Inui's reply is equally curt. 'Go to the Winton Palace Hotel right now.'

NANAO

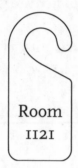

Room
II2I

'LADYBUG, YOU'RE MISTAKEN. You think I hate you? Why would I? If anything, it seems like you hate me!'

Soda says this with an exasperated sigh from his seat on the sofa. Nanao stands in front of him, his nerves stretched to their limit, ready for him to leap up and attack again at any moment.

After knocking him out in the hall, Nanao was left holding Soda's limp body in his arms and wondering what to do with it until, in a stroke of luck, he came across a keycard in the unconscious man's pocket. He started trying it on the doors of the rooms around him, and it was the door of Room II2I, the second from the end of the hallway, that ended up opening.

He dragged Soda's body into the room and sat him up on the sofa.

He meant to leave him there and escape, but, thinking it would be best to tie him up just in case, Nanao was still in the room searching around for something to use as rope when Soda's eyes popped open.

Nanao clucks his tongue with irritation, then leaps toward the sofa, ready for battle.

Soda raises his hands to ward him off. 'Stop, stop! What's your problem? You sure like to play rough, don't you!' His face distorts, and he reaches for his right leg with his left hand, whining, 'Owww . . .' Nanao didn't notice at the time, but it seems Soda must have twisted an ankle during their struggle.

'Is it broken?' he asks, to which Soda answers, his brow furrowed, 'I don't know . . . You know, if this were a soccer game, you'd owe me a penalty kick.'

'Only if we were in the penalty area.'

'Weren't we? Anyway, you really took me by surprise. To think Ladybug would be so violent . . .'

'You attacked me! You were trying to kill me!'

'Me? Why would I? It's you who has it in for me!'

Nanao knows, as a professional himself, that the best way to get out of a sticky situation is to turn the tables on your opponent, to overturn their assumptions and destabilize them, so he can only assume that Soda's putting on a show by acting so innocent.

'Why do you think I have it in for you? You mean the food poisoning?'

'Of course!'

'That wasn't on purpose! How could I have known that yakitori was raw? I heard it caused major trouble for you on a job . . .'

'I was so worried about my stomach, but it was the bomb that blew up instead.' Soda turns his head to the side. Nanao can see burns running down his neck toward his back. 'Cola was so mad. I had to go to the hospital and everything.'

Nanao remembers reading on the internet that campylobacter

poisoning can lead to Guillain–Barré syndrome if it happens more than once.

'I ended up recovering, but the process was long. I had a lot of time to think. To borrow Cola's words, I "engaged in self-reflection." '

'I'm not sure those are really *his* words—'

'Recovery gave me time to read a proper book for the first time in my life. I read a bunch of them – self-help books. To get to know myself. One was called *Go Your Own Way!* and this other one was called *Live for Others!* I was so confused, I didn't know which to believe. But then I read them and it was clear: I should *go my own way* while *living for others.* Simple as that.'

'Is that . . . possible?'

'You know Cola and I are rich, right?'

'Maria mentioned something to that effect. Though it's rare to hear someone call *himself* rich.'

'That's because Cola and I, we're nouveau riche. Proper rich people never show it off – in fact, they don't even actually think they're rich. But people like us, who get a bunch of money all at once, we're different.'

'You really see yourself objectively.'

'I realized that there comes a point at which you have so much money, there's no real way to use it.'

'That's a line I'd like to get a chance to use myself. I'll start practicing now.'

'We bought all the expensive watches and shoes and cars we could at first. But it wasn't satisfying. You only can only wear two watches max when you leave the house, after all. You can only wear one pair of sneakers at a time; you can only drive one car at a time. Having so many of these things began to seem meaningless. We had money and could buy anything we wanted, but we couldn't really *use* it.'

'You wear two watches at once? One on each wrist?'

Soda laughs. 'Not anymore. It felt like it made time go by twice as fast.' He rolls up his sleeves to show Nanao. His left wrist has an elegantly elongated rectangular-faced watch wrapped around it. 'I love the design of the numbers on this one,' Soda explains, excited.

'I won't ask how much it cost.'

'Special order, special price.'

'You didn't happen to read a book called *Give Your Expensive Watch to Whoever's Standing in Front of You*, did you?'

'I don't think I got to that one,' Soda says, smiling. 'Anyway, I began wanting to help others, and that's when my urge to do a job came back. It was that raw chicken that allowed me to find my purpose again! And it was you who gave me that chicken, and that opportunity, Ladybug – if anything, I should thank you.'

'But didn't you go for my neck back there? How is that "living for others"?'

'All I wanted to do was thank you.' Soda seems genuinely upset that Nanao might think otherwise.

'That's not what it looked like.'

'Maybe I was just too excited running into you, Ladybug. Like how kids get overstimulated and act strangely. Cola says that a lot, that I'm like a child. I'm on a job anyway, so I didn't have much time. I felt like I needed to hurry up if I wanted to get a chance to thank you properly.'

'You're on a job? Here?'

As he says this, Nanao remembers something important.

Maria.

He needs to deliver the message that her theater seat is a trap. She is, of course, a longtime member of the profession (even if she's just a handler who leaves the dirty work to others), so she should be more alert to potential danger than your average

89

citizen. Even if someone tries to attack her, she may very well manage to escape.

Thinking it through, though, Nanao has doubts. She's too habituated to leaving things up to people on the ground like him, and she's enjoying a 'break' from her 'busy schedule' – it seems just as possible she'll be caught unawares when trouble comes for her directly.

He has no choice. He has to warn her.

But his phone is busted. Unease washes over him. He feels twitchy and restless.

'What am I gonna do? Cola's gonna be so mad at me . . .' Soda's expression is forlorn, but then he suddenly brightens. 'Right!' He raises his voice to get Nanao's attention. 'Say, Ladybug, do you think you could do me a favor?'

'A favor?'

'I was actually heading to Cola's room when we ran into each other. The plan was for me to wait here until he contacted me, but he never did. I send him messages but he doesn't respond, and even when I call him, he never calls back. I need to know what's going on. Could you go check on him for me?'

'Why don't you go yourself?'

Soda pulls a sad face and points at his ankle. 'It hurts too much. I can't walk.'

'Really?'

'I just know Cola's gonna be mad at me. He's never late, so I'm worried something might have happened. And if something happened, it'll make him even grumpier. If I show up with my ankle like this, he's gonna get so mad.'

'You think I want him mad at me instead? I'm sorry I injured you, but I have things I need to do, too.'

'Word is, there's an assassin-killer on the scene now. I can't help but worry that maybe something like *that* might have happened to him.'

'Assassin-killer?'

'You might want to pay more attention to what's going on in the trade, Ladybug.'

'I'll try.'

'There's been a series of professionals found murdered. Both shoulders dislocated.'

Nanao reflexively glances at his own shoulders, first right, then left.

'This assassin-killer was active before, apparently. Cola told me. The professionals' arms get dislocated, then they're tortured to death. Leaves a bad taste in my mouth – toying with helpless victims like that.'

'So you're saying this assassin-killer's back?'

'Could be the same person, could be a copycat. No one knows for sure.'

'Fashion trends come back that way too, in cycles.' Nanao's answer is purposely evasive, as he's already decided to leave. He turns his back on Soda on the sofa and heads toward the door.

His gaze lands on a suitcase sitting beside the door. At first he thinks pieces of clothing are haphazardly sticking out of it, but, looking closer, he realizes it's covered with a multicolored array of small objects. *What on earth?* He looks away, but then can't help but look again.

'They're lucky charms,' Soda explains. He must have sensed that something had caught Nanao's attention. 'One of my self-help books said I should take a greater interest in spiritual matters. Though another one said I shouldn't rely on religion to solve my problems.'

'Very enlightening.'

'So, I started making little pilgrimages to temples and shrines. I got into collecting charms and amulets. They're things you can't just buy, right? You have to actually go to a place on your own two feet to receive them.'

Some of the charms are a little bigger, others a little smaller, but overall they're basically the same size and shape. There are indeed some amulets among them. 'You bought all these?'

'Ladybug, these are not things you "buy" and "sell." You "bestow" and "receive" them.'

'I wonder if they fight among themselves.'

'Fight?'

'All these powerful objects from different temples and shrines, they might not get along – don't they conflict with each other?'

'Gods don't fight each other like that. They're charms – they're *charming*, just like it sounds. They confer luck and protection. And look! Unlike with shoes and watches, you can use all of them at the same time!'

'I see,' replies Nanao, though he doesn't really see at all.

'Anyway, Ladybug, do you know Koko?'

'Koko?' *Chanel?*

'She's like a one-woman Witness Protection Program. A little old lady hacker.'

There's a Charlie Parker song called 'Koko,' right? Nanao thinks. *Does that mean there's someone out there who goes by 'Donna Lee' as well? I bet there's even someone calling himself 'Oleo,' too, after the Sonny Rollins tune—*

'Koko's in this hotel right now, helping someone get out of a jam. She hired Cola and me as bodyguards.'

'Bodyguards?' Nanao points a finger at Soda. 'I thought you were an explosives guy.'

'She only asked us yesterday. And the fee she's offering isn't much. There aren't a lot of professionals willing to do a job on such short notice, especially one that doesn't pay well, right? But Cola and I just had a client cancel on us, so we were free, and we don't care that much about money. We can handle a little body-guarding, after all – we're better equipped for it than your average Joe, at the very least. I don't mean to toot my own horn, but Cola and I, we're known even among other professionals as guys able to handle ourselves, right? So we decided to try to help Koko out of a tight spot.'

'Besides, you have so many sneakers you can't wear them all.'

'Exactly,' says Soda, nodding solemnly and pointing at his own feet. The high-top sneakers he has on clash with his suit, but they surely come in handy when he needs to move freely or suddenly. Nanao's never seen the design before. He imagines they must be an exclusive, hard-to-come-by model.

'Limited edition. Well, in any case, Cola and I got rooms here yesterday.'

'You came the day before the job started?'

'We can case the joint a bit, and then, if anything comes up, we'll have a home base to go to. As well as a place to stow our stuff.'

'If you have so much money to throw around, you could buy me a phone.'

'Don't you have one?'

'I broke it just now.' Nanao pulls the busted piece of electronics out of his pocket to show Soda.

'Oh man! You should take better care of your stuff.'

Whose fault do you think it is that it's broken? But Nanao resists the urge to voice his thoughts. There's nothing to be gained from confrontation at this point. 'I always use burners, so it's not like there's a bunch of important data in it. But now I can't contact Maria.'

Checking the time, Nanao realizes that he has about an hour before Maria's show will start. Imagining her taking her seat and then being taken by surprise by whatever weapon whoever's sitting next to her might be wielding, Nanao's mood grows dark.

'Do you want to borrow mine?'

'Actually, I don't know her number . . .' The number and email address for communicating with Maria was contained in the phone. He hasn't even memorized it. He knows it would be unfindable via a Google search as well.

The only real way left to prevent the attack is to go to the theater and warn her in person. In other words, he needs to get out of this hotel as quickly as he can.

Anxiety washes over Nanao again, making him want to crawl out of his own skin to get away, but another voice inside speaks up reassuringly, telling him that everything will work out fine if he just calms down. Leaving a hotel is no hard task. Regular people, guests of the hotel, do it all the time. All he needs to do is avoid complicating things unnecessarily – all he needs to do is make conversation with Soda for a little bit, then leave.

And try not to think about the time when all he needed to do was get off a bullet train at a particular station and couldn't.

'Anyway, what were we talking about again? Cola's not responding to you?' The first thing to do is shift the conversation back to the subject at hand.

'It's Cola who's been talking to Koko about the job – without him, I don't know what I'm supposed to do! I was on my way to Room 2010 – that's where he's staying – to talk to him. But then I ran into you, and here we are.'

'Wait – what was that number again?' Nanao asks, hoping against hope he's heard him wrong, but when Soda replies, '2010,' it's no real surprise to realize he hasn't.

I've already been there! But of course he can't say that. Nor can he explain that he went there by mistake, as he was supposed to go to Room 2016, and ended up watching the man he met there lose his life.

He'd figured that the guy in Room 2010 might be a professional when he went for Nanao's neck, and it seems he was right. Now that he thinks about it, the guy *had* been wearing a super-expensive-looking watch that looked a lot like Soda's.

Soda beseeches Nanao again. 'Can't you please go to his room instead of me? Just to see what's going on?'

Nanao shakes his head: *No.*

'Oh shoot, I said it wrong!'

'Said what wrong?'

'I read in one of my books how to get someone to do something for you. You shouldn't say "do it!" – rather, it's more effective to say "don't do it!"'

'Is that so?'

'Okay, let's try this again. Ladybug, please *don't* go to Room 2010. I'm begging you!'

'Well in that case, no problem. I won't.'

Soda gets a quizzical look on his face, shaking his head and muttering, 'That's odd . . .'

'All right, fine. I'll go.'

'Really?' Soda's eyes light up.

'I'll go to Room 2010 for you. Cola will tell me what you should do next, and I'll relay the message.'

Nanao naturally has no intention of going to Room 2010. He tries to put a lid on the guilt boiling up within himself, inwardly repeating, *It's just a little white lie,* like a mantra.

I need to get out of here now! Out of this room, then out of this hotel! This is the sole desire animating him.

Nanao naturally wants to prevent Maria from being attacked at the theater, but even more than that, he's becoming increasingly convinced that there's something cursed about this hotel – he needs to escape it as quickly as possible to save himself as well.

'Thanks so much! Just tell Cola I asked you to check in with him in my place. If you could call me and let me know what's going on as soon as possible, I'd really appreciate it.'

Soda seems to have already forgotten that Nanao's phone is busted. A convenient untruth. 'I will, as soon as I get a chance.'

'Thank you. You're a good guy, Ladybug.'

'I wouldn't go that far—'

'A man at a temple once told me that this world contains within it both fortune and misfortune.'

'All I've ever seen out there is misfortune, to be honest.'

'It's so hard to receive good fortune. And so easy to lose it. All it takes is being ungrateful. Those who ignore the blessings they're given end up abandoned by fortune entirely.'

'I'll remember that.'

Nanao resists the urge to run out the door, forcing himself to walk slowly, casually, as he makes his exit.

Once out of the room, though, his pace quickens.

KAMINO

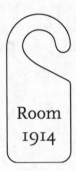

Room
1914

KOKO'S AT THE TABLE, tapping away at her tablet as she erases all
the security camera footage containing Yuka Kamino she can
find. 'It'll seem suspicious if I erase *all* the recordings,' she
explains as she carefully chooses each file and deletes it.
'So this might take some time.' Kamino sits patiently, watching
her work.

Some time passes, and then Koko exclaims, 'Oh!' Kamino
stands up and walks over, drawn by Koko's outburst.

'What's wrong?'

'There's been an unfortunate development.'

'Unfortunate?'

'I recognize these two.'

'Acquaintances of yours?'

'It could be just a coincidence, but . . .'

Koko turns the tablet so Kamino can see the screen. 'I'm looking through all the footage available,' explains Koko. 'This is the
feed from the camera mounted on the ceiling of the lobby. It's

live, not a recording. You're looking at what's happening down there in real time.'

Two women in pantsuits are standing against the wall near the lobby. One is small-statured and delicate, while the other is noticeably taller, with a hulking frame.

'You know them?'

'We can see two of them here, but there's a good chance their friends are somewhere around too. They're part of a team, called the Six. The ones we see here go by Heian and Nara. Nara's the big one – like the Great Buddha, right? Easy to remember.'

Kamino hardly needs the mnemonic, but decides not to say anything. 'What kind of group is the Six?'

'They do wind work.'

'Wind work? They play instruments?'

'Blowguns. Like this.' Koko demonstrates by making a tube with her hand and bringing it to her mouth, then blowing a short, strong puff of breath through it: *foo!* 'You put a dart – or really, more like a needle – in one end, and then blow it at your target. They make the tubes and darts themselves, apparently. Quite scary. They can hit their target in the blink of an eye. In the neck, in the face . . .'

Kamino reflexively brings a hand to her own throat as she listens.

'They have all sorts of darts: some that put you to sleep, others that kill you instantly. A rainbow of flavors to enjoy, you might say.'

'That kill you instantly?' Kamino finds she's now able to say the most horrible things quite casually.

'It's pretty clever, to be honest.'

'Clever how?'

'It's hard to get your hands on a gun in Japan, and harder still to walk around with one. Blades work, but you have to get close to your target to use them. That's where blowguns come in – they're not so big, making them easy to conceal, and you can dispose of them quickly if you need to.'

'Koko-san, have you actually met these people? You said you knew them . . .'

'I worked with them once. Only once, mind you. A terrible experience. I don't like to think of it even now.'

'Terrible . . . physically?'

Koko shakes her head. 'I found them repulsive. And felt guilty, too, having worked with them. All six are, on the outside, quite attractive. They say you shouldn't judge a book by its cover, but we all know the world doesn't work that way. If you look good, people will treat you well, like you belong to a special class – like you're better than everybody else. It's an advantage to be beautiful, right? No matter how people try to deny it. But the thing is, the Six think they really *are* better. They look down on everyone they meet, as if other people were no better than insects.'

'Really?' Koko's words sound like a joke to Kamino, and she wants to laugh – but Koko's expression is deadly serious.

'They treat their fellow humans like bugs, as if hurting them was no different than pulling the wings off a fly. They even seem to enjoy it.'

Kamino tries to imagine this group of blowgun-wielding sadists, but with little success.

'The worst was when we were actually on the job. It was a college party, with everyone drinking and having a good time, and they blew their darts into the scene. They purposely used a poison that drew out the suffering of their targets. Made me sick to watch, like if I worked with them any longer, the gods would punish me. So I left as soon as I could. It's not easy knowing there are people like that out in the world, you know? Much less six of them.'

'I can't believe . . .'

Kamino presses her hands to her temples. She can't believe

there are people out there who enjoy hurting others – but at the same time, hearing about the Six inevitably makes her think of Inui. In both cases, these are people who are not only completely indifferent to the suffering of others, but even take pleasure in it.

'Do you think that these, uh, *people* are in the lobby because of me?'

'I wonder. It's very possible Inui hired them to look for you. His network is vast, so he may well have gotten info on your whereabouts from somewhere. Oh dear, Kamino-chan, don't look so frightened! What we need to do now is get you out of this hotel as soon as possible.'

'What?'

'I know I said I'd keep you here for a while, but it seems we don't have that luxury anymore. If the Six are here for you, that's a worst-case scenario. We must act now, before they find out any more. You know what our one advantage is at the moment, right?'

'No – what is it?'

'That we know they're here. They don't know that yet. They're assuming you're just hiding out here in your room, unaware of their approach.'

Kamino nods, her face grave. She can't help thinking, though: *In a place like this, with staff and guests everywhere, it's hard to imagine a better way to take someone out than with a silent dart.*

THE SIX

The ground floor

YUKA KAMINO IS STAYING in Room 1914.

Having gotten this information, the Six regroup. It would attract attention if they huddled up physically, so they do so via their earpieces. Kamakura's back in the underground parking garage, changing out of his deliveryman uniform and into a suit inside the SUV, as they discuss their next move.

'Kamino's a civilian, right? And she doesn't even know we're here! I could go take care of her myself, alone,' says Asuka. 'I bet if I went to her door and rang the bell, she'd poke her head out to see who's there.'

'She's on the run. I think we can assume she won't just come to the door like it's nothing.'

'You worry too much, Heian.'

'I like to think ahead is all.'

'Anyway, Edo – do we have that thing with us?' Asuka redirects the conversation. 'That door-breaker thing?'

Kamakura knows what she's talking about. It's a tool that can open a door with a keycard reader, using a type of strong magnet to disable the sensor. It works on roughly eighty percent of the keycard-enabled doors in Japan.

'I'll give it to you once we're done here.'

'Then what are we waiting for? Let's finish this and go home already!' To Kamakura, it seems like a job that could be taken care of with a simple elevator ride up to the nineteenth floor.

'But listen, we have to think of the timing. This hotel has four elevators – what if she's going down in one while we're going up in another?'

Sengoku chimes in. 'Not only that, but she could easily decide to take the stairs instead.'

'Then let's send someone up the stairs! If they run into her, they can just nab her there!'

'Are you serious, Nara? I, for one, am not climbing nineteen sets of stairs for this . . .'

'Should we all go up, using different methods? Then one of us would definitely see her no matter how she tries to go down.'

Edo cuts in. 'This is how it's going to go. Asuka and Kamakura will ride the elevator up as a team.'

'Why them?' Nara pouts. *Does she want to do it herself?* wonders Kamakura.

'You and Sengoku are too big, people might notice you.'

'Don't judge people by their looks!'

'I have to! That's the way it works! In any case, Asuka, Kamakura: go up together to the nineteenth floor.'

'And me?'

'Heian, you'll keep an eye on the bank of elevators down here. Make sure Kamino doesn't pop out of one. Nara, you and Sengoku will do the same with the doors to the emergency stairs. There's one to the west and one to the east. If Kamino ends up coming out of one of them, I'll trust you'll be able to stop her. I'll go to the front desk and try to find Inui's mole. He's supposed to help us get access to the security camera system. Any objections?'

'I think I should be the one to go to the front desk,' says Heian. 'I'll arouse less suspicion than you, Edo-san.'

'You've got a point,' agrees Edo. 'All right, you go to the desk, Heian.'

Asuka and Kamakura ride up to the nineteenth floor, then get out of the elevator together.

'Why are hotels always so dimly lit?' muses Asuka. 'For the atmosphere?'

'Bright lights are exhausting. Hotels are to sleep in, right? That's why most people are here, they don't need any more light than this to get to their rooms.'

'It's so fucking quiet, too.'

'Sure is,' agrees Kamakura, sliding a hand into the inside pocket of his suit and withdrawing the small tube inside. His blowgun. 'Let's get this over with.'

'What, you've got a hot date after this? Anyway, I think we'll be done without breaking too much of a sweat. We just need to go to Room 1914 and grab her. Still, though, it feels good.'

'What does?'

'The porter who gave me her room number is definitely a Good Samaritan, right? He thought he was helping a damsel in distress find her sister, and that's why he made sure to tell me. Growing up, I bet his mom always told him to be kind to others. And now, as a result of that very kindness, Yuka Kamino's about to have something horrible happen to her. How fun is that? One nice person putting another nice person in danger. Like two idiots. And to think, all their good intentions were foiled by two not-so-nice people like us!'

'When you put it like that, it sounds so sad. That there are so many people out there who can only imagine getting through life by trying to be as *good* and *nice* as possible.'

'Okay, looks like 1914 is that way.' Asuka points left, following the arrows on the floor map posted on the wall in front of her.

'So, what are we supposed to do if she's really in the room?' Kamakura pitches his question to those listening in on his earpiece.

Edo's voice responds. 'Keep her there and make sure she keeps quiet. Don't let her escape. We'll head your way as quickly as we can. If she resists, feel free to inflict pain. All Inui told us was to deliver her with her head and mouth functional.'

'"Head and mouth," huh? I wonder what he wants out of her,' muses Asuka. 'He also said we need to avoid doing anything that would make the police show up.'

'Police would be a problem for sure. We need to fly under the radar. Keep us posted, all right?'

Kamakura and Asuka head down the hall side by side. Light fixtures mounted at regular intervals above their heads provide what little illumination there is. Five doors line the hall on their left, six to their right. It's completely silent, as if every sound were absorbed completely by the carpet and walls.

'What should we use?' asks Asuka in a hushed voice.

She means what kind of dart. Some paralyze the victims, others knock them out; some induce intense pain, others vomiting, then death.

'The knockout dart would be the easiest, but we're supposed to keep her mouth and head functional. So I wonder.'

'Maybe we should try to subdue her without darts.'

Kamakura has lost count of how many women he's been intimate with – indeed, he's completely uninterested in keeping track – but he's always loved the moment when a woman looks at him, despair in her eyes, and asks, 'Why are you doing this to me?' Nothing provides more pleasure for the betrayer than the look on the face of the betrayed. He doesn't know Kamino, and Kamino doesn't know him, but still he wonders: *Will I get to see her face as all hope dies, once and for all?*

Kamakura starts checking the numbers on the doors in the hall.

KAMINO

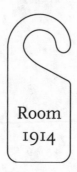

Room
1914

KAMINO STARES FIXEDLY AT KOKO as she goes about 'clickety-clacking' on the detachable keyboard set up on the round table in Room 1914. Koko, perhaps realizing that her expression has been awfully serious as she works, consciously softens her features and turns to Kamino, saying, 'These days, I specialize in this kind of "clickety-clack" work, but you know, ten years ago I didn't even know how to use a computer.'

'Really?'

'Life begins at fifty, they say!'

There's a world of difference between using a computer and becoming a hacker, thinks Kamino.

'My son is a pitcher, you see.'

'A pitcher? In baseball?' *Quite a change of subject . . .*

'That's right, a baseball pitcher. A pro.'

'A pro? What's his name?'

'Now Kamino-chan – that's confidential.'

It sounds like a joke, but she also knows Koko will never

actually tell her. Still, she hears herself asking, 'It is?' before she can stop herself.

'So, you know those baseball video games? The kind you play on your home system or on your phone?'

'Um, yes . . .'

'I tried playing one, and of course I chose my son's team to play on. Just as I expected, my son was the starting pitcher. The way these games work, they take all the stats on each player and load them into the game, but when I looked at my son's data I was shocked. My son's control was rated "E." In the game, "A" is the best and "E" is the worst. In other words, they were treating him like a pitcher with no control!'

'And that's not true in real life?'

'He's not an "E"! I mean, I can't say his control is *perfect*, he allows a lot of walks, but come on. He's at least a "D"!'

Sounds like a matter of opinion, thinks Kamino, but she decides not to say it. 'So, then what happened?'

'I talked to someone who knew the game better than me, and he told me that the stats are drawn from a database and then applied to each player in the game. Of course, I hardly even knew what a database was at the time, but I understood enough to know that somewhere in it, my son was rated "E."'

'You don't mean you—'

'So, all I had to do was get in the database and change the rating, right? And that's what put me on the path I'm on now. A shop in my neighborhood had a poster advertising an "Intro to Computing" course meant for old ladies like me, so I signed up and took it. That was step one. Then I bought a bunch of books and really got going. I started all this to help my son, but I also discovered I had a bit of a talent for programming, to the point that I became more and more obsessed with it. I'm a stubborn lady, you know? Very stubborn. And I had all the time in the world. I did a lot of internet research, too, staying up nights exploring the deepest, darkest parts of the Web. Even an old dog can learn some new tricks, right?'

How much of this story is true? Maybe she's just talking about her past to help lighten the mood. Kamino decides not to ask if she ever managed to go in and actually change her son's stats in the game.

'After that, I started taking jobs, thinking that now that I had this skill, I might as well use it to help people. People began relying on me to do things for them. Also, my husband had run up all these debts, so I felt compelled to take on more and more dangerous jobs to pay them off. It's scary, you know – once you step a foot into this world, there's no going back. You'd be surprised at some of the horrible stuff I've seen. Life can be a fearsome thing.'

As silly as it seems, it makes a certain amount of sense that Koko might have started down this road out of a simple desire to rectify her son's reputation. But it still isn't clear how that led to her becoming an expert in helping people restart their lives from zero to escape the trouble they've gotten themselves into.

'With your powers of memory, Kamino-chan, I bet you'd be great at computer work! Breaking codes and so on.'

'I don't know,' replies Kamino weakly. 'It's true I can easily memorize various codebreaking patterns, but you still need a certain spark of inspiration to really use them. And I'm afraid I don't have any talent for that at all.'

'I guess you have a point.'

'Inui was disappointed in me, too. The only types of codes I was good at breaking were super-simple ones, like acrostics.'

'Acrostics? Oh, you mean like those games you play at school, where the first parts of each line combine to form a message?'

'He laughed at me, saying I wear my gift like a pig wears pearls: uselessly.'

'It's awful to talk about people that way. As either useful

or useless, like they're just tools for him to pick up or throw away.'

That's true, thinks Kamino, but even as she does, she also thinks, *But I never really felt badly treated by him.*

She says as much to Koko, who shrugs in response, a sympathetic look on her face.

'You say that, but he made you memorize all those passwords, and now he's planning on erasing them by erasing *you*. You sound like a woman talking about her husband who beats her – saying, "Oh you know, he's not such a bad guy deep down."'

I wonder if she's right . . .

'You really don't see that people can be completely different on the inside than they are on the outside, do you?' Koko presses the subject. 'For example, let's say you see a man taking photos of a cute kitten. He takes picture after picture, the flash bathing the kitten in light. You'd think he's a cat lover, right?'

'Isn't he?'

'Say you approach him and ask about it. And he answers, eyes sparkling, that if you flash light in a cat's eyes long enough, you can make it go blind.'

Kamino can feel her face twisting at Koko's words. 'What do you mean?'

'A camera flash can be a weapon, is what I mean. That's what he was exploring.'

'How horrible!'

'Right? So even a smiling man taking pictures of a kitten might, if you take a look inside him, be hiding a gallery of horrors. And you know—'

'What?'

'That was a real man. That was Inui.'

'Really?'

'Really. I saw him taking pictures of a kitten and asked him about it, and that's what he said. I brushed it off as a weird joke at the time, but then I started to hear the rumors. You know the ones. And then I realized it wasn't a joke.'

Kamino finds herself at a loss for words.

The days she spent working for Inui, while not necessarily happy, were relatively stable and quiet, especially compared to other times in her life; she even remembers sharing little jokes with him and laughing together. She knew she was doing work that fell outside the law, but she comforted herself by imagining that he wasn't such a bad guy, really. But now, all her assumptions have been turned on their head.

Just like her entire life. She mutters inwardly, *I just want to disappear.* But at the same time, another voice within her speaks up, one unable to stand the idea of giving up.

If you let yourself disappear, you'll regret it.

THE SIX

The nineteenth floor

ASUKA AND KAMAKURA FIND it hard to discern the exact color of the walls around them. Are they brown? Beige? In any case, a color with a distinct heaviness to it. Doors run in both directions along each wall. The light is low, making everything a bit murky.

It's so silent, they can't help but wonder: *Shouldn't I at least be able to hear the sound of my own breathing?*

The silence is broken by Edo's disembodied voice in their earpieces.

'We've got a message from Inui.'

Kamakura and Asuka stop and look at each other.

'What did he say?'

'Just checking in, wondering what the situation is.'

'I hope you told him to sit, spin, and be patient.'

'He knows that if we haven't contacted him, it means the job isn't over yet. What's he so hot and bothered about?'

'The deal's about to go through, I think,' says Edo.

That's right, he did mention something on the phone about a deal, thinks Kamakura.

'Asuka, Kamakura, it's time to grab her.'

'We'll let you know as soon as it's done.'

'And I repeat: don't kill her.'

Kamakura and Asuka exchange glances once more, then head together toward the end of the hall. Once they're standing in front of Room 1914, Kamakura produces an unusually thick card from his back pocket. There's a small aperture interrupting its surface; he holds it up to the door's sensor while at the same time flicking a tiny switch on the card's underside. After a few seconds, there's a noise. Kamakura feels a rush of joy, not unlike the feeling he gets when he's able to suss out the weaknesses of someone trying desperately to protect themselves and make them taste the pain and humiliation of their own downfall. The sound means the magnet in the card successfully disabled the lock.

He slips the card back in his pocket and withdraws his blowgun. It's already loaded with a dart. The dart's smeared with a poison that slows the brain function of the victim, putting them into a state of near-sleep. Asuka has her own blowgun in her hand, loaded with the same flavor of dart.

He pushes the handle down, then slowly opens the door. He's ready to blow a dart at the slightest hint of a human presence. Asuka slips ahead of him. Is she deliberately courting danger? Or is she merely eager to hunt down her quarry as quickly as possible?

The suite is spacious, comprised of two connected chambers.

They walk through a living area with a sofa and a round table in it. Kamakura puts the tube in his hand to his mouth, inhaling and then holding it as he advances.

He heightens his senses, alive to the possibility that someone might be hiding anywhere not immediately visible – behind the sofa, behind the curtains – as he proceeds toward the bedroom.

Asuka moves toward the bathroom, her own blowgun held ready as she checks the room for anywhere a person might hide. In the bedroom, Kamakura drops quickly to the floor to see if anyone's under the bed. But Asuka and Kamakura's initial survey turns up no sign of Yuka Kamino anywhere.

He lowers the tube from his mouth, then picks up a suitcase on the floor by his feet and throws it on the bed. 'The woman's not here. Her luggage is, though,' he reports into the mic.

There's no lock on the suitcase, so he opens it and starts rifling through the contents.

'Did she just step out?' asks Edo. 'Or is she onto us?'

'Hard to say.'

'Kamakura, Asuka, you two stay there for a bit. If Kamino returns, grab her.'

'Roger that.'

'I want to see what the security cameras show. Heian, are you close to being able to check them?'

KAMINO

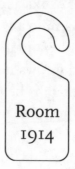

Room
1914

'SHIT,' GROANS KOKO. Unlike the light tone she took while recounting her baseball story, her voice is now colored with darkness.

'What's wrong?' Kamino's stomach tightens. 'Did something happen?'

'It's the Six. There's two of them waiting for the elevator on the ground floor. I think they're the ones called Asuka and Kamakura. A couple of real lookers.'

'You don't think they're coming here, do you?'

'Well, there's that porter you talked to . . .'

'You think he would tell a total stranger which room I'm staying in?' She never considered, in this age of strict information security, that a hotel employee might do something as thoughtless as pass along that kind of intel to anyone who asked.

Koko shakes her head ruefully. 'There are ways to get people to talk. He wouldn't tell someone who seemed suspicious, of course, but there are plenty of stories you can make up to give him a reason to trust you. So we can't assume it's impossible for them to have gotten your room number. Look at me – I could easily pretend I'm looking for my grandchild, all in a panic. If you seem like you're in genuine distress, people will try to help you however they can. It's like hacking into a server – there are always ways to get information if you really need it.'

'I guess . . .'

'We should be as careful as possible.'

'What about those bodyguards you mentioned?' Kamino's referring to the men Koko said she hired. She's been wondering when they'll join up together, if only to coordinate her escape from the hotel.

Seeing Koko's expression grow even more troubled, Kamino feels a sharp pain in her stomach.

'They're supposed to be waiting for us in a separate room. I sent them a message suggesting we meet up, but that was quite a while ago and there's no sign they even read it.' Koko gets out her phone and starts typing. Kamino can hear Koko's call go through, but no one's answering. 'Dammit,' Koko mutters.

'Could they be sleeping?'

'They're professionals. They should be waiting for us in Room 2010. I wonder if something happened.'

All Kamino can manage in response is to breathe, 'What are we going to do?'

'I think it might be best to get out of this hotel as soon as possible. Before the Six get here. Are you ready to go, Kamino-chan?'

'Uh . . . yes,' replies Kamino, nodding. Her body responds before her head fully registers the urgency of the situation, her heart beating faster and her limbs, as if in sympathy, starting to shake uncontrollably.

'Um . . .' Kamino only belatedly realizes she's started speaking. 'Do you . . . do you think we'll be able to get away?'

It's not that she doubts Koko. It's just that death has become suddenly palpable to her, as if something physical is clawing its way up the inside of her body, filling her with terror. She doesn't want to face the distinct possibility that her life may very well end in this hotel.

'You're going to be okay.' Koko smiles. 'You're going to get out of here, Kamino-chan, and then you're going to enjoy a long and lovely life. Don't think of it as leaving everything behind, think of it as starting over. You'll be able to do whatever you want – go back to work at a pastry shop, or start down the path to becoming a lawyer. That's what I'm here to give you.'

Koko's words might be simple, but they nonetheless manage to banish, at least for the moment, the paralyzing fear of death that has by now reached all the way up to her throat. She feels a sense of calm spread through her, replacing it.

'You know, I . . .'

'What is it?'

'If I *am* able to get out of this—'

'Yes?'

'I want a friend.'

Kamino is surprised at her words even as they come out of her mouth. It's unclear to her if a friend is what she really wants – it's possible she just wanted to say the words.

Koko's eyes narrow with merriment.

'How lovely.'

They emerge into the hallway. Kamino carries only a small backpack as luggage.

We might have to run, so be ready. Take only what you absolutely need – leave your suitcase here.

Koko, carrying a small bag as well, hurries down the hallway looking at her tablet. To the casual observer, they look no different from any mother–daughter pair on a trip together.

Koko proceeds purposefully, her pace steady.

They reach the bank of elevators and push the 'down' button. A bell rings almost immediately, and a light goes on over the last door in the line, indicating that an elevator is about to arrive.

Koko stands waiting, her eyes still glued to her tablet, while next to her, Kamino finds herself getting more and more impatient for the elevator to come. It doesn't. It seems to be stuck. *Come on, come on!* Kamino prays inwardly, impatient for the doors to open.

Please – my life hasn't been particularly blessed up till now, can't you afford to lend me a little luck now?

This is Kamino's prayer.

Please let the elevator arrive soon!

'We're too late, Kamino-chan.'

'What do you mean?' Kamino looks over and sees Koko, her eyes still on her tablet, shrug her shoulders.

'Those two are already on an elevator. I guess theirs came faster than ours is coming. They're on their way up.' Koko's still watching her tablet as she says this. 'Let's use the stairs.'

Koko starts walking back through the hallway, heading east. Kamino follows after her, as if dragged by an invisible net. They soon reach the door to the emergency stairs at the end of the hall.

'Once we're in there, be as quiet as you can,' says Koko as she turns the doorknob and slowly opens the door. 'The sound echoes.'

The air in the stairwell is chillier than in the hall. The emergency stairwells frame the hotel like bones frame a body. Koko gingerly moves one foot, then the other, as she begins her descent, as if even the tiniest sound made by her foot leaving the ground and then touching back down will be relayed by the floors and walls to alert the whole building to her presence.

Don't rush. Take your time. Yet, hurry. Kamino repeats this contradictory advice to herself as she carefully places her feet one after another on the stairs.

Koko urges her on. *We have to go down.* Kamino wants to ask, *What will we do once we get to the bottom? Is there a back way out?* But she's afraid to speak.

Koko, leading the way down the stairs and perhaps still looking at the tablet's screen as she descends, makes it about four floors down before she stumbles slightly. The sound of her shoe hitting metal rings out, and she barely stops herself from yelping in surprise.

Kamino puts her hand to her own mouth in sympathy as her eyes meet Koko's. Shock is written all over the other woman's face as well. Koko nods slightly to signal that she's all right.

Koko is now motionless, her eyes glued to the tablet. 'They got off at the nineteenth floor, just as I thought. The cameras in the hall near the elevators caught them.'

'They're here for me, aren't they?' Kamino feels as if she's about to lose her footing entirely and fall into space. She's been hoping and praying they are here for some reason that has nothing to do with her, but it's impossible to imagine that they've ended up going straight to the nineteenth floor by mere coincidence. 'They must have gotten my room number.'

'Whatever the case, we need to get to the ground floor as fast as we can.'

Kamino tries to voice her assent, but no sound comes out. She begins to descend as fast as she can, inwardly chanting, *Now or never, now or never,* all the while.

She feels herself about to stumble and fall so many times during the descent. The sound of her own footsteps pursues her, threatening to make her tumble down the stairs as she pushes herself to outrun them.

They reach the landing at the fourth floor when Koko stops. Kamino thinks she might be tired, but instead she says, 'We have to check out what's going on down there,' fixing her gaze once more on her tablet.

Kamino realizes she's the one who's winded. She bends over, resting her hands on her thighs as she catches her breath.

'Okay, one of them is coming this way.'

'What?'

'The camera down there shows a man coming over to the staircase. He just opened the door.'

'What door?'

'The door at the bottom of the stairs.' Koko's whisper diminishes even more. She points down. 'It's a guy called Sengoku. One of the Six.'

Kamino is suddenly gripped by terror, as if by the ankles. She's on the verge of collapsing into a crouch, her head between her knees.

'Do you think he's going to come up here?' Kamino breathes, her voice as faint as she can make it.

'Maybe. Sengoku's big, built like a fighter. Take a look,' says Koko, showing Kamino a photo on her tablet. 'Even among the Six, he's the most ruthless. He loves to destroy.'

'Destroy what?'

'Everything. Anything. People.'

Kamino feels like she's about to literally faint dead away on the spot. If she's honest with herself, she almost wishes for it, as it would release her from her terror.

She imagines the man throwing open the door at the bottom of the stairs and then bounding up them in an instant, taking several steps with each stride. Kamino's head feels struck by a tornado that threatens to whisk her up to rip off her limbs one by one.

Koko walks over to Kamino and points up. 'Down's no good. What a pickle we're in. Okay, let's go back up.' Her whisper is barely distinguishable from the sound of her breath.

But, Kamino wants to reply, *they're up there, too, on the nine-teenth floor! Both up and down are no good! We're trapped!*

'Let's go up one floor and hide out there for the time being.'

Kamino nods, then starts creeping back up the stairs. Her legs are trembling from fear and adrenaline, and she almost stumbles again and again despite the relatively short distance. As soon as she makes even the tiniest noise, the face of the man coming up toward them appears in her head, which only makes her legs tangle with each other even more.

Once at the fifth floor, they open and close the door as carefully as they can, and then they're in the hallway. Released from the compulsion to maintain complete silence, they let out their pent-up breath all at once in a rush of relief.

What are we going to do now?

Kamino wants to voice the question, but once again, she finds herself unable to make a sound. Koko strides purposefully ahead. She stops near the bank of elevators and looks back at Kamino. Seeing her face, Koko says, 'It's okay. Neither Asuka and Kamakura on the nineteenth floor or Sengoku coming up the stairs know we're on the fifth floor. As long as that's true, we have an advantage. There's no reason for them to come here anytime soon.'

Kamino imagines how pale she must be from the sheer terror coursing through her body, and understands that Koko's just trying to calm her down. *I understand,* she nods.

'We can always use the staff elevator . . .' says Koko, pointing at a nearby door with a sign on it reading EMPLOYEES ONLY.

The staff elevator's on the other side of that door?

'Can we really?'

'If we have a universal keycard.'

'So, that's out . . .' says Kamino, her shoulders slumping.

'The bodyguards were supposed to get one for us.'

'They were?'

'The idea was to be prepared for anything.'

Koko crouches down and begins working on her tablet.

Barely a moment passes before the elevator bell rings. A scream threatens to escape Kamino's throat, as if a gun were suddenly held to her head. Koko puts her tablet to the side and rises to her feet, standing at the ready with her back to the wall.

Do I hear children? Kamino barely has time to have the thought before they appear: a family of what appear to be ordinary hotel guests, a young couple with two small kids. They pass right by Kamino and Koko. 'Good afternoon,' they say as they pass, but only Koko has the presence of mind to return the greeting.

'We need to get in a room so we can figure out our next move in peace.'

'True enough . . .' *But surely we can't go back to Room 1914!*

Koko crouches down again, murmuring, 'Where to go, where to go . . .' as she busies herself once more with her tablet in that rather strained position. Almost instantly, she says, 'Okay! Room 525 it is!'

It takes a moment for Kamino to realize what she must have been doing: hacking into the hotel's reservation management system.

'Room 525 is vacant, so I just reserved it for us.'

'You what?' Kamino finds she's still a step behind.

'I put in information to the effect that we've been there since yesterday for a stay of three days and two nights.'

'We have?'

'Of course not. I mean, according to the data. Even if we've paid no money and made no such reservation, I can put some numbers in the database and it'll be like we have.'

'I guess that's true . . .' says Kamino, but still has doubts. They may well be in the database as guests staying in Room 525, but they still don't have a keycard, for example. It seems clear that no key equals no access.

'If you're worried about how we'll get in, don't be. We'll just call down to the front desk and explain that we lost our keycard – would they be so kind as to bring up a replacement for us? The data will show that we're paying guests, so there won't be any problem. The staff at a fancy hotel like this are trained to bend over backward to please their guests, after all.'

Kamino simply gazes at Koko, so able to think of ways to get them out of whatever predicament they find themselves in, while she herself is unable to do anything but stand around quivering in panic.

THE SIX

Behind the front desk

'I FINALLY MADE IT BACK here – I'm looking at the screen now,' says Heian, staring at the computer display in front of her. The front desk's 'backyard' is bigger than she'd imagined. There's a table, along with a set of shelves for storing various pieces of equipment.

Heian sees a small '27' written at the corner of the screen, which must mean it's a twenty-seven-inch display. The screen is divided into nine sections, each showing a different part of the hotel.

She senses someone approach and starts to take out her blow-gun, but then realizes it's just Inui's mole.

He taps the touchpad at Heian's fingertips, moving the cursor on the screen before them, explaining, 'Click here to switch between the views.'

'Oh wow, that's amazing! Thank you!' Heian claps her hands with joy, her face lighting up as she thanks him. The man's nose

123

flares with self-regard. 'Let me know if you need anything – I'll be right out here,' he says as he leaves the room.

Edo, hearing this exchange, speaks up in Heian's ear. 'Was that the man Inui said would help us?'

'Yes. It was so easy,' says Heian, lowering her voice.

This man, who's presumably helping them in order to get a bit of money from Inui, spoke to the rest of the staff without explaining much of anything to them as he brought Heian into the office behind the front desk, acting for all the world as if she were there for some reason to do with 'maintenance.' He showed her the computer and said, proudly, 'Go ahead!' as if treating her to a nice meal.

'How does it look? Do you see Yuka Kamino anywhere?' asks Edo.

'Just a second, I'm still getting the hang of using this thing. Okay, it displays nine views at a time, and I can switch from view to view. Hmmm . . .' says Heian, playing with the touchpad to change what's showing on the screen. 'It looks like there are cameras above the banks of elevators on each floor. And some in the hallways too. I can also see the area in front of the restaurants and the lobby – aha! I can even see you, Edo-san!'

On the screen in front of her, Edo looks around and above himself, searching for the camera.

'So, do we know if Yuka Kamino has checked out already?' interjects Kamakura from where he's still waiting on the nineteenth floor.

'When he looked into it for me, he said she hadn't yet. So, if she's not in her room, that means she's probably either on her way down in an elevator or coming down one of the stairwells, right?'

'Nara and Sengoku are heading up the stairs,' says Edo. His voice is followed by the voices of the two in question.

'I've just started up.'

'Me too. I don't really want to go up all nineteen flights, but I figured it would be a good idea to start climbing now rather than later.'

'Yes, go up now.'

'She could have left the hotel without checking out, right? Before we even got here, I mean.' This is Nara.

'That would be a real pain,' says Sengoku, his voice fluctuating rhythmically in time with his steps.

'Even if she did, she'd come back to this room eventually, wouldn't she?' asks Asuka.

It's at this point that Heian catches sight of something on the screen as she switches from view to view. 'Aha!'

'What is it, Heian?'

Heian furiously taps the touchpad, trying to find the camera feed again. *Not that one . . . not that one . . .*

'The emergency stairwell cameras caught someone – I think it was a woman. I flipped past it too fast, I need to get back, but I can't seem to find it again. Ugh, this stupid machine!'

'If she was on the stairs, she must be still coming down them. Couldn't you just start with the camera on the ground floor and go up? Maybe hit rewind a little to try to catch her . . .'

'It's easy to give advice when you're not the one doing it!' retorts Heian as she finally locates a menu allowing her to control the display parameters; she selects the emergency stairwell cameras to be the only ones shown. The screen suddenly fills with samey views of the stairs from the first to the ninth floors, both east and west.

'However,' says Sengoku, his words accompanied by the sounds of his footfalls as he climbs, 'if she's using the stairs to go down, it means she knows the elevators aren't safe. Which means she knows we're here, right?'

'It might.'

'Did she get some intel from someone, or does she just have a sixth sense about these things?'

'She left her suitcase in the room, which tells me she left in a hurry,' says Kamakura.

'This Yuka Kamino's no sitting duck, it seems.'

That doesn't mean we can't catch her, though, thinks Heian. *We may no longer have the element of surprise on our side, but if all six of us are after her, nabbing her should still be a piece of cake. Indeed, if she knows she's in danger, the powerlessness she'll feel when we get her anyway will taste all the sweeter, upping the thrill of the hunt.*

'Sengoku, Nara, stop a moment and listen. If she's using the stairs, you might be able to hear her.'

'That's true.'

'Roger that.'

Even if she knows she's in danger and that's why she's using the stairs, she's bound to run into either Sengoku or Nara anyway, thinks Heian.

'And have your blowguns at the ready regardless.'

As Edo gives his instructions, Heian catches sight of something on the screen that makes her lean in to peer closer. Her brain floods with the pleasure of a predator closing in on its prey.

'I'm going through the recorded footage, and I just found them going down the stairs a few moments ago.'

'Them?'

'Yeah, there's another woman with her.' Heian squints at the small-statured figure heading down the stairs ahead of Yuka Kamino. 'Oh! I know who it is! It's that old lady, Madam Clickety-Clack.'

'Madam Clickety-Clack?' Asuka asks, perplexed.

'She's a hacker. Clickety-clacking on her keyboard all the time. Get it?' Nara explains the joke before Heian has the chance.

'Koko? She's still doing jobs?' says Edo. 'I thought she'd be slowing down by now at her age. In any case, sounds like Kamino hired her.'

'I guess when you want to disappear, you hire a magician.'

'That old lady knows her stuff,' says Heian as she gazes at Koko on the screen in front of her. She watches the older woman carefully picking her way down the stairs, her eyes glued to the tablet in her hand, and feels a certain sympathy for her. 'Though I'm not sure how that's going to help her now.'

In today's world, the best way to get ahead is through the information war, flooding the zone with fake news and disinformation. Which means Koko's talents have real power in a variety of situations – save for when you have to confront your enemy directly, in the flesh. That's when bodily strength and cunning come back into play. No matter how high-powered a hacker you might be, it all becomes meaningless once you're punched in the face and find yourself bound hand and foot. At that point, even the great Madam Clickety-Clack becomes an old lady again, just like any other.

NANAO

The eleventh floor

NANAO LEAVES SODA IN ROOM 1121, closing the door carefully behind him, and then, after hearing the lock engage, hurries down the hall, making a beeline for the elevators.

I have to get ahold of Maria.

He reaches the elevators. The four of them sit silently together, two on each side, as if they'd agreed in advance to keep their secrets – none seem ready to open up to him. He pushes the 'down' button.

With all apologies to Soda, he never had any intention of going up to check on Cola.

The northeasternmost elevator dings, the light above it blinking on. As soon as he walks over and stands in front of it, the doors open. Nanao braces himself for some other unexpected danger to be waiting inside, but happily, it's empty. He jumps in and hits the button for the ground floor. Then he starts pressing the 'close door' button again and again, repeating a silent prayer as he does: *Please, you know I need this, let's just go, smooth as silk, easy as pie, all the way to the bottom.*

Nanao begins to breathe again once the elevator starts to descend. The floor numbers begin their countdown, getting smaller and smaller as he stares a hole into the display.

Keep going, keep going, that's it, just like that . . .

He feels the elevator start to slow, perhaps a bit too early to mean he's reached the ground floor, but he decides to chalk it up to nerves.

There's no reason for it to stop partway down, right?

The more he tries to reassure himself, though, the clearer it is that the elevator is slowing, and in fact is coming to a halt.

Will he encounter another problem from his past, like he did with Soda? He tries to calm his nerves, thinking, *Don't be a fool, there's not a chance,* but this is drowned out by another internal voice saying, in a resigned tone, *Get ready, that's probably what's coming.*

Nanao slips a hand into a bag he keeps strapped around his middle. It's always best to be prepared. He prefers to rely on his bare hands, not weapons, in close combat, but in this case, he'd really rather avoid combat entirely. His hand closes around a canister of pepper spray.

The doors open. Nanao hides the canister in his right hand, but prepares himself for whoever's waiting on the other side. If it's anyone who seems like they might mean him harm, he's ready to spray them without the slightest hesitation.

But contrary to his prediction, what's waiting for him on the other side of the opening doors is a woman he's never seen before. Dangerous people can be of either sex, of course, so he remains at the ready, not wanting to be caught unawares, but there doesn't seem to be any sign that this woman is up to anything. She strikes him as remarkably unremarkable, in fact, with an unassuming, serious face.

The woman walks right into the elevator and stands in front of the control panel. Nanao is relieved that he has no idea who she is. There's no reason why every time the elevator stops that it'll be someone from his past waiting to get in, after all.

He has to make it out. He must warn Maria. He doesn't quite know how he'll manage it, but what he does know is that he has to escape this hotel before he can do anything else.

He notices that the elevator has yet to move.

He then notices that the woman who got on is pressing the 'open door' button.

'Uhhhh,' says Nanao. Should he ask if she could kindly shut the door? But then he realizes that she must be waiting for someone. She's holding the elevator for someone lagging behind, that's all.

If so, maybe it would be best to get off himself. He starts to do so, but he's stopped by the woman's voice. 'I'm sorry to trouble you, but you're Ladybug, right?'

If he could cluck his tongue with his whole body, he would. *Of course this would happen!* he thinks, then amends his thought: *What exactly is happening?*

As Nanao stands mired in confusion, the woman continues. 'My name is Kamino. I'm on the run. I think I'm about to be caught. Will you help me?'

Nanao simply stares at her in response. There are too many impossibilities in her words to parse.

How do you know who I am? Why do you think I would help you?

'I'm very sorry, but I'm in a hurry myself. I have to get out of here too. Would you be so kind as to take your finger off that button?' *We can talk about this on the way down,* Nanao wants to add, but the woman is way ahead of him.

'Let me tell you my story before we get to the bottom? Please, I'm begging you.'

'You don't want to be with me anyway. No good will come of it, trust me. You should ask someone else,' replies Nanao, speaking quickly.

'I was with someone else until just a few moments ago. Someone specializing in helping people escape from bad situations.' The woman continues talking as if Nanao hadn't spoken. Her eyes fill with tears. 'Do you know her? Koko-san?'

'Koko-san?' He feels like he's heard the name before, but he can't immediately place it.

'She tried to help me escape, but . . .' She pauses, seemingly searching for the right words, but then gives up and decides to say it directly. 'She was killed just now.'

Nanao's brows furrow. *Killed* is such an ugly word. A word the average person would never say lightly. Yet she said it, as casually as one might say, *She tripped and fell just now.*

'Please help me – *please!*' repeats Kamino, beseeching Nanao with her eyes.

Nanao finds he can't help but stare at her fingertip as it presses the button, as if the pressure itself is expressing the urgency of her predicament, as if it represents the difference between life and death.

Somewhere outside the elevator's still-open doors, someone approaches.

YOMOGI

The restaurant on the second floor

'YOUR *TERRINE DE FOIE GRAS à l'orange*, sir.'

The waiter sets the plate on the table, then briefly explains the provenance of the ingredients.

Director Yomogi skillfully uses his fork to bring a bite of the terrine to his mouth with a bit of orange sauce on it. Ikeo tries to follow suit, his knife and fork clattering against the plate.

'You know, Ikeo, it's no small task trying to change things in this country for the benefit of generations to come.'

'Sounds like you speak from experience.'

A boyish grin spreads across Yomogi's face. 'The reason why is simple.'

'Is it?'

'No one wants to lose what they already have.'

Ikeo feels his expression relax. *That's so true*, he wants to say.

'Every young person will eventually become an old person. Which means, if a system's set up that makes things hard for older people, eventually every young person will be punished by

132

that system, too, if they live long enough. On the other hand, no old person will ever become young again, so if rules are made that make life difficult for the young, the old remain secure. No one will agree to a system that takes away a benefit they already enjoy.'

'I see.'

Ikeo doesn't actually know if he sees or not, but decides to pretend he does and nod.

'When you try to change a nation's laws or its structure, there are very few things you might do that would benefit everyone equally, that everyone would support unanimously. Someone always loses out.'

'Indeed.'

'A lot of people also think change is too much bother, so they oppose it for that reason. Which I'm quite sympathetic to! Any change that would make people have to do something they wouldn't have to otherwise will face opposition, which always takes the same form: *Explain!*'

'Explain?'

'"Explain!" they say. "You haven't explained enough!" But if you provide that explanation – if you say, "It will make this country's future brighter if you give up just a bit of what you have now" – they'll oppose it even more! The media will fan the flames, and the opposition parties will call for blood. So you need to think of an "explanation" that won't make anyone mad. But I've always thought that's futile. Once you start trying to reduce the cost to the people you're asking to give something up, or at least make it *seem* like you're reducing it, you end up changing this, changing that, until all these layers of administration and red tape build up around your proposal and make it cost more overall. Bailouts and relief measures add complexity to any program. So even though you started by trying to change things, after having to consider this and that and make various compromises, all that's left is a hollowed-out half measure and a pile of debt. It's heartbreaking. That's all my time as a member of Parliament brought me – heartbreak after heartbreak.'

Director Yomogi's way of speaking is so casual, his delivery so unemotional, that it's hard to know how much he means what he's saying.

'However,' he continues, 'it's not all hopeless. There are new ways this problem can be addressed.'

'Which problem?'

'The explanation problem. Think about it – we can have AI come up with these explanations now, right?'

It's true that, lately, people have increasingly been using AI to generate all sorts of things: the set phrases in formal letters, wedding speeches, instruction manuals, interview questions – the list goes on. Just a few years ago, AI could only produce awkward sentences and outlandish, uncanny content that would leave any listener speechless with discomfort, but these days, it's generating prose that not only provides a great springboard for writing, but also can even serve as the final product.

'The explanations it comes up with are infinitely more satisfying – neither too much nor too little – than the ones humans think up. So the brilliant minds in the Ministries can apply themselves to the real tasks at hand and leave the explaining to the machines.'

'I see.'

'Make no mistake – both meaningless questions *and* answers have been significantly reduced this way.'

'It's true that humans tend to provide feedback that's little more than trolling.'

'In that sense, AI may be better than humans.' Yomogi smiles again. 'It might even be the case that AI would be better at creating policy. And if that's so, then we would need far fewer politicians – talk about cost-cutting!'

'If artificial intelligence takes over governance, wouldn't that lead to a future like in the movies, where humans are ruled over by machines?'

'Things like machine-generated recommendations on shopping sites are already ruling over us, aren't they?' responds Yomogi evenly. 'What we should be considering is how best to make artificial intelligence work for us. We shouldn't be worried about AI taking our jobs – we should be thinking about how we can have AI do those jobs so we can live freely! That's one of the reasons I decided to move to the Information Bureau. The more information AI has to work with, the better its judgment will be. Information is its food, its fuel. Unhealthy info is like unhealthy food – feeding it to AI will harm it. This is what needs our attention, I realized. Happily, this realization occurred just as the Information Bureau was being created.'

'Wouldn't it have worked better if you'd become Information Bureau Director while still a member of Parliament?'

'Ikeo-san, a member of Parliament is subject to the public's will.'

'Okay . . .' Ikeo can't tell if Yomogi's still joking.

'The Information Bureau's work may well involve things that would anger people. I believe they're necessary for the well-being of this country and its citizens, of course, but parts of the process may invite public condemnation. I want to avoid being voted out and having my work end in failure before I can even complete it.'

'I see.'

'And besides, I got tired of campaigning,' adds Yomogi, this time in a tone that clearly shows he's joking.

Ikeo only has so much time with Yomogi. The various courses of the meal are proceeding apace. It's time to broach the interview's true subject. He places a morsel of foie gras in his mouth. The rich flavor spreads across his tongue; he feels its soothing power as it reaches his brain.

'Ikeo-san,' says Yomogi after a bit of time passes. 'You've been

135

investigating that accident, haven't you? The accident involving my family.'

He knows! Ikeo startles at the Director's words, finding himself at a loss to answer.

'You've been working so diligently on the matter that I decided to return the favor and do a bit of background research myself. Satō's been helping as well, looking into the matter to the best of his abilities.'

Ikeo glances over at the neighboring table to see Satō polishing his glasses, nodding apologetically. His neck seems so long. Like a giraffe's. Though as soon as the words pop into his mind, another inner voice pipes up to banish them. *It's not that long – pull yourself together!*

'Not a moment goes by that I don't think about the accident that took the lives of my beloved wife and son.' Yomogi's expression hardens. 'But I never know with whom I can share this pain. So I live as if cut off from it. That's why when I learned that you had such a keen interest in the matter, Ikeo-san, I was overjoyed. I felt hopeful again. That's why I'm talking to you now.'

'Thank you very much.'

'I would have preferred a setting more conducive to talking freely, but I have some business to take care of after this, so I had to insist on meeting you here. I apologize for that.'

'No, I appreciate it! To share such a lovely meal with you . . .'

'And besides,' Yomogi adds, scratching his head, 'it makes me feel better to be in a place like this, where I can see what's around me. I never know when someone might come for me, after all, or from where.'

Ikeo doesn't understand at first what Yomogi's talking about, but then puts it together that the Director means there are people out to kill him. He looks around, surveying their surroundings.

'When I was a politician, I received threats all the time. The majority of them were just people letting off steam, based on

136

some kind of preconceived notion or belief on their part. That's fine, really.'

'It's not fine!'

'But what I can't forgive is when fellow members of Parliament, or people connected to them, decide to go after people who get in their way. There is no way that could ever benefit the country. Going back to what we were just talking about, this is an area where an AI's judgment will always be better than a human's. It's never in the best interests of the country to concentrate one's efforts on taking out a mouthy fellow like me. Indeed, an AI would likely decide that it's the people who think only of themselves and try to protect their interests at the expense of others who need to be dealt with.'

'So, you're being targeted?' asks Ikeo. He immediately thinks, *Of course!* but restrains himself from saying it aloud.

'The people behind it would never do it themselves, you understand. They'd hire – or order – someone to do it for them. It's that kind of thing. I wouldn't be surprised if there was someone like that in this hotel right now.'

BLANKET

Room
405

BLANKET AND PILLOW WALK UP to the door of Room 405 in the Winton Palace Hotel, cleaning cart in tow, and stop. A small red light blinks next to the door handle – the signal meaning *Do Not Disturb*.

They're there to do the job Inui gave them.

Blanket looks over at Pillow, and, as their eyes meet, scenes from the past replay in her head. Scenes from when they first met Inui.

It all started that night, the night when Pillow had called her and said, 'I found him. I couldn't forgive him. So I did it.'

'I'm coming right now,' Blanket said, and then she left, hailing a taxi and taking it to the no-frills hotel where Pillow worked.

Blanket slipped in through a back entrance Pillow had told her about well before that night, and then she went straight to the room, where Pillow came out to meet her. Blanket pulled Pillow, who was crying so hard she was unable to speak, into an embrace and held her for a while. Her plan was to wait for Pillow to calm down a bit, and then they would use the cleaning cart to spirit the Bumping Man's body out of the hotel.

Fortunately, they ended up finding his car keys as well. The two girls walked around the parking lot next to the hotel pushing the remote control until a car responded.

Blanket next concentrated on convincing Pillow to return to work. *I can't!* she protested, but Blanket insisted. *It'll attract suspicion if you disappear halfway through your shift!* Eventually, Blanket managed to win out, and Pillow went back into the hotel.

Blanket got in the car alone.

She didn't know where to go.

What can I do with a dead body? She didn't know if she should stash it deep in the mountains or dump it in the sea; at a loss, she stopped the car on the side of the dark road and looked online. She did searches, clicked on links, and ended up on some rather unsavory sites. Everything in her head was fuzzy and indistinct; she felt like she was flailing around underwater, on the verge of drowning. Eventually, she realized she'd just posted a question asking, in thinly veiled language, for advice on how best to dispose of a body. She was losing all judgment.

Someone did respond to her question, though.

Inui.

I regularly go online and look for people about to break the law, or people who've already broken the law and are wondering what to do, and lend a hand. I'm doing a kindness, really. A drowning man will grab even a spindly piece of straw, they say, but what I'm offering is no mere straw — it's a strong, sturdy rope. All you have to do is grab on, and I'll pull you to safety.

139

And indeed, that's exactly what happened. Inui appeared, and Pillow and Blanket were saved.

He helped them dispose of the Bumping Man's body and offered a lot of other advice that proved quite useful, and as a result, the incident sank from view, never to rise to the surface again.

But of course, nothing costs more than something free.

He had them where he wanted them, and from that point on, Blanket and Pillow left their respective jobs and became, for all intents and purposes, his employees, living their lives at his beck and call.

It was true that their regret at the crimes they'd committed did irreparable harm to their psyches; at the same time, doing the work of removing bodies from hotel rooms and cleaning up murder scenes ended up numbing their senses of right and wrong quite a bit as well.

It was two years after they started working for him that they said the words: 'Inui, we want to quit.'

They'd heard the rumors by then and were scared. 'Haven't we done enough to pay you back for what you did for us?'

Inui's face betrayed no displeasure as he replied with a simple, 'Oh, is that so?'

They'd been scared that once they quit clean-up, they'd become useless to him and end up cleaned themselves, like two fishes under his knife. Happily, though, that's not what happened.

Maybe it was just that Inui had no special attachment to them, or that he simply had more than enough employees at the time.

'You want to go back to working legit again, then?' he asked, seemingly sincerely interested. He surely knew there was no way they could do that.

'No. We want to work differently – we want to do jobs where we pay people back for things they've done. For their victims, who can't do it themselves.'

'You want to help people get revenge?'

'You could call it that, I suppose. We want to do something about people who ruin other people's lives – maybe they're sex pests, or they abuse their power in other ways – and would otherwise get away with it.'

'You think that would make you able to work with a clear conscience?'

'It's worth a try.'

'We know it might be easier said than done . . .'

Inui shrugs. 'Okay – sounds fun.'

'Fun?'

'Yeah, fun! To stamp someone out as payback. In the name of justice.'

Thinking he was making fun of them, Blanket almost responded, *An Easy Streeter like you would never understand how hard it is for people like us!* But she stopped herself. Not because she thought better of her words, but because Inui, perhaps imagining 'stamping someone out,' had an expression of pure ecstasy on his face, chilling her to the bone. Even more than the clear sadistic pleasure he was feeling, it was the thought that this was the true face always lurking behind his usual affability that terrified her, showing her once again why they were right to try to distance themselves from him as much as they could.

'If we do this, we use hotels,' he added. He was just voicing his thoughts as they came to him, but they ended up having a profound effect on the subsequent course of Pillow and Blanket's lives and the kinds of jobs they ended up specializing in.

'Hotels?'

'You used to work in one, Pillow, so you know how they work behind the scenes. Once you get your hand on a keycard, you can put your target in a room and dispose of them there. Pretend you're part of the cleaning staff – you can use the cart to remove the body! Once that's done, other professionals can take care of the rest.'

They didn't really feel inclined to take direction from Inui, but Blanket had to admit his plan sounded like a pretty good idea.

'Housekeeping – we're coming in!'

Pillow's voice wakes Blanket from her reverie. The keycard in Pillow's hand passes through the reader on the door of Room 405, and Blanket hears the lock disengage.

Pillow slowly pushes open the door and slips inside, followed by Blanket pulling the cleaning cart in behind her.

They've done jobs like this countless times by now, but despite being old hands at it, their focus remains sharp.

They see a man standing in front of the bed with his back to the door, perhaps looking through his luggage. He's dressed nicely in a button-up shirt and slacks, but his hair is bleached nearly blond. Sensing their presence behind him, he turns quickly, his eyes widening reflexively as he catches sight of them, but then, as if accepting what's to come, his expression relaxes.

'I don't recognize him,' says Pillow. 'And what's up with the hair?'

'No idea.'

Blanket catches the sheet Pillow throws her, then advances toward the man. They play their mummification game together like always, switching places as they pass the edges of the sheet back and forth until, less than five minutes later, he's wrapped up nice and tight, like a parcel ready to be shipped.

He cooperates as they guide him into the cart together.

'I guess that's it! Almost a letdown,' says Blanket, shrugging.

'And to think he's trying to take out Yomo-pi!' Pillow agrees, sounding similarly nonplussed. 'I can't help but worry.'

NANAO

The fifth floor

NANAO SEES A MAN HURRYING down the hall toward the elevator where he's standing.

Is this who the woman's holding the door for?

As if to refute Nanao's unspoken guess, the woman starts pushing the 'close door' button as hard as she can. She pushes it over and over, as if to say, *Come on, close already, close!* She's pretty frantic. On the verge of panic, even.

Why were you holding the door open so long, then? wonders Nanao, irritated, and then he remembers that the woman had said she's on the run. If she's on the run, that means someone's after her. Perhaps the man in the hall isn't who she thought was coming, but rather an unpleasant surprise.

In any case, Nanao has to make a decision: should he stay or should he go? Like the famous fateful choice – behind one door, a tiger; behind the other, a wolf – except, in this case, behind one door is a man he's never seen before, and behind the other, an equally unknown woman.

He decides to stay where he is.

For one thing, if he stays on this elevator, it will presumably go down to the ground floor once the door closes, bringing him that much closer to his ultimate goal of leaving the hotel. If he gets off, he might find himself wrapped up in yet another dangerous situation. Not 'might' – he's sure he would.

The elevator doors start to close. As if mocking the urgency of the woman frantically pushing the 'close door' button, the right and left doors approach each other with agonizing slowness, as if caught up in a sentimental slo-mo reunion scene at the end of a movie.

The man begins to run. Nanao can see he's a slim man in a suit, apparently in his early thirties, but he can't get a good look at his face. This is because the man is holding his hand up to his mouth.

Is he stifling a cough? As soon as he has the thought, Nanao hears a metallic *ting* at his feet.

What was that? Nanao looks down in time to see the elevator doors judder back away from each other. The reopening is abrupt and violent, as if the right and left doors, instead of reuniting, got into an argument and are retreating to their respective corners.

The man is still approaching. He appears to have some sort of tube held to his mouth.

The doors begin to close once more, but as soon as they get near each other, they lurch back again as if mutually repulsed. Or as if they hit something on their way toward each other.

There must be something stuck in the rail where the doors slide back and forth. As soon as he realizes this, Nanao leaps through the reopened doors into the hall.

A blowgun!

It's the only explanation he can think of for the tube the man's holding to his mouth and the metallic sound he heard in the elevator.

Somehow, the man must have shot a dart that's now stuck in the elevator door rail, preventing it from closing. The man must have somehow aimed his dart carefully and then blown it hard enough for it to strike home. Is that even possible? But as soon as he has the thought, Nanao remembers that he's seen plenty of professionals perform seemingly impossible acts perfectly proficiently. People find ways to do what they can do.

The most dangerous thing for *him* to do, now that he's faced with a projectile weapon, is stay in one place.

The man may have been surprised when Nanao sprang at him, but he quickly recovers and adjusts the aim of his blowgun. Nanao pushes off the ground, jumping to the side. Another metallic *ting* rings out. A dart seems to have hit the back wall of the still-open elevator.

Nanao changes direction, crouching low to the ground as he tackles the man like a rugby player.

He grabs both of the man's arms as he does, flipping him onto his back. He's not nearly as heavy as Nanao imagined, not that he really had time to imagine much. The man's body strikes the floor hard. An earpiece pops out of his ear and rolls away.

Nanao's mind whirls, as if spinning in a centrifuge. Two clear choices emerge.

Should he get even closer to his opponent, or get away?

He imagines that he'd have the physical upper hand if he tries to pin him to the ground in close hand-to-hand combat, immobilizing him by restricting his airway or the like. But even as he goes to do so, Nanao suddenly stops himself and springs away.

Images from the past replay in his head from when he was trapped on that northbound bullet train. He almost died tangling with a fellow professional who dealt in poison darts.

This man is shooting the same sort of darts, isn't he? What would happen if one managed to hit him? Nanao doubts they're the kind that would improve his circulation or loosen his stiff neck.

So getting too close is risky. Even a tiny scratch could represent mortal danger. Nanao crawls hurriedly away from the prone man.

Still crouched low, Nanao looks back to see the man he tackled rise slowly to his feet. And then, like before, the man brings his hand to his mouth.

A dart flies just above him as he rushes the man once more, this time not crouched forward but sliding feet-first into the man's legs as if playing baseball or soccer, taking him down again. Nanao hears a dart hit the wall behind him, but also sees the tube slip out of the man's hand and roll across the floor. He hears something else fall to the floor, too, but he doesn't have a chance to look and see what it might be.

Nanao clambers back to his feet, feeling as though he were engaged in a life-or-death game of Capture the Flag. He must be up and ready faster than his opponent, or game over.

The man is scrambling to get up as well, but Nanao beats him. He slips behind the man, and then, before he even really has time to think about it, he wraps both arms around his neck and twists. He feels the man go limp.

Nanao lets himself sigh with relief, but there's no time to take a real breather. Guests could emerge from the hallway or an elevator at any time. His breath grows shallow again.

What's that?

Somehow, he hears Maria's voice.

You need to breathe, she says.

Nanao breathes in, then out, then in again.

146

NANAO

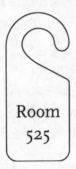

Room
525

'YOU HAVE SOME EXPLAINING TO DO.'

Nanao throws the body of the man he's carried into Room 525 onto the bed, then poses the question to the woman he met in the elevator, one Yuka Kamino.

Looking at the dead man, he sees that he's young and strikingly handsome, like an actor with a rabid female fan base, making it seem all the more unreal that he's just been trying to kill them.

'Where should I begin?'

'There's a lot of things I'd like to know.' Nanao sounds angry, but it's simply because there's so much he doesn't understand. At least he managed to learn Kamino's name. *First of all,* he begins, but then he can't immediately decide which question to ask first, vexing him even more. 'How do you know who I am? And did you know I'd be in that elevator, or was that a coincidence?'

There's no reason to think it was a coincidence. When the

elevator stopped at the fifth floor, this woman Kamino got right in as soon as the doors opened and betrayed no surprise at all that he was there – if anything, her manner was that of someone expecting to see him.

'I saw you on this,' says Kamino, showing him on her phone. Its screen shows several views of the hotel at once, as if it were a security guard's master screen. The views shift from one to the other at regular intervals.

'These are all from this hotel?'

'Thanks to some "clickety-clack" work, yes,' says Kamino before stopping and correcting herself. 'Koko-san hacked into the main system so we could monitor the situation in real time.'

'Who-who-san?'

What on earth is going on?

This was supposed to be a simple delivery job. Show up at a room, hand over a package, that's it. Instead, here he is still running around this accursed hotel – it's unbelievable.

'Koko-san. She was helping me get away.'

'Ah,' says Nanao as he hears this. He remembers where he heard the name 'Koko' before – from Soda. 'The escape artist?'

'Yes. You know her?' Excited that something she said finally got through to him, Kamino's voice grows louder.

'You need to get away, then? If so, aren't you already home free? This guy's not going anywhere.'

But Kamino dashes his hopes, saying, 'They're called the Six.'

'Don't tell me there's still five to go.'

'There's still five to go.'

'You owe me an apology.'

'Koko-san tried to use the security camera footage to help get me out of here. But it didn't go as planned . . .'

Nanao doesn't ask how the plan went awry – he doesn't want to stick his nose in this any more than necessary.

'She's the one who found you in the footage, Ladybug. She

told me that if anything happened to her, I should ask you for help.'

'Why?' Nanao can't help but voice his confusion. 'Why did she think I was someone you could trust?'

'She said I could rely on you because you survived a major incident that should've killed you. Though she didn't tell me what that incident was, exactly.'

'Ahh,' Nanao says, unable to stop his face from twitching at her words. 'It's something I'd like to forget, to be honest.'

'I see.'

'It seems like the things you end up remembering forever are the very things you'd like most to forget. Strange, right?'

Kamino freezes in response, staring back at him. Her eyes grow wet. 'They are,' she says, her voice quiet.

'They are?'

'Why is it that memories are something we have to live with forever? That's what's gotten me into this mess after all, the fact that I can't forget. And why Koko-san's no longer with us.' Kamino points mournfully at her own head. Her eyes overflow with tears, and at first she makes no effort to stop them. Eventually she tries to wipe them away with her hands, but it's too late for that, and she ends up using her sleeve instead.

Nanao waits for her to calm down, then says, 'Well, as long as you get free, you'll be okay.' He stands up from the sofa. 'I need to get out of here too. It's time for both of us to find our way home.'

'The thing is, Koko-san said she hired some bodyguards for us.'

I know, Nanao almost says. *Soda told me.*

Kamino grows silent once more. She seems to want to say something more, but the words won't come. She chokes back her tears, as if deciding that she needs to bring her emotions under control. She makes a sound like she's swallowed hard, then opens her mouth to speak. 'Actually . . .'

This doesn't bode well. Nanao raises a hand to stop her. 'You don't have to tell me—'

But to no avail.

'We were supposed to meet up with those bodyguards, but they stopped returning our messages.'

Nanao tries to nip the conversation in the bud. 'These things happen more often than you'd think!'

'So Koko-san decided to go up to Room 2010, where the bodyguards were supposed to be waiting for us. She had the keycard already.'

'Room 2010, huh? That makes sense,' says Nanao. This is where her story intersects with his. And with Cola slipping and hitting his head on the edge of the marble tabletop and dying, of course.

'They were supposed to have special cards that let us use employee-only areas of the hotel. She went up by herself to fetch it.'

'Koko did?'

'Yes.'

'Did it work? Or did she find a bodyguard dead in the room instead?'

Kamino's eyes grow wide, as if to say, *How did you know?* Nanao's afraid she might start to think he has some sort of special power, like second sight.

'Koko-san communicated the situation to me from the room. One of the men she engaged to be our bodyguard was indeed dead, but she was able to find the card anyway. She said she was on her way to bring it to me. But it seems that before she could, they caught up with her.' Overwhelmed with emotion again, Kamino fights to hold back her tears once more.

They. She surely means the blowgun-wielders. Did all six come to do this job, or just some of them? If so, how many?

'Koko-san gave me advice on what to do to the very end,' says

Kamino. 'She told me, "If anything happens to me, ask Lady-bug for help." She sent me your picture via text message. She also taught me how to access the security camera footage on my phone, in case I happened to be lucky enough to run across you.'

'And you were lucky enough. You found me.' She'd caught sight of him getting on the elevator and decided to nab him on the fifth floor. Of course, from Nanao's perspective, this was less luck than abject misfortune.

'Ladybugs are good luck, they say.'

'They fly toward the sun, taking the divine path to the god-dess. That's why they have seven dots on their back.' Nanao's heard this legend more times than he can count. It seems like nothing but cruel irony when juxtaposed to his own chronic unluckiness, and he's frankly a bit sick of hearing about it. 'Seven's quite an interesting number, really.'

'Yes.'

'There are seven days in a week, seven gods of good fortune, the seven seas. And of course the G7, and the seven wonders of the world.'

'And lucky number seven,' adds Kamino, looking off into the distance for a moment, as if gripped by a memory.

'If I were the number seven, I think I'd get tired of carrying all this baggage around with me,' sighs Nanao.

Nanao's words prompt a troubled look to cross Kamino's face. 'Will you help me? Will you get me out of here?'

He finds himself faced with a decision again: should he help, or leave? But it's not such a quandary, really. He has no duty to save her.

'Let me hire you properly. You're a professional, after all,' says Kamino, her tone tipping back into a plea.

'Everyone's a professional at something.'

'Think of it as a job.'

'I don't take jobs directly.' He could easily avoid this back-and-forth and just leave, but instead he finds himself giving her reasons for his refusal. *Why do I need to justify myself if I'm saying no?* It's a mystery even to himself.

'Who do I need to ask?'

'Maria,' says Nanao, and then he raises his voice. 'That's right! Maria!' He nearly slaps himself on the head, but instead checks the time.

Thirty minutes till curtain. He doesn't know exactly when Maria plans to get there, but he needs to communicate his message before then.

Even as he imagines the futility of explaining his arrangement with Maria to Kamino, he wants her to understand the position he's in, so he takes a deep breath and prepares to do so. But as soon as he does, Kamino stops him.

'Wait.'

Why are you cutting me off? I was about to give you the explanation you asked for!

Kamino thrusts her phone into Nanao's indignant face.

'There's two of them coming.'

'Coming?' *Who? Where? Why?*

Anticipating Nanao's questions, Kamino adds, 'Two more of the Six. They're on their way here. To this room.'

THE SIX FIVE

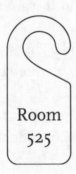

Room
525

NARA DESCENDS THE STAIRS. She knows flinging herself down pell-mell will only end in disaster, so she finds a rhythm instead, jogging down the stairs at a steady rate. Sengoku's in front of her, going down in much the same way.

'We just keep going up and down stairs,' she hears him say.

Yeah, thinks Nara.

Nara and Sengoku have just been up on the twentieth floor.

They initially headed up the emergency stairs hoping they'd run into Yuka Kamino as she went down them with Koko, but that didn't happen. Giving up, they'd started back down when they got word from Heian that Koko was stepping onto an elevator alone.

Heian managed to use the security cameras to see that Koko had gotten off on the twentieth floor, but she was unable to tell them into which room the older woman disappeared after that. Nara and Sengoku decided to split up and go door-to-door with their search, checking each room. It didn't take long before they found her in Room 2010.

Koko had plenty of information they wanted – which room Yuka Kamino was in now, why Koko herself was in Room 2010, whether or not they had other people helping them – so their initial plan was to interrogate her, but Sengoku misjudged his own strength during their first encounter, a fact he discovered when, after knocking her to the ground, he found she was no longer breathing.

Hearing about it, Edo said, 'That's too bad, but not the end of the world. It's Yuka Kamino who we need to keep alive at all costs. Inui's made that very clear.'

Her head and mouth need to be functional.

It was right then that Heian caught Kamino on camera. She was on the fifth floor.

'I'll be right there!' Nara heard Kamakura say happily.

'Go for it,' said Edo. 'Nara, Sengoku, stay there and search the room. I'd like to know why Koko went there. Kamakura should be able to easily handle Kamino now that she's alone.'

Minutes later Kamakura reported in. 'I have Yuka Kamino in my sights. She's standing in the hall in front of me. Oh, she's walking – I'm following her now.'

Nara expected that before long she'd hear Kamakura boasting – *Got her! Piece of cake, like always!* – but instead she heard him say, 'Wait, there's someone in the elevator,' his voice shaded with worry.

This was followed by the sound of intense fighting and then nothing more from Kamakura at all.

Edo said Kamakura's name again and again, trying to get a response, but none came. Nara and Sengoku exchanged glances, then bounded out of Room 2010 and down the stairs toward the fifth floor.

'Do we know what happened to Kamakura?'

Hurrying down the stairs while making sure not to miss a step and go tumbling down them, Nara pitches the question to the

154

others through her earpiece. Her footfalls sound like the beating of the hotel's heart.

'Something unfortunate,' answers Heian from where she's still stationed in the front desk's 'backyard,' monitoring the security camera footage. 'Which isn't good news.'

Nara and Sengoku stop, silencing the sound of their steps. When they start down again, they do so with caution. When Heian says something 'isn't good news,' it generally means the news is actually 'terrible.' In other words, something terrible must have happened to Kamakura.

'He didn't get taken out, did he?' asks Sengoku, incredulous.

'He might have been,' says Heian. Nara swallows hard.

'Didn't you say she's a civilian, Edo?'

'According to Inui, she's just a normal woman.'

'It wasn't Kamino, it was the other guy. He was stronger. I saw it on camera.' Heian's voice has lost its usual sangfroid. 'The guy from the elevator attacked him.'

She informs the others that the fifth-floor security cameras showed what happened. It was all over in an instant, she adds.

'Who was it? I thought Kamino was supposed to be alone,' asks Nara.

'It looked like a guy who just happened to be riding in the elevator.'

'A guy who just happened to be riding in the elevator wouldn't suddenly jump Kamakura like that,' retorts Nara.

'Perhaps *he's* the professional,' says Edo.

'It's very possible. In any case, I couldn't get a good look at his face, so I'm not sure who he is or where he came from,' says Heian. 'He carried Kamakura's body down the hall and they went into one of the rooms. Judging from what I can see from the hallway cam, I think they're in Room 525.'

'Nara and I are already heading there.'

'Which floor are you on now?'

155

Nara steps onto a landing and looks at the sign. 'We just reached the twelfth.'

'Maybe I should join you,' says Edo, but Heian stops him. 'The bigger the group, the more attention we attract. The rooms aren't that big, either, so there's a real chance you might not be able to get out of the way of each other's darts. You should stay where you are, Edo-san, and direct us from there.'

'Who's directing who, again?'

'Nara, Sengoku, you should be careful too,' adds Heian. 'He seems to have dodged a number of Kamakura's darts.'

'Is he really dead?' asks Asuka.

'It looks like the guy snapped his neck. I can't confirm any more than that from here.'

'If his neck's snapped,' says Asuka, her indifference palpable in Nara's ear, 'it's unlikely he survived.'

Kamakura's death doesn't evoke much emotion in Nara, either. It's not like she has dear memories of him to cherish. Though she does think fondly of talking with him about being attractive. 'We're the chosen ones – is there even any point in comparing ourselves to others?' She remembers Kamakura saying something like, 'When I'm breaking up with someone, it's always a nightmare when she knows she'll never have a chance with anyone at my level again. Girls like that get so desperate, it can be a real drag. It's better to try to get someone closer to your own level,' to which Nara remembers replying, 'You're so right!' and them bursting out laughing.

They bound down the stairs to the fifth-floor landing. The noise echoes throughout the entire stairwell, like a gong struck to shake them out of any grief they might feel over the loss of their comrade.

A dead teammate is no longer a teammate at all. Letting yourself linger on their loss is a trap, an enemy waiting to trip you up. Or at least that's how Nara thinks of it. Whenever she finds herself starting to think about Kamakura, she sternly tells herself, *Knock it off!*

They leave the stairwell and emerge into the fifth-floor hallway.

'That guy might be someone Koko hired to help them,' says Nara as they make their way toward Room 525.

'Could be,' agrees Sengoku as he leads the way down the hall.

'Okay, we're here. Room 525.'

Voices fill their earpieces.

'Get in there!'

'Don't be too hasty!'

'Be careful!'

Nara reaches around Sengoku to hold the lock-breaker up to the sensor on the door's card reader. There's a small noise. The lock is disabled.

Nara has her blowgun in her hand already. It's loaded with a dart that induces paralysis. If their only target was the man who attacked Kamakura, they could have used darts smeared with a nerve toxin that induces a state of shock that's very close to death, but Yuka Kamino's there, too, and must be captured alive and conscious. As long as there's a chance she might catch a stray during battle, paralysis darts are the only real choice they have.

Sengoku pushes down the door handle with his left hand, his right hand gripping his own blowgun.

Imagining that there might be someone pointing a gun on the far side of the door, they crouch to half their normal height.

Nara follows Sengoku inside. No gunshot rings out – in fact, there's no sound at all, nor any trace of human presence. They close the door and stand up.

Heian's voice sounds in their ears. 'Both the man and Kamino are likely still in the room.'

Likely? Heian's choice of words troubles Nara. The hallway security cameras surely have blind spots, though. So their grip on the situation isn't absolute.

Could they be hiding somewhere? Nara realizes she and Sengoku don't know what kind of weapons they might have, either.

The room is dark. Maybe they turned out the lights on purpose. There's a switch near the door. Sengoku turns his head to look at it, as if to ask, *Should we get some light in here?*

The pros and cons of turning on the lights race through Nara's mind.

If they do turn them on, then they're alerting their targets that they've entered the room. But they should probably assume they know that already. With the lights on, it'll be easier for them to find their targets. But the reverse is also true.

In her experience, Nara has always been able to keep track of her target's movements even in a darkened room. She sees a shadow, blows a dart, and that's that. The problem with guns is that the sound of a shot can expose your position, but there's no such worry with a blowgun.

In that sense, darkness is their friend.

Nara shakes her head, and Sengoku nods as if to say, *Agreed – no lights*. He moves away from the switch.

It's a bit of a tight squeeze near the door, forcing them to proceed single file. They're unable to see the entire bedroom in front of them.

They move carefully, putting one foot in front of the other as their nerves sing. A hotel room has only one entrance. There's no escape, except out the window.

It's a blind alley.

Where could they be?

Sengoku, leading the way, moves over to the closet to the right and slides open the door. Nara takes a peek inside, releasing her breath at the same time. There are two bathrobes hanging in the closet, and the darts she blows strike them both right in the collar.

Where is the bathroom?

Sengoku slips into the bedroom proper, followed closely by Nara. She's ready to launch more darts at the slightest hint of movement, but all that's in the room are twin beds set crosswise to the entrance.

Sengoku stands next to one.

'Between the beds, or under them,' whispers Nara, wanting to check off the list of places where they might be hiding. They need to be ready.

'The bathroom is in the back.'

Setting the identity of the man aside, they know that Yuka Kamino, at least, has never received any special training. *If we make a sudden sound, she'll probably scream and give herself away,* thinks Nara. But the man may well have his hand over her mouth to prevent just such a thing from happening.

Thinking someone could be hiding behind the curtains, Nara studies them carefully, trying to detect any unnatural movement.

The man may very well be carrying a projectile weapon as well, like a gun. If Nara's previous experiences facing gun-wielding targets have taught her anything, though, it's that her darts can stop someone with a gun in their tracks well before they have a chance to shoot. This is because there's almost zero need to prep a blowgun before firing it, unlike a gun.

She imagines scenarios: the man jumping up from behind the bed in front of her and pointing a gun in her face, or throwing something at her head. Or maybe he'll launch himself at her in an attempt to tackle her. But whatever the case, she and Sengoku will surely be faster in their attack.

She surveys the bedroom. There's the sideboard, the refrigerator, the TV. But nowhere to hide.

I'm going in.

Sengoku whispers to Nara, then takes a step away from the bed. That's when they hear the alarm.

It comes from one of the nightstands next to the beds – it's hard to tell which has a clock on it – and as soon as she hears it, she launches a dart in that direction. Sengoku does the same, and they hear their darts hit the nightstand nearly simultaneously.

Nara turns her gaze again, blowgun still at the ready and scanning the room for movement, and takes a step.

By the time she has a moment to think *Dammit!* she's already pitching forward. Her foot is caught on some sort of rope. The sound behind her drew her attention away from her immediate surroundings. As she falls, she brings her hands up; they're close to hitting the floor when she sees it's covered in tacks, spikes facing up.

In the nick of time, Sengoku lends a hand, preventing her from hitting the spiky ground. Her head fills with rage at falling into the trap in exactly the way the target must have planned. A shadow jumps out from the edge of the bedroom – was this part of his plan? Nara's blowgun is far from her mouth, so she can't launch a dart right away. Sengoku, his hands occupied supporting Nara, can't either.

The man in front of them moves his arm. Is he throwing something? There's no gunshot. She feels no immediate pain, so she at first thinks he must have missed her. She goes for her blowgun, but stops as a tiny explosion of pain erupts on her face. It feels like burning as it spreads across her face and eyes and head.

It's water! Boiling water! That's what he must have thrown at them. Sengoku has his head down, too, and is wiping his face with his hand.

But he's also working to steady himself as he shakes his head violently back and forth. Something more than water must have struck him. The electric kettle! Nara senses something else coming at her, but she manages to duck it. The object hits the ground behind her. A hairdryer.

He's not going to miss the next opportunity! He must be coming for her. Nara frantically puts the tube in her hand to her mouth and blows.

But it's deflected. She sees that the man has a chair in his hands. He's holding it in front of him as he advances.

Nara brings her blowgun to her mouth once more. Sengoku reaches out. Is he trying to grab the chair?

The man waves the chair back and forth, leaving his torso exposed. Just as she predicted. Nara takes aim and blows as hard as she can.

She senses her dart hitting home. The man's movements should be slowing down, but he's still moving toward her.

Right then, another sound splits the air, a series of loud bangs from the back of the room like electricity shorting out – *batchi batchi batchi!* A string of firecrackers?

Her eyes are drawn momentarily by the sound. *Dammit!* She turns her gaze back to the man just in time to see him strike Sengoku in the head, and then, almost immediately, something heavy hits the back of her own head. Brightness explodes in front of her eyes, followed by darkness.

She falls forward once again, tiny spikes piercing her as she hits the tacks arrayed across the floor, but she's unable to get back up.

NANAO

The fifth floor

NANAO HURRIES OUT OF ROOM 525. He pulls Kamino with him by the hand; they close the door quickly as soon as they're both in the hall.

He managed to execute every part of his plan, from A to Z. He boiled the water in the kettle, set the alarm, gave Kamino some firecrackers, and hid. The alarm went off exactly when he wanted it to, then he picked up the chair and managed to hit both of them with it. The only thing he didn't manage to do was finish them off.

There were two of them: a well-built guy who looked like a martial artist, and a woman about the same height as Nanao himself.

It's a good thing he knew they'd be armed with blowguns. If he hadn't, he'd very likely have been hit with a dart right off the bat, and that would have been that. As it was, he stuffed his clothes with pillows in case he got hit with a stray dart.

He used the chair on the man and then hit the woman in the

162

head with it, but the chair slipped from his grasp after that, and he was left with nothing else to use as a weapon. Maybe he should have taken the time to grab each of their heads and twist, snapping their necks. But the man hadn't lost consciousness entirely, and was already trying to get back on his feet to come at Nanao again. He decided the best course of action was to get as far away as possible at that point.

It's true that the guy was dazed enough that Nanao figured he could still take him, but there was also Kamino to consider – her presence made everything that much more dangerous. There was also the possibility that the woman might wake up, too, while he was busy dealing with the man.

So it was time to flee the scene.

In cases like this, Nanao trusts his gut.

They hurry down the hall. He looks over at Kamino walking beside him and notices she's holding a cushion.

'Ah!' Kamino looks as surprised as Nanao to find it still in her hands. Embarrassed, she holds it up to show him, and then they see a dart-like object stuck in its center. 'This is from when we went out the door. I thought I heard something and looked back, and held this in front of me.'

The big man must have shot it at them as they left. The cushion was a lifesaver.

As they approach the elevators, Nanao debates inwardly if they should use them. The man might catch up with them as they're waiting for one to arrive.

'The emergency stairs are this way. I was just there.' Kamino rushes ahead. They have to hurry – they don't know when a dart might come flying at them from behind.

Partway down the hall, Nanao notices something on the floor. An earpiece. He picks it up, guessing it belonged to the man he tangled with near the elevators.

Out in front of him, Yuka Kamino reaches the door to the

163

emergency stairwell and opens it. They slip through, closing it as quietly as possible behind them.

They begin going down the stairs, but then Nanao stops them.

'Should we go down to the ground floor, or should we find another place to hide out first?'

His thoughts have been so occupied with saving Maria that he's been unable to focus on anything else but getting out of the hotel as quickly as possible, but he recalls the advice he always gives himself in these situations: it's when you're most in a rush that you need to be at your calmest.

Of course, even when he manages to follow this advice and act calmly, misfortune finds him. But if he acts rashly, he'll regret it, wondering, *Maybe I should have thought before I acted*, when things inevitably go wrong. If things go wrong even after he considers his actions calmly, he has an out – he gives himself permission to say, 'Oh, I'm just unlucky.' That's what he's learned so far in this life of his.

'What?' Kamino looks perplexed by his question, as if she's thinking, *You want me to decide?*

'If I decide myself, I know it'll all go to shit.'

'I don't—'

'It's a long story, so just trust me – it's better if anyone else but me decides what to do now.'

'Well, if we go down, there's surely more of them waiting for us on the ground floor.' Kamino slides the bag she's been carrying off her shoulders and puts it on the ground. Did she intend to get her phone out and start looking at the security camera footage again?

'We don't have time for that!' interjects Nanao. 'Just choose: up or down. Go with your gut.'

Even as he pushes her, Nanao still thinks that going down would be the best choice, but he repeats his own advice to himself: if we act rashly, no good will come of it.

'I think those two people up there figure we're heading down. To get out of the hotel.'

'I see.'

'Which means we should go up. We need to be a step ahead of them.'

'Got it!' Nanao immediately starts back up the stairs, then stops again. 'But where are we going?'

Only one place comes to mind.

NANAO

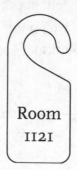

Room
1121

'I APOLOGIZE, LADYBUG. The truth is, I'd started to doubt you.' Soda is sprawled on the sofa, scratching his head. 'Now I know how Selinuntius felt.'

'Selin-who?'

Nanao and Kamino have climbed the stairs and now they're here, the only place Nanao could think of to hide out in: Soda's room. Soda and Cola were hired by Koko to protect Kamino in the first place, after all. So saving Kamino is, properly speaking, Soda's job.

'How's your ankle?' asks Nanao.

As soon as he does, Soda winces. 'Still pretty bad,' he says as he hastily makes a show of reaching down to massage it. Seemingly forgetting which was the bad one, he massages both ankles. 'You know, I had a moment there when I thought you might have broken your promise and left the hotel. You really seemed to want to get out of here.'

'I do.'

'So I was left here to wait, just like Selinuntius in "Run, Melos!"'

'You've expanded your reading beyond self-help books?'

'It was in a textbook in school, I read it then. But anyway, I'm sorry. I should never have doubted a friend.'

'We're not friends.'

'And look, you're even doing bodyguard duty for me!' he continues, pointing at Kamino. 'I'm sorry to have doubted you. Are you gonna hit me? Like Melos did?'

'I'm not going to hit you. Not like Melos or anyone else.'

'Anyway, how's Cola? And Koko? Are they off doing something on their own?'

Nanao hesitates, wondering whether he should tell him, but only for a split second.

'They died. Both of them.' No need to sugarcoat it. Professionals losing their lives is hardly rare, after all. 'At least, according to her,' he adds, pointing to where Kamino sits clutching her cushion. Staring blankly into the middle distance, she doesn't react.

'What?' Soda stiffens.

'They died.'

'Cola's . . . dead?'

Nanao fills in the blanks: Koko went to Room 2010 and found a body there that seemed to belong to Cola, and then Koko herself was attacked and killed.

'Koko-san was talking to me when I heard someone come for her.' Kamino had been silent, paralyzed by either fear or sorrow, but finally, haltingly, she begins to speak. 'After what sounded like a struggle, I heard the voices of a man and a woman telling their friends that Koko-san was dead.'

'Were they the ones who killed Cola too?'

'Maybe . . .' Nanao plays dumb. After all, he's hardly in a position to say, *Well, actually, I was in the room when he slipped and fell and hit his head on the table.*

Soda begins doing something on his phone. Nanao barely has

167

time to wonder what before he holds it up to show him a picture. 'This is Cola.'

'Yeah, that's him,' says Nanao without thinking. And indeed, it's definitely the face of the man he met in Room 2010.

Dammit! All is lost if Soda thinks to ask, 'Wait, how would you know what he looks like?' After all, he already explained that it was Koko who discovered the body in Room 2010. His story doesn't add up.

But Soda seems to accept Nanao's words anyway – or, perhaps, he's simply too shocked to question them. 'I see . . .' He slumps, as if all strength has left his body.

He turns pale and sighs deeply again and again. Is he preparing to start tearing out his hair in grief? 'That must . . .' he mutters to himself, trailing off before starting again. 'That must be why he never messaged back.'

Nanao finds himself at a loss – he can't say either, *I know how you feel,* or, *I don't care.*

Soda remains silent for a while longer, then breathes in and out deeply, as if attempting to bring himself back under control. Is he thinking back on his time with Cola? Nanao can't imagine what it might be like to lose someone you've worked with for years, but he does know that the two of them surely took the lives of others on more than one occasion, which might help him accept the loss.

It feels like forever before Soda speaks again. 'What a way to go,' he says listlessly, and then adds, 'Who did this?'

'Not me!' insists Nanao before he can stop himself.

Soda sighs, his expression clearly saying, *Of course not you,* and then points at Kamino. 'Koko was helping you escape, right? So it must be the people trying to stop you who killed both Koko and Cola.'

'The Six,' mutters Kamino vacantly, as if unable to accept reality. 'That's what Koko-san called them. She said they use blowguns.'

Nanao doesn't miss that Soda's expression grows dark at her words. 'You know them?'

'The Six? Yeah. They're serious business.'

'They're that good?'

'You know Edo?'

'Edo? Is that someone's name?'

'Look, Ladybug, I said this before, but you really need to start paying more attention to what's going on in your own profession. Edo's a guy who used to work on his own. I think he's in his mid-thirties now. He likes to hurt people, you now? What people call a sadist. He's assembled a group of like-minded young people to work with him – five of them. And yeah, they use blowguns.'

'They certainly do,' agrees Nanao. The man in front of the elevator used one, as did the man and woman who broke into their hotel room. He takes pains to describe his experiences without making it sound like a swashbuckling swords-and-samurai adventure.

'They shower you with darts, right? Cola always said knives and guns were better,' says Soda. 'Cola knew so much about everything,' he adds, lost in his thoughts again.

'You never know when they fire the darts – you just notice when you hear them hit something. By the time you think, *Oh, they got me!* it's too late.'

'Yeah, it's just like – you know.'

'Like what?'

'Time's arrow.'

Nanao doesn't know how to respond to that.

Soda goes on. 'But you managed to get away without them getting you! Classic Ladybug.'

'I don't know how "classic" it was, I barely escaped. In any case, I just did what I had to do to survive.'

'You took three of them out!'

'No, the last two survived. It was all I could do to get out of Room 525 alive.'

'I think the guy you took out first was the one called Kamakura. Young, handsome, slim, right? From what you said, the two that came to Room 525 were the big ones – Sengoku and Nara.'

'You really know your stuff.'

'Cola always told me I needed to know the names of our professional colleagues,' shrugs Soda, before suddenly breaking into a smile.

'What so funny?' asks Nanao.

'I was just remembering something else Cola once said to me. You know, we were partners for ten years and did all sorts of things together, but for some reason, all I can think about right now was when he talked about stone guardian dogs.'

'Guardian dogs? You mean like the ones they put in front of shrines?'

'Yes, exactly. If you're facing the shrine, the one on the left will have its mouth closed, like it's going, *Ohmmm*. That's the guardian dog. On the right, there'll be another one, this one with its mouth open. That's the guardian *lion*. The two of them side by side. So cute.'

'I thought they were both dogs.'

'Sometimes it's two dogs, but a lot of places have both. Cola really liked it when it was both, a dog and a lion together.'

'In front of a shrine?'

'Yeah. He looked at me once, dead serious, and asked, "Do you like it better when the dog and lion face forward, their backs to the torii gate, or when they sit looking at each other?"'

Soda holds up his hands, curled to make animal mouths of them, and holds them so they face each other, saying, 'Like so?' as he does, and then he turns them so they both face Nanao, saying, 'Or like *so*?'

'It's true, you see them both ways,' Nanao says.

'He looked so serious that I assumed he was about to say something really important, so when it turned out he was just asking about guardian dogs, I burst out laughing. "It's hard to choose, they're both so cute," I said. Anyway, that's the first thing I thought of when you told me he's dead.' Soda falls back into silence, as if overcome by emotion. He rubs the corners of his eyes.

With Soda, who just lost Cola, and Kamino, who just lost Koko, on either side of him, Nanao doesn't quite know how to feel – it's almost as if he should have lost an important person in his life, too. A rather cart-before-the-horse kind of feeling. He awkwardly tries to manufacture an appropriately humbled expression.

'Well, it was bound to happen sometime,' says Soda, seemingly addressing himself. 'Cola told me that too, long ago. We inflict harm on others, so it's only a matter of time before that harm turns back on us. No use complaining about it. I think I read something like that in one of my books, too. *What goes around comes around.*'

Has he read any of these books past the title? Nanao has his doubts.

'I guess that's true,' he says, then puts one of his hands in his pocket. His fingers encounter something, and when he pulls it out, he sees it's an earpiece. The one that fell out of Kamakura's ear.

'What's that?' Nanao's movements haven't escaped Soda's sharp eyes.

'One of the Six had this in his ear. I think they use it to keep up with each other.' Nanao puts it in his own ear but hears nothing. He reaches up and realizes there's a switch – it's turned off. 'I wonder if we can use it to listen in to them ourselves.'

'That would be *very* useful.'

Hoping against hope, Nanao flicks the switch to 'on' and puts it back in his ear. Fearing that they might be able to hear him as well, he closes his mouth and holds his breath.

NANAO

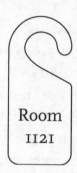

Room
1121

'HAVEN'T YOU FOUND THEM YET, Heian?'

A male voice is speaking through the earpiece in Nanao's ear. Nanao, looking at Kamino and Soda, puts a finger to his lips.

'I'm going back through the footage now. They were in the fifth-floor hallway, right? Both Kamino and that guy.'

'Who is that guy? Sengoku, Nara, did you get a look at him in the hotel room?'

'It was only for a second, I didn't have time to really see his face. I don't think he's a civilian, though. By which I mean, I feel like I've seen him somewhere before. I wonder where . . .'

'Nara, are you okay?'

'How can I be okay? He hit me in the head! And poured boiling water on me! I have burns! Burns!'

'Maybe you should take a breather.'

'Are you joking, Edo? When I say I'm not okay, I mean I'm *mad*. I'm not going to go through something like that and then just leave! I won't rest till I get my revenge, okay? I'm going to paralyze him and then pour boiling water over his head, at the very least.'

Nanao, listening in, can't help but scrunch his face up in alarm.

'We can't let them escape. Heian, keep an eye on the entrances and exits!'

'You don't have to tell me, I'm already doing it. There are three ways out on the ground floor – the front entrance and two back doors. I went through the footage from those cameras and didn't find any trace of Yuka Kamino using them. I believe she's still in the building.'

'Do we really need to spy on the entrance? If she makes a break for it, it won't matter if Heian's watching. Wouldn't it be better if we were there ourselves, keeping an eye out?'

'No. Sengoku, I want you and the others to concentrate on searching for her. It would be stupid to have you waste your time standing around at the entrance. A waste of firepower, if you will.'

'So what do you propose we do, Edo-san? If there's no one watching, she could just run out the door!'

'I've called in some reinforcements to keep an eye out for us.'

'"Reinforcements"? What are you talking about?'

'Wait, I think I see them near the front entrance. Those guys milling around out there – is that who you mean?'

'Professionals who come right when you call them are hardly professionals at all, but they're better than nothing. They can earn a little spending money watching the door as well as anyone.'

'Let the riffraff have their moment. Better them than us anyway.'

'Heian, can you look through the camera footage and find the guy helping Kamino? I want to send the guys watching the doors a pic of his face.'

Nanao, hearing this, reaches up and touches his own cheek.

'Got it. I took a screenshot, I'll send it to the group chat.'

'Let's send it to Inui, too, just in case. If he's a professional, Inui'll know who he is. Now, since the door's covered, Sengoku, Nara, Asuka: I want you three to scour the hotel and find them.'

'I really feel like I've seen this guy before . . .'

'Try to remember where, Sengoku!'

Nanao hears something ding in the background. A notification on one of their phones?

'You can't check every room in the place. Heian, the faster you can provide a clue as to where they might be, the better. They should be somewhere in the footage even if they used the emergency stairs, right? If we can at least narrow it down to which floor they might be on . . .'

'There's a lot of cameras, you know. It's not so easy to check both the recorded footage and the live feeds. It takes time to go looking.'

'What should we do with Kamakura's body?'

'Don't you think we should leave it in Room 525, Sengoku? I'd been planning to call Inui and get him to send a clean-up crew.'

'We can do that.'

'Take a picture first, though.'

'Of Kamakura?'

'There's demand for that kind of thing, you know. Faces of death.'

'All right, got it.'

'Um, what should I be doing?'

'Are you still in Room 2010, Asuka?'

'Yeah. Should we leave Koko's body behind too?'

'Oh, that's right. I think we can have Inui's people dispose of her as well.'

Nanao hears the notification-like sound again. Was it really from their phones?

'Oh, by the way, when we put Koko's body in the bathtub, we found someone else already there.'

'Someone else? Who?'

'Another body, I should say. I don't recognize him. He's dead.'

'This is getting so complicated.'

'Did Koko take him out?'

'That's a possibility. Or maybe Kamino's guy.'

'Seems like when you check in to this hotel, you check out in a body bag.'

That must be Cola, thinks Nanao, sneaking a glance at Soda. He hears the notification-like sound go off again somewhere.

'Clean up Room 2010 the best you can, Asuka, then go down to join the others on the fifth floor.'

'Right, right, got it.'

Nanao takes the earpiece out and then, handling it as gingerly as if it were a piece of precision machinery, he carefully switches it off.

'So? What did they say?' asks Soda.

'Everyone's pretty angry.'

'Well, thanks to you, Ladybug, they're no longer the Six – they're the Five. Of course they're angry.'

Nanao then summarizes what he overheard to Soda and Kamino. The Five have called in reinforcements from somewhere to watch all the ways out on the ground floor.

Kamino's face goes white. Nanao almost asks if she'd like to lie down for a bit, but then thinks better of it – no need to go out of his way to be kind.

'They seem to have someone checking the security cameras all over the hotel. So, we should too. Can you show me the cam feeds?' He directs his question to Kamino.

'Oh – yes, of course,' says Kamino, startling as if from a deep sleep, momentarily rejoining the world to pick up her phone. Nanao leans in to look, followed by Soda.

'There are some fishy-looking guys out by the back entrances. At the front, too.'

A group of guys in tracksuits are indeed visible in the live camera feed from the front. They're standing around where they set their luggage on the ground, slightly apart from where a hotel doorman manages the taxi stand.

'Couldn't they be regular guests?' asks Kamino, seemingly unwilling to believe they're there for her.

'Maybe. But they could very well be riffraff.'

'Riffraff?'

Nanao explains that one of the Five used the term to refer to the guys they called up to help them.

'I hate that,' says Soda, drawing Nanao's attention.

'You hate what?'

'When people say stuff like that. They think they're so different, that they're not just *riffraff* too.'

'That's true.'

'They can only be happy by feeling superior to others,' adds Soda, pouting.

'What do you mean?' asks Kamino.

'What do you mean, what do you mean? I meant exactly what I said. I asked Cola once, "Don't you ever get jealous of people? Or want what they have that you don't?" After all, I knew I did. Like, I'd watch sports and see someone perform some amazing feat, and I'd think, *Oh man, if only I could do that!* or, you know, I'd get depressed, thinking, *Oh man, I could never do that in a million years.* So I figured Cola must be the same. But he just looked at me and said, "No. Never."'

According to Soda, he was shocked at Cola's response, raising his voice to ask, 'Really? You never get jealous, ever? Of anyone?' To which Cola, puzzled, replied, 'What point would there be for a plum tree to want to be like the apple tree beside it? A plum is perfectly a plum; an apple is perfectly an apple – what good would it do to want to be a rose?'

Aren't we getting a bit off-topic? Nanao almost points this out to

176

Soda, but at the same time, he realizes that Soda's story about Cola is starting to get to him. He's spent countless days cursing his own unlucky life, consumed by envy of others' relative good fortune. More than once he's thought that if he could only live the life of someone else, he'd be able to pass his days in peace and harmony.

An apple is perfectly an apple. So what if an apple can't bloom like a rose? The words echo in Nanao's head.

Kamino is staring at Soda as well, rapt, but he doesn't seem to notice. 'Ahh, that reminds me,' he says, leaping from one subject to the next. 'Have you noticed that these days, when you wait for an elevator, it doesn't tell you which floor it's on before it arrives?'

Nanao doesn't understand the intent behind the question, but it's true that the Winton Palace elevators are made that way – there's not even a place for such information to be displayed above the door.

'I heard they're doing that to cut down on customer irritation.'

'Irritation?' Nanao doesn't understand what he means. After all, if you know where the elevator you're waiting for is, you can predict how long it'll take to arrive. Wouldn't that be less stressful than not knowing?

'Elevators don't always stop to take everyone in order, you know. Sometimes one passes by someone waiting for it so as to bring everyone where they want to go more efficiently. But if someone sees an elevator pass by without letting them on, they'll get mad, right?'

'I guess that's true.'

'So they made it so you can't tell where the elevators are until they arrive. That way, it can pass you by and you'll never know. From the point of view of the person waiting, being passed over is no different to not being passed over. Oh, there's a theory about this! Cola told me about it once, what was it?'

'A theory?'

'Quantum theory, I think he called it. It says something like, the position of something isn't decided until it's observed. Until then, it's like it's not in any position at all – or in all of them at once. This is like that. It doesn't matter where the elevator is until the moment you observe it.'

Nanao's sincerely impressed. 'You really know some complicated things.'

'Cola said something about a cat, too. When we were talking about this.'

'A cat?'

'Isn't there a cat? A quantum kitty?' Soda turns to Kamino. 'Do you know what I'm talking about?'

'Do you mean Schrödinger's cat?'

'Yes! That's it.'

'It's a thought experiment where you don't know what state the cat is in until you look at it.'

'That's what Cola said, too. You don't know how the cat's doing until you look. Well, I'm not sure what it all means, really, except one thing. There's one thing that's always true.'

'What thing? What's always true?'

'Whether you look at it or not, one thing's sure – that cat's gonna be cute!'

'Oh—' Kamino seems at a loss for words.

Nanao sighs, similarly defeated.

'There's no debate. You don't need to observe it to know that.' Soda nods, the picture of confidence. 'Didn't Schrödinger get it? You don't have to look at a cat to know it's cute.'

'What were we talking about again?' Nanao can no longer be silent. Why were they spending all this time talking about observing things? But then, out of nowhere, inspiration hits. 'Wait – what if we use the staff elevator?'

'You think?'

'We'll be harder to find if we use the staff elevator, right?' There'll be fewer cameras than in the guest elevators, surely. Which means they'll be less likely to be *observed*.

'That might be a good idea. But you need a special keycard to get into the area where the staff elevator is. The staff who have access to the guest rooms use them to pass back and forth between the "back of the house" and the hallways.'

'Oh!' exclaims Nanao. He looks at Kamino. 'Isn't that what Koko went up to Room 2010 to get?'

Kamino nods: *Yes.* Nanao sees that her eyes are starting to well up, perhaps from memories of Koko helping her.

'Cola brought it with him. He was always prepared. Always two steps ahead.'

Two steps ahead till he fell on his head, thinks Nanao guiltily, remembering the incident in Room 2010. No matter how prepared you might be, unexpected accidents still happen.

'Even this watch was his idea,' says Soda, showing off the time-piece on his wrist again.

Nanao recalls that Cola was wearing a similar-looking watch on his own wrist. He can't help but ask, 'What's a person who says things like, "An apple is perfectly an apple," doing wearing a fancy watch like that?'

Soda shrugs. 'I'm the one who bought them, wanting to show off. I think Cola was just being nice by going along with it. Though he did say he liked the design. Since we had so much money all of a sudden, maybe he just wanted to have the experience of buying something fancy. Though in the end, it didn't seem as though he enjoyed the experience all that much.'

'So what was his idea?'

'It's for when we find ourselves surrounded.'

'How do they come in handy, then?'

Is it so you can offer to give them the watch so they'll let you go? The thought occurs to Nanao, and as soon as he voices it, Soda laughs. 'Yes, exactly. One of the useful things about an expensive watch is that a materialistic person will want it!'

'So that was the idea?'

'It could come in handy in other ways, too.'

Nanao stares up at the ceiling, faintly appalled. *Is it really such a good use of our time to listen to Soda try to explain things?* He feels like he's looking up not just at the ceiling above him, but all the way up to Room 2010. 'Is there a way we could get up there and get that card?'

'Don't you think one of them will be there?' asks Kamino, visibly frightened. She's surely afraid of ending up the same way Koko did. Her voice shakes as she speaks.

'When I was listening in, a woman named Asuka was there, but it sounded like she was about to head down to Room 525.'

'Sounds like there's a chance, then,' says Soda.

'No,' says Nanao, remembering something important. 'Think about it. Going up to Room 2010 carries just as much risk of being seen as going anywhere else. We'd be caught by a security camera no matter what we do.'

Even access to the staff elevator might not be worth the risk of going up to get the card, Nanao thinks.

Suddenly, Soda rises to his feet. 'All right,' he says.

Nanao stares at him, wordlessly asking, *What's with you?*

'I think I can do it,' Soda answers.

'What do you mean?'

'You two are busted – they know your faces. If they see you on camera, they'll be onto you and send someone right away. But they don't know me, right? I can go up and get the card out of Room 2010 no problem. In fact, you could say I was left waiting in this room up till now just to be able to do this!'

'All right,' agrees Nanao. 'But it's still dangerous. It might be less likely they'll know who you are, but the chances they might come for you aren't zero.'

'If they come for me, they come for me. I'll deal with it then. I might even welcome the chance to get even with them, for Cola's sake.'

Nanao decides not to tell him that it was the corner of a marble table, not the Six, who robbed Cola of his life.

YOMOGI

The restaurant on the second floor

'YOUR *POMFRET POÊLÉ*, SIR. Beneath it, you'll find a *coulis* made with *céleri-rave*. Please make sure to enjoy them together.'

The fish course is served.

As soon as the waiter leaves, Director Yomogi says, 'Aren't you nervous? Personally, I hardly dare even breathe!'

Is he talking about the danger to his life? Ikeo looks around the room. The restaurant is spacious, with the other guests seated well away from them.

'It's like he's performing a sacred ritual every time he explains a dish! I feel like I have to pay attention to every word before I'm allowed to eat,' continues Yomogi, laughing.

'Oh, you mean the explanations of the food!'

'You know, when I was in Parliament, I once accidentally called the Prime Minister the Prime Minestrone.'

'What? How could that happen?'

Ikeo understands that Yomogi is trying to lighten the mood.

Yomogi picks up his knife and fork. Ikeo follows suit, slicing his knife into the elegantly plump cut of fish on his plate.

'I looked into the accident. The one three years ago, that took the lives of your wife and child. It might be indelicate to say, but it's possible that it was no accident – that someone meant for it to happen. Or at least, I've heard rumors to that effect.'

Slowly, carefully, Ikeo raises his eyes to look at the Director. His face shows no sign of disquiet, as if he's heard this kind of thing before. But he also seems to be taking Ikeo's words to heart. 'They blamed the accident on a drunk driver,' adds Ikeo.

'Yes, they did.' Yomogi's words have force behind them. The Director generally acts unbothered by everything, speaking casually as if he's heard it all before, but it's possible that this is simply a performance, and that he's constantly fighting to suppress his real emotions. *Will I finally get to hear from the real Yomogi?* Ikeo can't wait.

Yomogi goes on. 'I will never forgive the driver for what he did. Nor for dying in the accident, either.'

Ikeo nods, scooping up the last piece of *pomfret* on his plate and putting it in his mouth. His hands are shaking, and he stares at them as if they're someone else's as he readies himself to open his mouth once more.

'An acquaintance of mine saw the driver right before the accident. I only found out about this recently.'

'Really,' says Yomogi, seemingly a bit surprised.

Yes! thinks Ikeo. Offering people information they don't already know is the best way to get them to value you.

'He was standing a few hundred meters away from where the accident happened, he said. Right beforehand, he'd taken out his phone to take a picture of a billboard he thought was funny. The car is in that picture. He told me he only realized it now.'

'Is that so?' Yomogi suddenly seems closer. Perhaps he is – he seems to have leaned forward at some point. 'That car?'

That car, he says, as if saying, *That infernal machine, the one that stole my whole family in an instant?*

'It appears it wasn't moving – it was stopped at the side of the road.'

Ikeo takes out his phone and pulls up the picture, then shows it to the Director. 'This is what he sent me.'

Yomogi points at the screen. 'There, on the sidewalk! That's—'

'Yes. A man.' Ikeo realizes that his voice has gotten louder. *This is why I'm here!* he wants to shout. The picture shows a well-built man standing next to the car. It's an import, with the steering wheel on the left side; the man appears to be leaning over, talking to someone on the driver's side. 'Of course, this may have nothing to do with the accident at all. Maybe it's just someone he knows that he met by chance on the street. Or maybe, since he was drunk, this is some other incident that happened before he started to drive again.'

'Of course. But it may very well *be* related, too.' Yomogi's expression is grave. 'Isn't that right?'

'That's right. Furthermore, there's only one business in the area with a security camera that might have caught the incident on tape: the liquor store across the street. I asked to see the footage from it.'

'And?'

'And it appears the camera was broken.'

'Really.'

'Yes. Broken. Apparently, the owner hadn't checked on it in a while, so it's impossible to say when it broke, as it wasn't set up to keep the footage it takes for more than a day.'

'One might think there's something suspicious there.'

Ikeo nods.

Behind the façade of this accident lurks someone's ill intent – that's the message Ikeo wants to get across. And, it appears, he's succeeded.

KAMINO

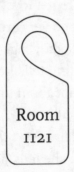

Room
1121

YUKA KAMINO IS TRYING to regulate her breathing. *Deep breathing and stretching can be surprisingly effective!* It seems like a million years ago that Koko said that to her.

'Why don't you sit down and take a minute?' says Nanao, but she finds she can't sit still.

'You know, I'm so grateful.'

'You realize I'm not doing this to be nice. All I want is to get out of here too.'

'Oh, I'm sorry, I didn't mean you. I meant that other fellow. Soda-san? Is that his name?'

'Ahh, him,' replies Nanao. 'Yeah, he's something to be thankful for. Who would have thought he'd take it upon himself to go up and fetch that card for us?'

'He's a good person.'

A troubled expression crosses Nanao's face. 'He's a professional like me. That makes him most decidedly *not* a good person. Soda, me, even your precious Koko – we all work outside the law. It's dirty work. None of us are good people.'

'Well, I . . .'

Kamino looks down at the phone in her hand. The feeds from the security cameras fill the screen, but she notices that the phone's battery is starting to get low. She mentions it to Nanao, who says, 'There must be a power cord around here somewhere,' and starts rifling through Soda's bag.

Don't think about it, Kamino tells herself. Not about Koko, not about when she met Inui, not about the 'unsettling rumors' she's heard about him since. She knows that the moment she begins to think, she'll lose it entirely. *Don't think deeply about anything, just take things at face value,* she tells herself. *Please, for the love of God, don't think!*

The screen is split into sections showing different views of the hotel. The top left shows the bank of elevators on the twentieth floor, while the view next to it is a continuous feed showing the hallway on the fifth floor where they barely escaped with their lives.

'Soda-san made it to the twentieth floor. I see him.'

As she speaks, her phone dings, notifying her that she has a message. It's Soda telling them that he made it to the right floor.

'So conscientious.'

'He could have easily abandoned us and made a run for it. I can't believe he actually kept his promise and went all the way up there!'

'He's just doing the job he was originally hired to do, you real-ize. I, on the other hand, was minding my own business when I got all wrapped up in this!' Nanao looks down at his watch and looks concerned. 'By the way, I never asked – why are the Six after you in the first place?'

Kamino realizes now that after meeting in the elevator, barely escaping Room 525, and then rushing up here to Room 1121, she never had a chance to explain to him what's going on. She more or less strong-armed Nanao into saving her. It's the first time in her life that she's ever asked for someone's help so brazenly.

'It's not really the Six who are after me – it's Inui. Inui's the one who hired them to find me.'

'Inui?' Nanao looks up at the ceiling as he searches his memory. Seeing him struggle to remember, Kamino can't help but feel a bit jealous. Even things she desperately wants to forget end up lodged in her brain forever.

'Do you know him? I used to work for him. I have a talent for memorization.'

'Memorization?'

'Or, I guess, just memory. I'm much better at remembering things than most people. I remember everything that's ever happened to me.'

Nanao stares at her as she talks.

'So, I have everything Inui told me about his business memorized.'

'For example . . .'

'For example, bank account numbers, credit card numbers, email addresses, messages – everything he ever showed me.'

'Really?'

'Really.'

'That's really something.'

'Really something horrible.'

'I guess it would be. Horrible.'

Kamino's surprised. Most people, when they hear about her good memory, say they're jealous.

'I mean, it's not like I can imagine how hard it is for you. I

187

don't really like to think about things like that. But there are plenty of things in my life I'd like to forget. To remember every single one of my failures and unlucky breaks with perfect clarity – it makes my blood run cold.'

Ahhh, thinks Kamino. It might seem overblown, but she's genuinely moved. She feels as though she's met a soulmate, someone who might actually comprehend how hard her life has been up till now.

'So anyway, Inui's after you because of your great memory, is that it?' Nanao doesn't seem to want to get into specifics. As long as he has the gist of things, the rest will work itself out on its own. 'And he put the Six on your tail.'

'That's right. I came here to the Winton Palace to hide out, and that's when I met Koko-san.'

It seems so long ago now that it's a shock to think it's only been a few hours. She's beginning to think that the Winton Palace's reputation as a hotel where you can't die even if you want to is pretty ironic. Things keep happening to her one after another, putting her in ever greater danger – it's more like a hotel where you end up trying as hard as you can not to die.

'Sounds like it's been pretty rough, what with that group of crazy dart-blowers after you.' Nanao's tone contains something resembling sympathy.

'You know, just once in my life, I'd like to hit the jackpot,' says Kamino without really thinking.

'What's that?' Nanao turns to look at her.

'Playing a slot machine, when three sevens line up, that means you won the jackpot, right?'

'Yeah, that's how it works.'

'Someone once told me about how as a child, his father got him a little toy slot machine to play with. He pulled and pulled the lever, but he never got a jackpot. So he went to his father and asked him, "Is it okay that I'm so unlucky?" He was sincerely worried about his life, if this meant that he and his father were going to have a hard life.'

Is this how it's going to be from now on? What's gonna happen to us, Dad?

It's gonna be okay. We don't need that luck right now.

'It's like that with me, too. I know exactly how that kid felt.'

Nanao's response is filled with genuine feeling, surprising Kamino. 'Really?'

'So much it hurts. Anyway, what's the rest of the story?'

'I don't know, he didn't tell me any more than that. My life has been that way, too – not simply without jackpots, but without a single seven ever coming up.'

A life of pulling the lever on a broken slot machine unable to get a win.

'My life has been like playing a slot machine and having the lever come off in your hand.'

'So you're unlucky too?'

'So unlucky that if I order cheesecake, I wouldn't be surprised if it came sprinkled with shichimi togarashi.'

'That might actually be good,' replies Kamino unthinkingly.

Nanao stares blankly in response.

'Yuzu pepper's good, too.'

Nanao makes a face. 'I don't know. I guess the only way to find out is to taste it for myself, but I think I'm going to stick with the standard kind for now.'

'You should really try it, at least once.'

'If I get the chance,' says Nanao. He goes on to ask her, 'By the way, what time is it?'

She answers, and he sighs.

'Do you have something else you need to do?' she asks, despite knowing it's a dumb question. It's not like she checked with him to see what his schedule was like before she blurted out 'Save me!' in the elevator.

'If I did, would you give me leave to go?' Nanao sighs again, longer this time. 'I'm mixed up in this now; I don't think I'm going home anytime soon.'

'I'm sorry.' All Kamino can do is apologize. 'To think it would end up like this.'

'Wait.'

There's something in Nanao's voice that makes her think he's had a sudden flash of inspiration. A thrill runs through her body.

'You said you had all the information about Inui's work in your head, right?'

'Yes.'

'So that means you must know how to get ahold of Maria.'

'Who?'

'Maria's a colleague of mine, we do jobs together. Well, not a colleague exactly, she receives jobs and then gives them to me. Well maybe not *gives* them to me, it's more like she orders me to do whatever she wants me to do.' Nanao's words are less about explaining things clearly than reevaluating their arrangement aloud. 'They're both in the trade, so I figure Maria and Inui must know each other. Which means you might have memorized how to reach her.'

'I don't know if it's her, but I do know the email address of someone named Maria.' The information had popped into her head as soon as he said the name.

Nanao claps his hands in triumph. The sound surprises even himself. 'Can you give it to me? Or, wait, can you send her a message from your phone? Mine's busted.'

Nanao then explains the situation with Maria, how she might be attacked at the theater and that he needs to warn her before that happens.

He doesn't seem to be lying. And she can't think of any reason why he'd think up such a lie in the first place. Before she quite knows what she's doing, Kamino finds herself typing the address into her phone from memory.

'So, it's okay?' Nanao seems as surprised as she is that she's willing to do this. Which makes Kamino worry.

'Is it not?' Kamino hurriedly lifts her fingertips from the screen.

'It is, it is. It's just that if it were me, I'd make sure you agreed to help me first before I helped you, you know? I'm just shocked that you'd do it right away, no questions asked.'

'I see,' nods Kamino. It never even occurred to her to bargain like that. 'I guess that would make more sense.'

'Well, I mean, you don't *have* to . . .' Increasingly agitated, Nanao starts waving his hands back and forth.

'It's fine. Someone's life is at stake; we have to reach her.' Kamino writes the message and sends it with no further delay. 'I hope it reaches her and she reads it in time.'

Nanao, still surprised, brings his hands together in thanks.

'You don't have to thank me so much for something like that,' she assures him, but he replies, 'I can't thank you enough. You really saved the day,' his voice filled with sincerity.

Flustered, Kamino looks down quickly at the phone in her hands to hide her embarrassment. Then, catching sight of the screen, she lets out a shriek.

'What's wrong?' Worried, Nanao leans close to look.

Two people, a man and a woman, pass through the view of the camera in the fifth-floor hallway. 'They're on the move again.'

'Yeah?'

'The camera showed them leaving the room and going down the hall.'

Nanao peers at the screen, then scrunches his face up in displeasure. 'Wait a second. Where could they be going?' He takes the earpiece out and puts it in his ear. He concentrates on their words, then takes the earpiece back out of his ear. 'They don't sound like they're making a big move right now. It seems like they don't know what floor we're on yet.'

'But there they are in the cameras. They just went to the elevators.'

Nanao looks over at the screen again. 'It's those two from before, all right. What were their names again? Sengoku and Nara?'

'I wonder if they're going down to meet the others.'

'If they're going up, there's a chance they might be coming here.'

The image on the screen is too small to see if the call button they pushed was for 'up' or 'down.'

'I wonder if we made a mistake,' whispers Nanao, as if to himself.

'What mistake?'

'I wonder if we should have kept Soda here instead of sending him up for the card. Then he'd be here to help us if it comes to that. As backup.'

'What are we going to do?'

'All we can do is pray that they're not on their way here.'

'But say they are coming – how would they know where we are?'

'I wonder if they went back through the security cam footage and saw us on the eleventh floor.'

'They weren't talking about that, though, when you listened in just now, right?'

Nanao nods. 'I thought that meant we were safe. So naïve.'

'You think they didn't talk about it on purpose?'

'Maybe they caught on that I was listening in. If so, they could just keep talking about whatever while they made their real plans via text message. And now that I think about it—' Nanao's tone turns regretful '—I did hear a lot of dings, like notifications of incoming messages, while I was listening to them talk. How careless of me.'

Kamino realizes that her heart is racing so hard it's making her whole body thrum.

Are they really coming here? Will she have to face them again? Remembering what happened in Room 525, she feels like she can't breathe. She hid like Nanao told her to and waited for them to come. Her entire body had been gripped by fear and anxiety. Even when it came time to run, her knees threatened to give way beneath her, and she had trouble making her legs move properly.

I have to go through all that again?

She feels faint just thinking about it. She managed to survive the first time, but will her luck hold out again?

'What are we gonna do?' says Nanao. He's not asking her, he's asking himself.

Kamino reminds herself that Nanao knows what he's doing. Even while they were pressed for time in Room 525, he thought to boil the water in the kettle and set up the trip line on the floor. He went into the washroom looking for 'something to throw,' and when he came back out, rather than a bunch of little bottles of shampoo and body soap stuffed in his pockets like she'd imagined, he was carrying a hairdryer, weighing it in his hand to see how best to throw it. Later, when Kamino froze in terror, he pulled her along with him out the door. It really seemed as though Koko was right – she could trust this man to get her out of this alive.

That said, her time in this hotel has been nothing but one dangerous situation after another. She can't expect each encounter to go her way, but if even one thing goes wrong, she's dead. *What am I gonna do? What am I gonna do?* The words repeat nonstop in her head, like an alarm she can't turn off.

They hear a sound somewhere outside the room.

Kamino cries out shrilly once again. She could swear she saw the door opening. But she was wrong – it seems the sound had come from next door.

Nanao has already moved to the door to look out the peephole. 'You want to make a break for it?'

'What?'

'Five guys just left their room next door. I saw them before, there's a big group of them, I think they're old school buddies on a trip together. They're on their way out, looks like. We could mix into their group and ride the elevator down with them.'

'Mix into their group?' If there were ten or twenty of them, maybe, but five people would hardly provide enough cover to hide them. 'Why can't we try the stairs again?'

'Why would we?'

'Elevators are traps – there's no room to maneuver, no escape.' If one of the Six got on the elevator with them, it would be all over.

'Stairs aren't much better. Maybe if I were alone, but with you there too, there's a limit to how much I could move around in there. These are professionals with silent projectile weapons. Even spacious settings are no problem for them – in fact, those work in their favor.'

'But if they get on the same elevator as us . . .' *Wouldn't close quarters spell disaster?*

'If there are civilians there, too, I don't think they'd make a reckless attack. They don't want to hit someone with a stray.' Nanao is speaking quickly. 'Besides, stairs take time. The more time passes, the higher the chances that something unpredictable might happen.'

'Something unpredictable? Should we contact Soda-san?'

'There's no time. We need to get out there now and mix ourselves into the crowd to get out.'

'Okay,' agrees Kamino. Then, out of nowhere, Nanao asks, 'What did you think of what he said before?'

'Which part?'

'The part about how an apple is perfectly an apple.'

'Oh.' Her expression softens. Her unusual powers of memory have naturally meant she's spent a lot of time envying others. She's asked herself, *Why me?*; she's imagined that if only she were just a little prettier, people would be more willing to help her out.

She replies, 'I think it's true – unhappiness begins the moment you start comparing yourself to others.'

THE FIVE

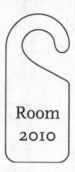

Room
2010

A MAN JUST ARRIVED on the twentieth floor. Tall, thin, with what looks like a perm. Wearing a blue suit. Not the guy with Yuka Kamino who killed Kamakura. Warning: he appears to be heading for Room 2010, where Asuka is.

Asuka is lying on the bed in Room 2010, perusing the room service menu, when Heian's message arrives.

She's just moved Koko's body into the bathroom. She's already taken a picture of the dead man she found there and sent it to Edo. Edo replied, *Look through his luggage if you find any.* What a bother. She picked up his suitcase, ready to search it, and saw that it was secured with a combination lock, then she lost her will to do anything more about it.

Not wanting to be alone, she said she wanted to join the others in Room 525, but Edo messaged her, saying, *Stay there a little longer.*

Oh my god, this is so annoying! Asuka fights the urge to complain aloud. Messaging all the time is so cumbersome, and there's a time lag as well. Why do they even have these earpieces? It's so much easier just to talk!

Edo was the one who first caught on that someone might have picked up Kamakura's earpiece. He sent a message to the whole group: *We need to assume there's someone listening in. All conversation from here on out will be a decoy.*

Do they really have to go to all this trouble? The whole thing irritates Asuka no end, but on the other hand, Edo's love for taking precautions has saved their lives on more than one occasion, so she has no real choice but to go along with what he says now.

Asuka rises lazily from the bed.

There's a knock at the door.

Really? Asuka slips behind the bed and crouches down. She checks her eyeline to the door. It's a bad angle to make a shot, so she gets up, rolls across the bed, and hides behind the sofa instead. She peeks over it, making sure it's a straight shot to the door.

She messages the group: *Someone's entering the room.* Then she slips a tube from her pocket.

It's already loaded with a paralyzing dart. She doesn't know who's coming in the door, so she decided against a lethal one just in case. Stopping whoever it is in their tracks will be enough.

She has her blowgun to her mouth, ready to shoot. The door opens. She hears a male voice. 'Eh?' He's probably surprised the door's unlocked.

Asuka stares at the door, the blowgun at her mouth pointed straight at it. She's like a sniper with her sights on a target. If the guy's clothes are padded, the dart might not penetrate. So she aims for the neck. Either neck or head – Asuka aims up, factoring in how tall she imagines an adult man might be.

The handle moves again, and then the door opens all the way. She's ready to blow her dart at the first sign of someone coming through it, but no one does. The door stands open. For a while, nothing else happens. Then, after no one enters, the door closes.

The door just opened and closed with no one passing through it. Or at least, that's what it looked like.

But she was wrong.

The man who opened the door was down on his hands and knees, crawling through it.

Like a spider – both creepy and comical. Finally she notices him, but she's too shocked at first to react.

He's skittering across the floor toward her at a rapid rate.

Asuka recovers and belatedly blows a dart at him, but he's apparently anticipated that and rolls to the side, dodging it. He's unsettlingly quick.

She blows again, hard. The dart hits the floor next to the man. She clucks her tongue, annoyed, and brings the next tube to her lips.

But he's too close. The man is suddenly right in front of her face. Asuka pushes off the floor, cartwheeling over the sofa. The man is quite tall. He changes direction and rushes her.

Asuka throws herself to the side to get away. She hits the table on the way, but there's no time even to say *ouch*.

What she does say, though, without even realizing it, is, 'What the fuck?'

A voice sounds in her earpiece. 'Asuka? What's going on?' It's Sengoku. 'Where are you?'

'I'm still in the room,' she answers quickly. 'There's a guy here.'

'Who?'

'A professional?'

'Lanky. But he can move. Permed hair. In a suit. Blue.'

'Of course – it's that guy I saw on camera!'

The man is coming for her again. A blowgun's no good at

close range. She puts the tube back in her pocket and grabs a dart instead. It's smeared with a deadly dose of nerve poison. The man is clearly no civilian from the way he moves. There's no reason to hold back.

Asuka flips the table in front of her, then runs sideways, hopping on the bed. She tries to spot the man so she can turn and stick him with her dart, but he's already launched himself at her. She bends her knees instead, then shoots upward as if off a springboard. She hits the man with quite a bit of force, knocking him backward off his feet. She hears him cry out in pain – did he fall on the table? In any case, she sees that the table's broken.

Asuka jumps to her feet and hops off the bed. The dart is in her right hand. Aiming where she thinks the man is still lying on the ground, she throws it.

She sees it hit him in the chest as he struggles to get up. Asuka's head lights up with exclamation points as she exults in her victory.

She doesn't think she let her guard down, but suddenly, her head spins. Does the room look darker? Or did he attack her again? It's the latter – the man rushes her as hard as he can. Asuka flies back, her head hitting the wall.

Anger rips through her body like fire.

Who do you think you are? Asuka leaps to her feet. Her arms and back hurt. Inside her head, she screams at the top of her lungs: *You think you can do something like that to me?*

The poison should be working by now.

But the man simply stands there, no foam coming from his mouth yet.

Should I rush him again, or put a safe distance between us? Asuka has yet to decide what to do when she notices something hit the floor at her feet.

Picking it up, a chill goes down her spine at the thought that it might be something dangerous, but then she sees that it's a small, flat, elongated hexagon wrapped in cloth. The words *May Your Deepest Wish Come True* are embroidered on its surface.

'Don't open that!' yells the man, his body beginning to tremble and shake. He succumbs to a seizure and falls to the ground.

Asuka breathes a sigh of relief. 'You can't tell me what to do,' she says, undoing the string on the lucky charm in her hand. She peels the cloth back to look inside. There's a faint sound, like a tiny bang.

And then Asuka's consciousness leaves her, her last sensation a rush of heat that hits her like boiling water as her face blows apart.

BLANKET

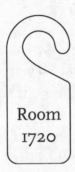

Room
1720

BLANKET AND PILLOW RIDE the staff elevator up to the seventeenth floor and get out. They enter the guestroom area with their cleaning cart, now heavy with the weight of a man, in tow. The Employees Only door closes behind them as they head toward their destination.

It's the first room on the west end of the hall. Pillow knocks on the door. No response. She knocks again. Once again, no answer; there's no sound at all. Blanket comes up behind her and pushes the button to sound the bell.

They're not expecting anyone, but it's best to make sure. Time passes, but there's no sign of anyone.

Pillow uses her card to unlock the door, and they slip inside.

'Look at how big it is! And there's another room, too.'

They pull the cart through the door.

'One, two, three!' They haul the man out of the cart. His

201

hands and feet are bound, and there's a towel wrapped around his head.

'Where should we put him?' Pillow surveys the room. 'What do you think?'

'It shouldn't be where you see him the moment you come through the door.'

'Right.'

'We don't want Yomo-pi to be shocked. What if he opens the door and shouts, *Who did this? Unacceptable!*'

'He might praise us, you know. If he knows the guy's an assassin hired to kill him.'

'Depends on if he knows we're with Inui.'

'So, should we tie him to the desk? Maybe that would be best, like we're saying, *Look, we got him for you!*'

The man starts to struggle where he lies on the floor, as if in protest at the plan. *Don't tie me to a desk!*

'We could always put him on the bed in the other room.'

'Then he might say, *This man tried to take my life, and you tuck him in like a baby? Unacceptable!*'

'I don't think so . . .'

'It's amazing, though, right? Just think, we're doing a job related to Yomo-pi!'

Blanket and Pillow combine forces to put the man on the bed – though, strictly speaking, it's more of a cooperative three-person game that gets him there.

Should they lay him face-up or face-down? They go back and forth, then decide to leave him face-down.

They follow Inui's instructions on how to bind him and put a pillowcase over his head. Then they place a small item under the bed.

Finally finished, they take some refreshments out of the refrigerator. 'Mineral water's free, right?'

Blanket's phone rings.

'Who is it?' asks Pillow.

'An unknown number. Hello?' Blanket puts it on speaker so Pillow can hear too.

'It's Inui,' says the voice on the other end.

Blanket asks why he's calling. It's so unexpected, she can't help but laugh.

'What do you mean, "why"? I need you to do something! I'm not allowed to give you a call?'

'Of course you are,' replies Blanket, still laughing. 'We already did the job, though. We're finishing up.'

Blanket and Pillow look toward the bed at the same time and shrug.

'Something came up. I need you to do another job for me. There's a body in Room 2010. Go up and take care of it.'

'What? Are you joking? We have to go to another room?'

'Please, I'm really in a bind here. I've been told there's a corpse in the bathtub in Room 2010. I need it disposed of before anyone notices.'

'Who's this job for?'

'It's for me. The people I hired to find that woman ended up leaving a corpse.'

'And you want us to clean up after them?'

'I trust you two.'

'Is this really the time for that?'

'I don't care what time it is or isn't! This needs to get done! I *told* them not to do anything that would attract the police.' Inui seems irritated. 'Anyway, I want you to take care of that body. I'll compensate you, of course.'

'Of course!'

'All right. We'll do it.'

'Thank you!' Inui's tone turns light again, as if he's thanking a girlfriend who's lent him some money. 'All you have to do is bring the body to the parking garage; someone'll be there to take care of the rest. Okay, bye!'

'He really does get everyone to do everything for him.'

'But honestly, what's going on in this hotel? Corpses every-where . . .' Pillow mutters under her breath.

'It's like a plague god checked in.'

NANAO

The eleventh floor

THE FIVE YOUNG HOTEL GUESTS are talking merrily among themselves as they wait for the elevator, seemingly completely
oblivious to Nanao and Kamino's deadly seriousness.

They seem like regular guys in their mid-twenties making the
most of a long-awaited reunion trip. Maybe they're old classmates. The tallest of them starts complaining about the overtime
rate at his company, to which another replies, 'Still, for that
much . . .' His tone both reproachful and proud, as if to say, *You
think you have it bad?* Nanao can't help but think, *I have it worse
than any of you!* But at the same time, he hears Kamino quoting
Soda in his head: *Unhappiness begins the moment you start comparing yourself to others.*

Kamino, standing next to him, has her eyes glued to her phone.

Nanao moves his eyes without moving his head, checking the
position of the dome-shaped security camera above them.

The elevator arrives. Its doors slide open.

There might already be someone dangerous in there, so he

and Kamino don't move to enter right away. Instead, they hide behind the gaggle of new young friends. But the elevator's empty. Nanao and Kamino let the men go first, then file in after them.

The man nearest the control panel is pushing the 'open door' button for them. Nanao takes Kamino's hand and leads her toward the back of the elevator. They push their way there, wedging themselves in, but the men are too absorbed in conversation to do anything other than glance at them briefly as they pass.

There's a mirror on one of the walls, making the interior look bigger than it is. A second control panel, oriented horizontally rather than vertically, is mounted on the wall near Nanao.

The doors begin to close.

Nanao looks up at the screen displaying the floor numbers. He considers saying a little prayer that they'll make it from the eleventh floor to the first without incident, but then reconsiders – with his luck, he should pray first that the doors close at all. You never know what might happen, after all. He laughs at his own anxiety, then stops.

I knew it!

The doors are reopening.

The young man is pushing the 'open door' button.

Nanao clucks his tongue. Kamino sighs.

He sees immediately that the person getting on is one of the Six. The woman he threw boiling water on in Room 525, Nara.

Faced with her height and rather forbidding bearing, the men step back in unison, bumping into Nanao. He doubts that Nara would go on the attack right away; she surely wants to avoid doing anything that would attract attention. Their eyes meet for no more than an instant, but it's more than long enough to communicate her murderous intent like a laser aimed straight at his head.

Nanao edges closer to the secondary control panel next to him and extends a finger to start tapping the 'close door' button, but to no avail. Nara makes it in.

Surveying the bodies crowded into the elevator, Nanao mentally rehearses scenarios to judge the best way to react if Nara launches an immediate attack. But Nara pointedly turns her head away from Nanao, wordlessly nudging the man away from the main control panel near the door and hitting the 'close door' button herself. Not yet, it seems.

Nanao and Kamino are standing in the corner of the elevator diagonally opposite Nara.

Anxiety envelopes Nanao like a silent shroud. His every sense is alert, primed to catch even the smallest movement Nara might make, and the same is surely true of her. He finds that when he turns slightly to the side and looks over his shoulder, he can see the whole elevator at once.

Strikingly tall and dressed like a model, Nara cuts an unusual figure, augmented by the red, swollen patch on her face and her ice-cold stare. The young men seem unsettled by her, their conversation faltering.

Humming with tension, the elevator descends.

Will she make her move when they reach the ground floor?

Nanao reaches into his pocket and flips the switch on a small box he keeps there. It's a device that scrambles cell signals. It emits electromagnetic waves that prevent phones from working, if only temporarily, within a radius of about five meters. He wants to make sure Nara can't communicate with her fellows.

The elevator descends as if falling through the air.

What should I do? What can I do?

Nanao slips a hand into the bag strapped to his midsection. Is there anything in there that might come in handy? His finger encounters a small container. It's a little bottle of shampoo he swiped from one of the rooms.

Could be useful. After all, shampoo contains both water and surfactants. If it spills across the ground, things could get very slippery very fast.

As soon as he has the thought, he notices Nara move. She brings her hand in a fist up to her mouth, as if to stifle a cough.

Blowgun!

The moment he sees her, Nanao moves too. He pretends to trip over his own feet, bumping lightly into the young guy in front of him. 'Sorry, lost my balance there for a second,' he says apologetically.

He needs to create a situation in which she can't predict who a dart might strike if she launches one. He's sure they don't want to get any civilians involved if they can avoid it.

The guy Nanao bumps into stumbles. Nanao leans further into the other men's personal space as well. Kamino, concerned, moves to help Nanao. He wobbles back and forth, as if about to fall down.

One of the men turns toward him. 'Are you okay?' He seems equal parts worried and suspicious. He probably also senses that something unusual is happening and instinctively wants to get away.

As he predicted, Nara's having trouble getting a fix on her target. Nanao makes sure to keep his eye on the deadly instrument in her hand.

All the while, the elevator keeps going down.

He thinks about what to do if they make it all the way to the ground floor.

There's a good chance there will be other guests waiting in front of the elevator when it arrives. Could they mix into them and escape that way? Nara is standing right next to the door, and as long as she is, they'll have to pass right by her to get out. Could he manage to sidestep her with Kamino in tow?

All-or-nothing scenarios are the worst. There's always a way for something to go wrong that no one could predict.

If it's not a sure thing, he'd much rather bet on his abilities, whether technological or physical, than on his luck.

So thinking, Nanao presses a button on the secondary control panel. The one marked '4.'

The elevator's descent slows. Everyone looks up at the number display to see if they've reached the ground floor. Nanao raises his voice and addresses the room. 'Excuse me . . .'

They've stopped at the fourth floor. 'Sorry, but I think I spilled some shampoo on the floor . . .'

What? The five young men start looking around on the ground, murmuring among themselves. *He did! What's going on here?* 'Sorry, so sorry,' Nanao apologizes. After all, it was never his intention to make these guys uncomfortable or scared.

Nanao pushes the 'open door' button and holds it, keeping the elevator doors open. 'I think it might be best if we all get off here and let the cleaning staff take care of this,' he says. Despite clearly not being hotel staff of any kind, his officious tone makes his request land anyway; the men obediently file out of the elevator. 'Guess we should . . .' It's likely also the case that they don't want to spend any more time around clumsy, accident-prone Nanao, making it an easy decision to get off.

'So sorry, so sorry.' Nanao continues apologizing, but he does so without bowing his head. Instead, he stares at Nara as she stands in front of the main control panel.

Nara, perhaps realizing what Nanao's up to, is absolutely still.

As soon as all five men clear the elevator, Nanao and Nara hit the 'close door' button simultaneously. Nanao pushes Kamino into the corner behind him as he steps forward to face Nara directly.

The elevator doors begin to slide toward each other. The men who just got off, even as they check the bottoms of their shoes for shampoo, stare back in through the narrowing gap. Maybe they're still a bit suspicious, but Nanao no longer cares about that.

The doors slide together. The instant they meet, Nanao makes his move. He knows the quickest draw will be the winner. He's already chosen where he needs to land to avoid slipping on the shampoo. He reaches Nara in a heartbeat, grabbing her arms to immobilize them. After all, the slightest prick from a dart and it's all over for him. He squeezes hard as he holds her. In response, Nara pushes off from the ground and kicks Nanao with both legs.

Nanao flies backward and, due to the size of the elevator, slams against the far wall. Knowing that she'll try to launch a dart at him the moment any space opens up between them, Nanao pulls himself together and tries to rush her, but the shampoo he spilled, once his ally but now his enemy, sends his legs flying out from under him, and he falls forward instead.

Nanao reaches out as he slips, clutching at Nara's arms. At the same time, his head butts her torso. He doesn't know if these moves are intentional or simply the consequence of flailing out of control.

Nara grunts at the blow. He wrenches her body to the side, throwing it against the elevator wall. Seemingly dizzy from the impact, Nara staggers, trying to regain her balance. Nanao reaches up from behind, intending to snap her neck, but Nara looks back in time and swings her fist to stick him with a dart.

She misses by a hair's breadth. Nanao reverses course, pulling back from her. He then slides the opposite way, narrowly avoiding her as she tries to land another kick.

Nanao then leaps at her from behind once more, and this time he succeeds in breaking her neck. The sound of it coincides exactly with the ding of the elevator. They've finally reached the ground floor.

The door opens, and Nanao walks out holding Nara's body up as if comforting her. He addresses the crowd of hotel guests waiting to get in, saying, 'Be careful, someone spilled some shampoo in there!'

Passing by the guests as they file into the elevator, Nanao looks back at Kamino and signals with his eyes that she should head for the lobby. He wishes he could just drop Nara, but he needs to avoid the uproar the discovery of a corpse would cause.

But wouldn't that create a diversion, allowing me to get away?

An inner voice pipes up, urging him to go for it, but he can't go along with it. If the police show up, all will be lost. With the number of dead bodies there are in this hotel, there's no way they'd let him go scot-free.

As Nanao adjusts his position to better carry Nara's body, he catches sight of a man in a suit standing slightly apart from everyone else. The man raises a fist to his mouth. *Another blowgun!* Nanao quickly swings Nara around so her body covers his. He feels a dart hit her back. It all happens so fast, no one else in the area seems to notice.

I have to get out of here.

How far could I make it using Nara's body as a shield?

A group of seven foreign tourists approaches. Laughing and talking and unable to hide their high spirits, they steam past, cutting between Nanao and the man with the blowgun. Nanao works to keep his gaze on the same place, trying to keep an eye on the man's position.

According to the information Soda provided, this must be the one called Edo. The man who assembled the others. The unrepentant sadist.

The head of a team of like-minded individuals – like the young CEO of a venture-backed start-up?

The tourists are passing by shoulder-to-shoulder with Nara's corpse, but fortunately, they don't seem to suspect a thing.

Less fortunately, though, one of the group ends up slipping and falling. Maybe some of the shampoo Nanao spilled in the elevator got tracked out into the lobby. The man cries out as he goes down, attracting others to come to his aid and get mixed up in the situation.

The ensuing brouhaha – which, after all, is his fault – momentarily flusters Nanao, and when he recovers, he sees that the man in the suit has disappeared.

Did he get me? Nanao panics. *Was he able to get a clean shot? Do I have a dart in me?* He searches his body but finds nothing, and nowhere on his body hurts even slightly.

He's lost sight of the enemy. The word *mistake* appears in his head.

He looks up and sees an elevator standing open.

The man in the suit is inside, along with Kamino. A petite woman stands beside them.

He lost sight of the enemy, and now they have her. His eyes meet those of the man who must be Edo, and then the elevator doors slide shut.

But right before they close entirely, the man raises his hand. He holds up three fingers, then he folds down all but one, which points up.

The third floor. That's what he must mean. But Nanao keeps his cool.

First things first – I have to find a bathroom to stash this body.

YOMOGI

The restaurant on the second floor

'*RUMSTECK DE BŒUF WAGYU GRILLÉ, à la sauce aux truffes.* On the side, you'll find asparagus and *poireaux gratinés*. Please enjoy.'

After his pronouncement, the waiter in his white shirt and black waistcoat adds, 'This will be the final course before dessert.' Then he leaves.

'So your friend, the one who took the picture you showed me from right before the accident – did he come to you because he recognized the man in it?' asks the Director.

'No, he didn't seem to have paid much attention to that. It's more that he thought it was cool that he'd happened to take a picture of the car right before the accident – or, I mean, not *cool*, I don't want to—' Ikeo, flustered, waves his hands to ward off confusion. He's let his excitement about how *cool* this article is going to be run away with him. 'Um, anyway, that's why he showed it to me.'

'And seeing this stimulated your imagination, Ikeo-san? And you began digging?'

'I did, but I still don't really know anything. The security camera footage doesn't exist anymore, so all we have is this photo.'

'Do you recognize this man?'

'I tried to enlarge the image, but it got too pixelated. I couldn't make out any distinguishing features.'

'I see, I see,' says Yomogi, letting out a little sigh. His expression softens. 'So you're simply sharing this for my benefit, then?'

'Yes. It's beyond the scope of what I can do as a lone journalist, but if it could act as a catalyst for getting to the truth, then I thought it was important to bring to your attention.'

Suddenly, Ikeo notices Satō right next to him. His bulk rocks the table, rattling the dishes.

His bulk.

Right there.

Rocking the table.

'Would you mind if Satō has a look, too?' Yomogi turns the phone on the table toward Satō.

Extending his neck to bring his face closer to the phone's screen, Satō's body – its very proximity – makes Ikeo feel like the world's closing in on him.

Wait! an inner voice cries out.

When does he realize? Even Ikeo doesn't know.

Before the thought even forms in his head, Ikeo looks at the man in the picture, then looks back at Satō. He looks back and forth, first at one, then the other.

No! he thinks. *It can't be!* He tries to deny it, but in the end he can't.

The man's face in the photo is unclear. But his body isn't, and neither is the way his neck extends – both recall Satō exactly. *Like a giraffe!* he thinks, before again correcting himself. *It's not that long.*

Ikeo shivers, as if a cold liquid just slid down his spine.

Director Yomogi! he wants to yell out loud. *The man in the photo is your own assistant, Satō!*

Is Satō secretly working with the other side? Against Yomogi?

But he can't say anything while Satō's around. Perhaps after dinner?

Ikeo's mouth opens and closes, like that of a fish drowning in air.

At this, Director Yomogi begins to speak again. 'It's always struck Satō and me as so strange.'

Ikeo looks up at Yomogi.

'Why are those who wield the most power so often the weakest among us?'

'What do you mean?'

'At first blush, it makes sense that the most physically strong people in a group would hold the most power. Right? No matter how smart you are, if you're hit, or immobilized, that's it for you. Which means the most important thing in life should be firepower – the ability to deal out violence. But this isn't how human society has actually evolved. I've always found that strange. Politicians, ministers – they aren't strong people. Yet they hold power. What if we gathered together the truly strong among us and overthrew them? What then? Why doesn't anyone try? We make laws and regulations specifically to pre-vent this. We call this "order." A system built to protect the intelligentsia.'

'The intelligentsia? What system do you mean?'

'And so, I thought, why not cross over to the other side and see what I could do? That was about fifteen years ago now.'

'The other side?' Ikeo is confused. 'What are you talking about? What does this have to do with the picture?'

'Becoming a politician and getting elected was the first hurdle. The truth is, neither Satō nor I had done much to be proud of in our lives up till then. Indeed, we were the kinds of guys who might take someone's life just for fun.'

Is this some kind of sick joke?

'We gave ourselves new identities, the right qualifications and such, but that's not enough to get elected.' Yomogi's way of speaking – his way of making everything he says sound both sincerely felt and as if he's joking around – is the same as when he's answering questions at a media scrum.

What does he mean by 'gave ourselves new identities'?

'So we needed an incident, like the one on that train fifteen years ago. We needed to get my name out there, to be associated with something good. We needed to build trust and get the public to support me, so we found a guy to do the job for us. He was up to his gills in debt, and all we had to do to convince him to do it was hint that his children's lives might be in danger if he didn't. And what a success! As you well know, Ikeo-san. I had no trouble getting elected after that.'

Ikeo feels himself gripped by the shoulders. *I have to get out of here!* He tries to rise from his seat, but Satō's already behind him, pressing him back down.

'I had no trouble once I was elected, either. I simply removed whoever was in my way. I did some housekeeping, and soon enough I'd found my place in the opposition party. That accident three years ago was just one more link in the chain.'

'Link in the chain? You don't mean—'

'I realized that there was a limit to what I could do as a politician. I had a pretty good idea what they do, and what they want to do. From my perspective, these things all seemed pretty boring. For better or worse, Japanese politicians are generally good people. Half-assed as they are, they mean well. There are enemies and allies, and they try to steer any benefits they get to their allies. They squabble with their enemies, they investigate

216

them, they hound them. And that's it, just that over and over and over again, forever. Nothing more than a power game. And not only that, you get nothing out of it! What I wanted was real power. So I devoted my efforts to creating the Information Bureau, setting myself up to run it. That's where the accident comes in – I needed a way to smooth my transition from member of Parliament to Director.'

'What do you mean?' Ikeo realizes he's been repeating essentially the same sentence for a while now. 'The accident?'

'A member of Parliament who's lost his whole family in a tragic accident and vows from then on to devote himself to preserving the nation's peace – what a story, right? Anyone would accept it. Human beings love stories. They love to support a man working diligently for the people even when beset by tragedy. And then, even better, people started coming out of the woodwork claiming it was no accident, that it was the work of my enemies! People like you, Ikeo-san. You invented enemies working against me, making me even more sympathetic! It was all so easy, and so instantly effective.'

'Wait a minute,' says Ikeo, finally finding his proper voice again. 'Wait just a minute.'

'I'm waiting.'

'That was your *family*!' Ikeo forces the words out.

'What do you mean?'

'You sacrificed your family just to get popular?'

'I'll turn it around to ask you: why, exactly, shouldn't I have done that?'

At that, the Director picks up Ikeo's phone and looks at the time. 'I'm waiting for someone to get ahold of me, and I'd like to wait for his call here. Should we finish dinner now? I mean, it's the meat course. And we still have dessert. Which I'm sure will be delicious!'

Ikeo can't seem to think anymore, as if his entire head is empty. His body is covered in sweat, but he feels chilled and can't stop shivering.

'We'll let you have the use of your arms until dinner's over, don't worry. You'll be able to eat everything right to the end.'

'My arms?'

'It's kind of our specialty, *disarming* people. Oh, don't look so worried! It's not like we break them. Relax and enjoy your meal.'

BLANKET

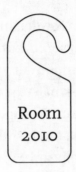

Room
2010

PILLOW PASSES HER KEYCARD over the sensor by the handle on the door of Room 2010, and then looks at Blanket, as if to say, *What's going on?*

Blanket's unsettled too. There's no sound to signify that the mechanism unlocked. They wave the card past the sensor again and again.

Did something happen? Blanket grabs the door handle and pushes down. The door opens. She looks at Pillow again. The lock is broken. But this in itself isn't so unusual, even if she can't shake her unease. After all, Inui asked them to come here to dispose of a body, so it's hardly shocking that something out of the ordinary might have happened here – a broken lock is no big deal in the greater scheme of things.

Blanket pushes the door open and steps inside. Pillow follows, pushing the cleaning cart. She closes the door and throws the bolt.

They walk past the closet, and as they get further in, they're able to get a good look at the room as a whole.

'I thought it was *one* body,' mutters Blanket.

A glance at the room reveals that there are in fact two bodies. There's a broken, overturned table in front of the twin bed, and next to it, the body of a woman propped up against the wall, as if sitting against it. Opposite her, a man in a blue suit lies face-up on the ground.

There's the smell of gunpowder in the air; Blanket searches for the source. She finds some burnt cloth on the woman's stomach – perhaps the gunpowder had been wrapped in it. It looks like the remains of a small explosive. The woman's face is burnt and broken, her features completely indiscernible.

The man in the blue suit, on the other hand, has his face perfectly intact, and almost appears to be sleeping. Looking for a possible cause of death, Blanket searches his body until she finds something stuck in his chest. It looks like a needle.

'Must be this,' says Blanket, thinking Pillow's right behind her, but when there's no answer, she whips her head around, but Pillow's nowhere to be found. 'Hello?' she says, her voice breaking.

When did she disappear? Loneliness overtakes her. As if Pillow had never really been with her, all this time. But then Pillow reappears, saying, 'Sorry, sorry, I got curious and checked the bathroom!'

'The bathroom? But the bodies are out here.'

'There's some in there, too!'

'Really?'

Their back-and-forth becoming absurd, they pause and take a breath.

Blanket and Pillow then go into the bathroom together.

The black-and-white patterned walls and the full-sized, spacious bath lend the bathroom a sense of high-class luxury, but the bodies crammed haphazardly into the tub make it seem more like a piece of contemporary art.

'They're all different, aren't they?'

'Different how?'

'Different ages, different genders . . .'

The man in the blue suit next to the bed appears to be in his mid-thirties, while the woman against the wall seems more like she's in her mid-twenties. The man in the bathtub, dressed in a white shirt and chinos, looks young for his age but is nonetheless probably in his late forties or early fifties, while the woman lying beneath the showerhead seems to be quite a bit older. 'They don't seem to have anything in common.'

'Could they share a special interest of some kind? Like they're some sort of club of aficionados? Was it a suicide pact?'

'I don't think so. The woman near the bed looks like she had her face blown off with a bomb. Not something you'd do on purpose.'

'Are we supposed to dispose of them all?' wonders Blanket.

'I'm afraid we probably are.'

The purpose of body disposal is to remove the evidence of trouble, leaving no trace. It doesn't make sense to dispose of some bodies and leave behind others. 'Inui's really pushing it.'

'I guess we could start by moving the bodies in the bathroom out here,' suggests Blanket, and Pillow agrees. It's the only way to get through a difficult, complicated job: take things one at a time. *A journey of a thousand miles begins with a single step* – words of wisdom that have guided the girls since their time in the basketball team.

'One, two – three!' They work together to lift the man in the white shirt out of the tub.

'Why ask petite people like us to do a job like this?' mutters Blanket as she hauls the man out to the bed. She drops him on the floor, where he sprawls as if deep in sleep, his body flopping onto that of the other dead man.

It's not like it's a problem if they lie on top of each other, but it

221

still bothers Blanket, so she lifts the man back up and turns him so his back is propped up against the side of the bed.

'I don't see any obvious wounds . . .'

'There, on his head – I think that's blood.'

'You're right! Okay, and this guy has a needle in his chest. Or maybe I should say, a dart.' Pillow points at the blue-suited man at her feet.

'A dart? Oh yeah, look at that.'

Pillow walks over to the door to the hall, then comes back. 'I unbolted the door. I decided to bell it instead.'

If they're going to have to carry corpse after corpse out of this room, having to bolt and unbolt the door every time would get quite annoying. In cases like these, where the clean-up job might take some time, they often hang a bell off the door handle instead to alert them if someone tries to come in.

They hear a ding – a message notification? Blanket looks around, then notices a phone in the hand of the woman with the blasted face. Its screen is lit up. She walks over, and using the dead woman's fingertip to unlock the screen, sees that a message just arrived. 'Heian? Is that someone's name?'

'What does it say?'

'"I figured out who went to Room 2010. His name is Soda. Part of a duo: Soda and Cola. Professionals. Cola might be the body in the tub. They're explosives specialists. Be careful." Got this message a little late, looks like. He blasted her,' says Blanket, glancing at the woman's body.

'Soda and Cola, huh? Is that who the men are?' Blanket looks at the man in the blue suit, then at the man in the white shirt. They weren't distant enough in age to be father and son, but they weren't the same generation, either.

'Like that other duo, right? Lemon and Tangerine?'

Now that Pillow mentions it, Blanket does remember people talking about those two. They were supposed to have died in the

E2 Incident. They left behind a host of rumors that may or may not be true.

'I wonder if they really kidnapped that soccer player.'

'What are you talking about? Is that a story from before they died?'

'Of course it is! It's the kind of story that's like, if you know, you know.'

'There sure are a lot of professionals who work as a duo.'

'Including us.'

'With three, you always have the chance that two will gang up on the other one. Two's the limit.'

Pillow lifts up the man in the blue suit by the shoulders, dragging him over to prop him against the bed next to the other man. Blanket wordlessly moves to help. She's afraid the corpses might topple over, but they don't. They sit quietly side by side against the bed, as if taking a breather together.

Blanket pauses for a moment, contemplating them. She imagines herself and Pillow in their place – is this how they'd look if they ended up losing their lives on a job? She likes the idea that if they had to die together, their bodies would end up side by side like stone dogs guarding a shrine. She reaches down to prop the man in the blue suit back up, and then sees Pillow doing much the same, straightening up the other man's white-shirted body.

'Don't guardian dogs usually face each other?'

Blanket asks the question without really thinking she'll get an answer, but Pillow seems to have been thinking the same thing.

'I've seen ones that both face forward.'

'Which way do you prefer?'

'Either is fine.'

More time passes, then Pillow says, 'All right, we'd better get the old lady in here too,' and returns to the bathroom.

Blanket follows her, and they lift the older woman out of the tub together. They carry her into the room and lay her out on the bed. Then she notices something.

'Oh!'

The woman appears to be breathing. She brings her face close to the woman's mouth. It's weak, but it's there – she's breathing. No matter that she's an old lady, she could still be a professional. Blanket jumps back – if she lets her guard down for even a moment, it could be the end for her – but Pillow comes up and stops her, saying, 'Oh, that's Koko!'

'What?'

'You know, Koko-san!'

'Oh, you're right!'

Many of Blanket and Pillow's jobs have involved spiriting a client away to safety, so they've engaged Koko's services on more than one occasion. She's not only unrivaled in her ability to manipulate IT and hack into security systems, but she's also very resourceful on the fly, always full of ideas. They were never particularly close, but Koko, seemingly divining their backstory and characters after working only a brief time together, told them once, 'You two are serious. That's what counts the most.' She's one of the few fellow professionals they like.

Pillow hurries over to the bed and prepares to perform CPR on the older woman, but at that very moment, Koko's eyes pop open.

'Koko-san? Are you okay?' Pillow says, but the older woman's eyes remain unfocused; she's barely conscious. It seems too dangerous to shake her, so all they can do is speak softly in her ear. Pillow looks at Blanket, wordlessly asking what they should do. And then a word escapes Koko's lips. 'Where—?'

Blanket, surprised, tries to wake Koko up, shouting her name and saying, 'Your son's pitching!' Koko often talked about her pro baseball player son, though they never knew if she was telling the truth. 'The game's starting!' she continues. 'There's two outs and the bases are loaded! You don't want to miss this!'

It's unclear if any of this has an effect, but eventually Koko comes around. Still bleary, she says, 'Who's there? Is that Blanket . . . and Pillow?'

She seems to be awake.

Thank goodness! Blanket and Pillow look at each other, their faces filled with happiness.

'Kamino-chan,' she says. 'Is she okay?'

'Are you on a job, Koko-san? There's a woman over there, but I don't think she's Kamino-chan,' says Pillow, looking over at the woman propped against the wall.

Koko shifts her body so she can take a look. Then, as if her battery has run out of juice, she collapses back onto the bed. 'No, that's not her. I think that's Asuka.'

It seems as though Koko's coming back to herself, though her voice is still faint, but Blanket is frightened that it might be like a candle flame flaring right before it goes out.

'Asuka?' asks Pillow.

'One of the Six. The dart-blowers,' says Pillow.

'I think I've heard of them,' says Blanket, searching her memory.

'They're six real Easy Streeter types – snobby assholes, all of them, from the way they look at you to the way they dress. They all seem like they had a great time at school, loving life and all it gave them. The total worst. There's Asuka, and then Kamakura and Heian . . .'

'And Sengoku, and Nara. Also Edo. He's like the Olympic gold medal champion Easy Streeter.'

Blanket remembers them now. Not as acquaintances, as she never met them on the job, but people talk, and a group of six sadistic dart-blowers is quite a story.

'You were fighting the Six, Koko-san?'

'If so, you know we're definitely on your side, right?'

But Koko's no longer talking. Her eyelids are shut. She's still breathing, though. Did she lose consciousness? Blanket's chest tightens as she realizes that Koko may never open her eyes again.

'Should we take Koko-san down first?'

'We need to get her to a hospital.'

'If Inui's guys are down there, let's ask them.'

Blanket and Pillow know these particular delivery professionals. They'll take any body you give them to the right place for disposal, or if you have someone who needs emergency medical attention, they'll take them to the appropriate hospital right away. They're another duo. They don't say much, but they're quick and reliable.

'If it looks like it's going to take too long, maybe we should find a way to take her to the hospital ourselves.'

Pillow pulls the cleaning cart up to the bed. Slowly, carefully, they lift Koko off the bed, almost taking her in their arms to embrace her, and then lower her into the cart. It would be better to let her rest quietly where she is, they know, but they don't have that luxury.

After packing Koko into the cart as if packing fragile goods in a box, they cover her gently with linens.

And then the bell rings.

THE THREE

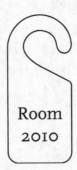

Room
2010

SENGOKU OPENS THE DOOR to Room 2010 and hears a bell. He looks down and sees it has been hung on the door handle, and it's now on the floor.

'What was that noise?' says Heian in his earpiece.

'A bell. It fell off the door handle. I just entered Room 2010.'

'That means there's someone in there. The bell is an alarm.' This is Edo.

Sengoku realizes this, too. 'How's Nara?'

Earlier, Heian went through the security camera footage and found out that Yuka Kamino and the man helping her were hiding in Room 1121. She saw them mix into a group of regular guests, trying to get away, prompting Nara and Sengoku to rush to catch them. When they were partway there, Edo called, saying, 'I can't get ahold of Asuka in Room 2010. Can one of you go up and check on her?'

That's how Nara ended up continuing to the eleventh floor while Sengoku went up to the twentieth. At one point, he heard her say, 'I'm getting on the elevator.' But he's heard nothing since.

'I haven't heard from her. She must be still riding the elevator down to the ground floor.'

Sengoku doesn't have a good feeling about Room 2010. For one thing, there's the bell. He feels as if all his nerves are on edge at once.

He has a blowgun ready in his right hand. Kamino's not here, so killing people shouldn't be a problem. No need to hold back. The dart in the tube is smeared with lethal nerve toxin.

And then, as soon as he steps in far enough to survey the room, it happens.

Two figures approach, one from the left, the other from the right. Following their movements with his eyes, he brings his blowgun to his lips, and he's just about to blow when his field of vision goes white. It's like a curtain fell on him – or a bedsheet. The dart he blew sticks in it.

There's two of them. He's sure of it. Two women. Children? No, probably just short.

The woman to his left must have thrown the end of the sheet to the other woman, who caught it, allowing the sheet to unfurl and engulf him. He decides against trying again with the blow-gun. He tries to rush the one to his right.

He can tell from how they handle the bedsheet that these are no amateurs. So, two professionals of some sort. He can tell they're quite used to working as a team as well. But no matter how clever or proficient they might be, simple physics dictates that if you hit something hard enough, it'll stop functioning, whether it's a human or a machine or anything else.

He crashes into the woman to his right. It's a solid hit. The woman tumbles backward.

Sengoku steps on the fallen sheet, approaching her. The other woman slides at him from the left, aiming at his feet. He almost loses his balance, but at the last minute, he jumps out of the way.

Just as he lands, the first woman rushes him and he kicks at her hard, as if kicking a soccer ball.

He's kicked people like this so many times in his life. He's stepped on people's heads, too, crushing them, tasting the joy of seeing a face split open like a watermelon beneath his foot.

The joy of doing what you will with the life of another.

But the woman rolls quickly away from him, leaving him kicking air.

Her escape makes him angry.

Once he gets his hands on this little bitch, it's over for her.

As Sengoku tries to close the distance between them, he realizes that the other woman is hauling the sheet back in an attempt to pull his legs out from under him.

You think you can knock me over so easily?

He turns and jumps at her, but, perhaps having planned it this way, the woman times it so that she rushes him right then, ramming into his lower body while he's still in the air.

His lower body flips up, causing him to somersault straight into the floor.

His head explodes with pain. He leaps back to his feet.

'I bet you're thinking, *Don't think you're going to get away with that, little lady!*' says one of the women.

The other one chimes in, shrugging her shoulders. 'Look at you – you're handsome, you're built, I bet you've had it easy your whole life!'

'And he's done some real bad things, too.'

'Absolutely.'

These tiny women are acting like they have all the time in the world as they taunt him. Sengoku can't understand it. They're like two hamburgers asking, *Why are you trying to eat me?*

229

What other purpose do you have? All you're good for is eating, or smashing to bits.

'I bet you've won every fight you've gotten into up till now. Do you wanna know why?' asks the first woman.

Suddenly, all he can see is white cloth. *Dammit.* Trying to scramble his reflexes, the women to the left and right of him alternately crouch down, then stand up again, as they quickly wind the sheet around him.

'It was all so you could lose one to the likes of us.'

Before he quite realizes it, his entire body, from his head on down, is wrapped tight.

'One, two – three!' As soon as he hears this, he realizes they're going for his neck. If they find the right angle, it won't matter how many muscles he has or how strong they are, his neck will snap.

He hears one of them say, 'Thank you, leverage!'

Sengoku flings his body back and forth as hard as he can, struggling against the sheet.

Pain floods his right eye. One of the women seems to have stuck her finger in it. He kicks his legs. He can't see where he's kicking, but he eventually feels a blow land. One of the women groans. He throws himself in that direction and runs right into her.

His head is flung forward. The other woman must have kicked him from behind. He turns and kicks in her direction. The kick doesn't connect, but he can tell he's driven her back. He concentrates all the strength he has in his body into his arms, attempting to loosen the sheet wrapped around him. He hears the cloth rip, and his field of vision clears slightly. Though he still can't open his right eye.

He concentrates again, as if trying to break a chain binding him, and the sheet tears further. He frees one hand and uses it to take the sheet off his head.

As soon as he's able to use both hands, he reaches into his pocket to get his blowgun.

His right eye still hurts and is useless, but he still has his left one to aim with. But he's too late and the two women are already disappearing out of the room. They have a cleaning cart with them, and are dressed in staff uniforms.

Noticing his earpiece on the ground at his feet, Sengoku picks it up and puts it in his ear. 'There were two women in Room 2010. They attacked me. No fun.'

'They got your number, huh?' laughs Heian.

Sengoku's head gets hot. He makes a fist, then punches a hole in the wall.

Why do I have to put up with two little bitches hurting me like that? That's what really makes my blood boil!

'They might have been here to dispose of the bodies. Edo, did you ask Inui to send them? Edo, are you listening?'

'You should come down here, too, Sengoku,' says Heian.

'Where's Edo? Did Nara manage to get Kamino?'

'Nara's dead. But we did manage to get Kamino. She's right here next to me. Can you come to the third floor?' Heian's voice fades in and out, perhaps because she's on the move too.

Nara's dead. Sengoku has trouble grasping the words that Heian said so blithely. 'The third floor?'

'Where the banquet rooms are. Go to the one in the back. The Maple Room.'

'That's where we're handing her off to Inui?'

'We've already contacted him. He said the final handoff will take place in Room 1720, so we'll take Kamino there. His client will meet us there too. But before that, we're going to go to the third floor and wait for the other guy to come for her.'

'The other guy?' Sengoku is still ripping the sheet off the rest of his body.

'The guy who's helping Kamino. I saw him again down in the lobby, and I finally remembered who he is.'

'Who is he?'

'He's Ladybug. The sole survivor of the E2 Incident.'

Sengoku doesn't immediately understand what she means. It takes Heian saying, 'E2, like the bullet train. He's the one who lived,' for him to finally remember.

'Ladybug, huh? The lucky bastard. You've seen him before?' All sorts of rumors swirled after that incident. After all, so many professionals lost their lives in it, even that famous duo everyone thought had retired from the biz. Things got so out of control, yet Ladybug made it through unscathed – he must be blessed with not only skills, but all the luck in the world as well. He became quite famous in the trade that way, but there wasn't much evidence he was still taking jobs; some said he'd let his fame go to his head, becoming choosy about what he'd take. 'So Ladybug's the one who took out Nara?'

'What's going on in Room 2010?'

Sengoku looks over at the two bodies leaning against the bed. 'There's two dead men, and a woman. I think that's Asuka.'

Walking over to where Asuka's body sits propped up against the wall, Sengoku crouches down and brings his face close to hers. 'I don't think she'll be able to brag about how pretty she is anymore. Her face is totally burnt off.'

'Wow, really?'

'I'll take a pic.' Just like Edo said, the world is filled with all types, with all sorts of needs. There's sure to be someone out there who wants a photo of the face of a once-gorgeous woman whose beauty was obliterated in death.

'Oh, I almost forgot. Is Madam Clickety-Clack's body there? Can you take a picture of her too?'

'I don't see her around,' says Sengoku. He doesn't see the body of an old woman anywhere. He looks back at the door. 'The two from earlier might have her. They might be taking the bodies out of here one by one.'

After ruining my eye, he doesn't add.

'Well, no matter. Leave the body disposal to them and come here to the Maple Room, Sengoku. Let's get even with this Ladybug guy.'

'We have the woman already – why do we have to worry about Ladybug?'

'He took out Kamakura and Nara. We can't just let him go. For all we know, he had something to do with Asuka's death, too. I'd say he owes us an apology.'

'It does sound fun, to make such a famous professional cry out in pain. We should take some video, too. People will want it.'

'You're right, there's definitely demand for something like that.'

As he listens to Heian, Sengoku imagines ripping the legs off an insect, then crushing it under his foot. He gets excited at the thought that he'll soon get to do the same to Ladybug.

NANAO

The Maple Room, on the third floor

AS HIS ELEVATOR HEADS TOWARD the third floor, Nanao talks to himself.

'You are one unlucky bastard, you know that?'

Of course, there's no point in saying it aloud, even to himself. Starting from when he was mistaken for a rich classmate and kidnapped when he was a child, his life has been one unfortunate event after another. The small ones are too numerous to count. If he buys a pair of white jeans, a passing car will splash muddy water on him the first day he wears them. Every check-out line he waits in grinds to a halt, never to move again; whenever he goes to a movie, it's guaranteed that the guy next to him will start snoring, and then someone else will pick a fight with him, thinking *he* was the one snoring. If he goes to a shrine for a ritual cleansing, the priest is sure to immediately slip and fall on his ass, then cancel the ceremony. Every step he takes ends with his foot in a puddle; every bird passing overhead leaves its shit on his face. He does a job and inevitably ends up surrounded by corpses that he has to find some way to get rid of. If he's asked to simply get on a bullet train with a suitcase, leave it there, and get back off, a troublesome man will appear at the door as he tries to get off and push him back on. If he's asked to fill up a car at a gas station, two other cars will pull up as well and they'll get in a fight, destroying his car and dragging him into the fray.

Would anyone be willing to trade places with a guy like that?

But so what? Nanao asks himself. *You've known you're unlucky your whole life. What are you trying to say, bringing it up now?*

What I'm trying to say, he answers himself as the elevator nears its destination, *is that you'd better watch out.*

Nanao nods at his own wisdom. *It's just as he said. There's no need to compare yourself to others. I'm me, I'm the one who knows me best. An apple should be content to be an apple.*

He thinks of Edo. He was standing in the elevator next to Yuka Kamino, holding up three fingers. *Get off on the third floor,* he was saying. *If you want her, come and get her.*

Nanao has ushered so many of the team Edo so carefully assembled to the next world, the guy surely doesn't want things to end without some sort of reckoning.

Why should I go? Leave me out of it!

Nanao found himself heading to the third floor anyway. Not out of a sense of justice, though, or of wanting to play the white knight.

The fact is, Nanao was in a jam and Kamino helped him right away, sending his message to Maria without a second thought. If he abandons her now, it will be a clear case of ingratitude.

Sheer ingratitude, no matter how you slice it or try to dress it up.

The ungrateful, who ignore the blessings they're given, end up abandoned by fortune. That's what Soda told him.

The elevator dings. The doors slide open.

He steps out onto the floor beyond. At that exact moment, the elevator next to him arrives too. The door opens, and a well-built man steps out.

Nanao is ready. This is his moment.

He's a man who's lived his life abandoned by fortune, everything he attempts going hopelessly south, even the safest of situations turning into deadly crises – of course he's stepping out of the elevator onto the third floor expecting something like this to happen. In fact, it would violate the order of the universe if it *didn't*.

So, Nanao is ready.

But Sengoku, riding down here from some higher floor, surely never imagined, not in his wildest dreams, that he'd arrive at the exact same moment as Nanao.

You're already late, thinks Nanao.

By the time Sengoku looks over and sees Nanao, his eyes growing wide as he scrambles for his blowgun, Nanao is already upon him, his hooked elbow jutting upward to catch the big man in the gut. Sengoku, taken by surprise, bellows his displeasure, but Nanao is already swinging around to attack him from behind. He reaches up and grabs his head in both hands, and then, without a moment's hesitation, he snaps his neck. Nanao pulls the earpiece out of Sengoku's ear and throws it to the ground, crushing it underfoot.

Sengoku's body sags, but Nanao catches its bulk in time, supporting it with his own body. *All I do these days is carry around corpses,* he thinks, sighing. Where will he stash this one? Another bathroom, most likely.

It was all over in a heartbeat.

Did I think I was really that ready? Nanao can't help but laugh at himself. *You're so used to expecting the unexpected, it's made you into a philosopher.*

Dragging Sengoku's body, Nanao heads off to look for a bathroom to stow it.

It's only when he's stuffing Sengoku into a stall that he notices the watch on his wrist. The design is familiar.

That's Soda's! It has the same elongated rectangular face. 'One of the useful things about an expensive watch is that a materialistic person will want it,' Soda said earlier, and he was right – Sengoku had snatched it the moment he got the chance.

Nanao takes the watch off Sengoku's wrist and puts it in his pocket.

It's not like he can wander around yelling, *Kamino-san! Kamino-san! Where are you?* Instead, he decides to make his way down the line of banquet rooms, taking a look in each one.

There are two larger halls and two smaller ones, according to the floor map. The first great hall he peeks into is spotlessly clean, and empty not only of people but even of furniture.

The next room has round tables scattered throughout it, with several hotel employees briskly circulating among them.

Nanao surveys the room, keeping an eye on how the staff are moving, but he detects nothing out of the ordinary. Neither Edo nor Kamino are anywhere in sight.

He sees a cart near the entrance with several stainless-steel trays stacked on it. Instinctively, he grabs some, tucking the stack under his arm to take with him.

The next banquet room is much smaller and has a single large table running down its center. Did they use this one for seminars? The double doors at one end are standing open, but a quick look reveals the room to be empty. He crouches down just to make sure, but there's no one hiding under the table, either.

If he gets to the last room and fails to find Kamino, he'll stop searching any further and go home. That's his decision, and it's final.

The last banquet room has a sign on it reading *The Maple*

Room. Only one of its enormous double doors is closed. Nanao approaches the open one to take a peek inside.

The moment he does, though, a dart flies at him. A sound rings out – *bang!* It's the sound of the dart hitting the stainless-steel trays in his hands. He's raised the whole stack up at once to shield himself.

Nanao steps back from the door, then slips across to hide behind the closed one.

It's obvious they're lying in wait like snipers, hoping to pick him off from a distance.

He crouches down, then peers cautiously around the edge of the door. Perhaps catching sight of the top of his head, they let loose another dart almost immediately, forcing him to whip his head back. He was at least able to see that the room is crowded with long tables.

There's no time to hesitate. Nanao prepares to take the first opening he sees and use it to dash into the room, but then he hears a male voice.

'Please enter slowly and calmly, or we'll make it so she can't use her legs.'

A woman speaks. 'All we need is for her head and mouth to work – the rest of her can be as useless as a ragdoll.'

'It isn't temporary, you realize. She'll be paralyzed forever.'

They're saying they have a poison that, while not fatal, can do a lot of damage. It's clearly a threat, but he doesn't think they're bluffing.

'Heian, feel free to do the honors anytime,' says the man.

Do what you want with her, I don't care. The words are almost out of Nanao's mouth before he swallows them back.

He only met Kamino today. Furthermore, she all but forced him to get mixed up in this – isn't he the real victim here? It's not his duty to save her.

But in the end, he can't let himself off the hook that easily.

Those who ignore the blessings they're given end up abandoned by fortune. The words repeat in a loop in his head.

Nanao decides to walk straight through the door into the room.

He walks slowly, his head bowed in defeat, as if raising the white flag of surrender.

Nanao passes between the tables as he advances. He sees Edo and Heian standing at the far end of the hall. Heian has her arm around Yuka Kamino, almost embracing her.

'I'm going to start with her legs!' Heian's voice is merry.

Nanao looks all around him. He knows there must be a dart trained on him. The moment it hits him, it'll be over.

It flies at him. As soon as he realizes, he shields himself with a tray. He can see Heian's face beyond it. The dart bounces off the tray with a bang. The next thing he knows, the tray is flying out of his hand. A second dart, this one from Edo, hit it with incredible force.

He has no time to wonder at the amount of power a blow dart can possess. He reflexively throws a tray, but he knows it won't reach them. He also knows Heian and Edo are ready to shoot at him at the same time. He swings his last tray up to shield his face. The dart hits the tray hard, almost hard enough to punch a hole in it, but he's ready for it this time and manages to keep the tray from flying from his grasp.

He advances further into the room, heading for the center. He holds his tray up with one hand and reaches into his pocket with the other. When he pulls it back out, it's holding the watch he took off Sengoku's wrist.

It was Soda's, so it's probably worth millions of yen. Maybe upwards of ten million.

He remembers the rest of the conversation he had with Soda back in Room 1121.

'You wouldn't think I'd mess around with a watch this classy, would you?'

'I'm not sure what classiness has to do with it. Did you set it up to explode or something?'

'Explosives are so yesterday, Ladybug. Blowing things up is barbaric. You destroy something and someone has to come and build it all over again. I believe in a sustainable society.'

'Hasn't society managed to sustain itself pretty well so far?'

'That's an illusion. All we've done is somehow manage to muddle through as we did whatever we wanted, like destroying the environment and starting a million wars. Though you could say we can't help it – starting wars and destroying the environment are what humans are built to do.'

'What were we talking about again?' He found himself saying this to Soda all the time.

'Explosions are out, heat and sound and light are in. This was Cola's design. If you push here, right in the middle, burning liquid squirts out!' Soda pointed at the center of the watch's face.

'Burning liquid? Like boiling water?'

'Hotter! It sets off a chemical reaction that produces an enormous amount of heat. And it sprays right out in a jet.'

'So you can spray it in someone's face?'

'That's not the best way to use it.'

'Really?'

'It only works once. So the best time to do it is when you're surrounded.'

'So you can spray them all at once?'

Soda shook his head: *No.* Then he pointed at the ceiling.

'You hold it up, then set it off.'

'And then what happens?'

'The hot spray goes up to the ceiling. All this heat, all at once. You'll get a response.'

'The fire prevention system?'

Sensing heat, it'll think there's a fire. Many places have automatic sprinklers that will go off once that happens.

Now it's time for Nanao to put Soda's plan into action.

Reaching the center of the room, he raises his hand, pointing the watch's face at the ceiling, and goes to press the button where the hands meet in the center. He imagines what will happen next. The sprinkler system, thinking there's a fire, will start spraying water everywhere. It will become hard to use the blowguns, as all the water will interfere with the darts as they fly.

At that moment, though, he notices Edo running right, heading for the far wall. He's planning on angling himself diagonally to get a shot off at Nanao. And as soon as he has the thought, a dart flies toward him. He gets goosebumps all over his body. He manages to deflect the dart with his remaining tray, but he can't do that forever. He's bound to get hit some time.

Anticipating his defensive move, Heian takes aim and blows a dart straight at him. *I'll never get the tray up in time,* he – or rather, his nervous system – thinks, dropping to the ground right on his ass.

His last tray flies from his hands.

Darts fill the air above his head. He crawls under a nearby table.

He hears the sound of rapid footfalls. It's Edo – it sounds like he's running across the tables toward him.

Still on all fours, Nanao sticks his head out from beneath the table and sees that Edo is right on top of him. There's a sparkle in his eye. He brings a hand to his mouth.

Nanao ducks and rolls, ending up under a different table.

He sees something stick in the floor beside him. It's the dart Edo shot at him. It's longer than anything he saw Nara or Kamakura use, and thicker, too, more nail than needle.

Nanao keeps crawling, heading for yet another table, when he hears a sound like wood breaking – and indeed, the table above his head starts to come down on him. One of the table's legs suddenly breaks. *Classic timing!* Nanao clucks his tongue and prepares to roll away again. Edo, anticipating this, jumps down and blocks him, closing in on his prone form.

Knowing that another dart is about to come his way, Nanao presses the screw in the center of his watch again. It's less his will than sheer instinct that guides him.

It only works once. Soda's words come back to him, but it's too late.

Edo falls back, his hands covering his face. The hot jet from the watch hit home. Edo overturns the table as he lurches up, then collapses.

The plan to use the sprinkler system to foil his enemies is now just seafoam, a bubble that's already burst.

Dammit! He begins to spiral, but stops himself. Now's not the time to have a breakdown. Nanao approaches the fallen Edo, hauling him up roughly. The shock from the hot jet hitting him square in the face seems to have knocked him out completely, but he's still breathing.

Heian's standing at the back of the room, facing him directly. Yuka Kamino sits beside her.

Nanao stands up, lifting Edo's unconscious body up with him to use as a shield.

There doesn't seem to be anyone else around. If he can handle Heian, he'll be home free.

Nanao wonders how close he can get to her using Edo's body as a shield.

'He's still alive. You can still save him,' says Nanao. He speaks loudly, hoping Heian hears him.

Edo's body suddenly jerks in Nanao's arms. Looking up, he sees that Edo's neck is bent at an unnatural angle, flopping over to the side. Blood sprays Nanao's face. Not just blood, but bits of flesh as well.

Heian blew a dart at Edo, aiming for his head. Not just any dart, but one of the heavy-duty ones.

The shock to Edo's body throws Nanao off balance, and he tumbles to the floor. He sees Heian drop immediately into a crouch. A split second later, he feels a dart hit his body.

She went low and got him. He's hit.

'I'm not one to forgive. I don't want to give you a quick death. I want to take the time to see you lose consciousness first.' Heian's voice is getting closer.

I need to get out of here! But fog is beginning to fill Nanao's head already. *Run, run!* He orders his body to obey him, and he starts crawling toward the door.

'You killed them all. I demand satisfaction. I need to see you suffer.'

He sees Heian's feet right next to his face.

He tries to get up. He pushes against the floor with his hands, but his movements are dull. He's starting to find it hard to move at all. *It's over,* he thinks, and at that moment Heian starts to shout.

Nanao hears the thump of hurried footsteps. Somewhere in his mind, he understands that Kamino has run away.

It seems she made it out, because Heian clucks her tongue in irritation, then runs after her.

It's now or never! Nanao rises to his knees, then to his feet, and then uses every ounce of strength he has left in his body to push the door shut behind Heian. He locks it from the inside, then starts sinking back down, the world around him distant and blurry, as if sealed behind frosted glass. His consciousness loses its footing entirely, everything turning vague and unreliable.

Did Maria go to the theater?

Even as he has the thought, though, Nanao is overcome by a feeling like drowning, and then he collapses completely.

YOMOGI

The restaurant on the second floor

'YOUR *SORBET AUX FRAMBOISES*, sir. Accompanied by *meringues fraises-chantilly*. Enjoy.'

The waiter sets the dessert before Ikeo, then elegantly pours coffee into the cup next to it before turning smartly on his heel and returning to the kitchen. Ikeo wants to tell him not to leave, but swallows his plea with a gulp.

The hors d'oeuvre platter that began this meal now seems like a distant memory. He wishes he could savor the rich flavors again, smacking his lips with relish, but the only thing smacking now is his heart against his ribs.

'This is really good, Ikeo-san!' He hears the Director's voice, but it seems so far away.

The story Yomogi told him blots out everything else in his head.

It's hard enough to believe that he'd use a mass murder in an express commuter train to get ahead, but to stage an accident that killed his own wife and son as well – Ikeo finds it almost impossible to accept the confession he's just heard. Yomogi has explained himself without a trace of regret or madness; rather, it's like he was simply explaining a strategy he's developed to optimize efficiency.

Satō speaks up. 'There's a phone call. Inui.' He reaches over from where he sits beside the terrified Ikeo, handing his phone to Yomogi.

The Director puts the phone to his ear and says, 'What good timing! We're just finishing eating now.' He then nods along with whatever the person on the other end is saying, making sounds to indicate he's still listening. 'Room 1720. Understood. We're on our way now.'

His call finished, Yomogi hands Satō back the phone. 'Seems they were able to catch her,' he says.

'Wonderful,' replies Satō.

'Sounds like Inui's on his way now, but we might not want to wait.'

'We can use my device to input the password.'

Yomogi turns back to Ikeo, who's been left to simply watch them talk, and smiles. 'He has some data regarding our past. Data – well, more like *evidence*. Of who we were before we became "Satō" and "Yomogi." It would be very annoying for us if it were to get out in the world.'

Who we were before we became 'Satō' and 'Yomogi.' It still sounds like some sort of joke.

'We need the password to delete the data. It seems they finally got their hands on it. That's what that call was about. When you came to me wanting to interview me, Ikeo-san, I admit I thought it might have something to do with this. The timing seemed to line up. I invited you here so I could dispose of both you and the data at once, here in this hotel. But it seems I was mistaken. You don't know anything about any data, do you?'

Ikeo's body has turned to stone; he has trouble making his

mouth move. *Dispose of.* The phrase sticks in his mind. How does Yomogi plan to *dispose of* both him and the data together?

'Let's finish our coffee and then head up to Room 1720. The keycard should be waiting at the front desk for us.'

'Are you . . . talking to me?'

'I think there might be some interesting things to show you up there. There was a professional who was sent to take me out. He's here in this hotel. They caught him, and now he's apparently in that room, waiting for me. I told you before, I have a lot of people gunning for me. There've been a few professionals who've shown up and tried to get to me during the past couple of years. Maybe because a security detail isn't around me as much, now that I'm no longer in Parliament. The thing is, though, while I know that Satō and I may be getting older, we still have some tricks up our sleeves.'

'Like that old one. The Mallet Handle,' says Satō, chiming in.

Director Yomogi throws his head back, laughing heartily. 'Exactly! That's what I'd love to show you, Ikeo-san. The Mallet Handle. You'll see, don't worry. First we dislocate someone's shoulders so they can't use their arms, then we beat them like a bag of sand. Doesn't that sound fun? You have to try it, then you'll see. There's nothing more fun in the world. One of life's great pleasures – to have your way completely with someone who can't fight back.'

BLANKET

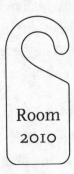

Room
2010

THEY'RE ON THE TWENTIETH FLOOR, having come up from the parking garage via the staff elevator, when it occurs to Blanket that returning to Room 2010 might be quite dangerous.

Right before they moved Koko, they had a confrontation with a man who seemed to be one of the Six. They wrapped him in a sheet and were on the verge of snapping his neck, but in the end, they didn't manage it and had to run away. So it seems unwise to go back there now.

But Pillow insists. 'We have a job to do,' she says. 'And besides, if the guy's still there, that just gives us another chance to finish him off. Otherwise, it's like he chased us off.'

'That's true,' Blanket agrees.

And so they're going back, vowing not to be defeated this time and planning how to render him immobile immediately. But when they go in the room, there's no one there but corpses.

Talk about an anticlimax!

'What happened?'

247

'Guess he ran away.'

'I hope Koko-san's gonna be okay.'

'She regained consciousness again; I think she'll be fine.'

They'd placed Koko, still out of it completely, in the cleaning cart and taken her down to the parking garage to hand her over. Inui had hired them for corpse disposal, but when Blanket and Pillow had explained the situation, the delivery guys had immediately known what to do. They even had some rudimentary medical equipment in their van, and they promised to do what they could to help her on the way to the hospital.

'There's three of them left, which means three more trips. Ugh.'

'Which one should we start with?'

They decide on the man in the blue suit, as he seems to be the heaviest.

Pillow takes the top half, Blanket the bottom, and together they heave the body into the cart. They pull his legs up and curl his arms around them, then cover him in a sheet.

As they're on the way out the door, they catch sight of someone standing just inside it. Blanket startles, gripping the edge of the sheet in the cart.

They should have thrown the bolt when they left. *All these weird things keep happening, it's thrown me off my game,* thinks Blanket ruefully.

Blanket and Pillow ready themselves for another attack, but they stop when they get a better look at who it is.

'Oh, look at this! Blanket and Pillow!' It's another professional, someone they've only seen a handful of times, who's raising her hand in greeting as if running into friends on the street. She's wearing a black blouse and a pair of pale wide-legged slacks.

'Maria!'

Pillow asks, 'What are you doing here?'

Blanket quickly balls up the sheet that had been in her hand.

'I'm looking for Ladybug, actually.'

'Ladybug? Oh, *that* Ladybug . . .' She's never met him, but Blanket knows who he is. He's kind of a celebrity among those in the trade.

'He came to this room for a job, but even though he was supposed to finish and go right home, I haven't heard from him at all. Well, except for this weird message he sent.' Maria holds up her phone.

'Weird message?'

' "Don't go to the theater tonight!" I thought it was some kind of prank at first, but to what end? And I hadn't heard from him at all otherwise. So I decided to come here and talk to him in person. This was the last place he told me he was going before he stopped talking to me.'

'Ladybug is here?' says Pillow, and then she brings her hand to her mouth. 'Oh!'

'Do you know where he is?'

'Maria, if he came to this room, I might have some bad news for you.'

'Bad news?'

'There are some dead men in here.'

The thought had occurred to Blanket as well. One of the corpses might well be Maria's Ladybug. They'd thought they were Soda and Cola, but that was just a guess.

Blanket doesn't know how close Maria and Ladybug might be. But it's never good news to learn that a colleague's been killed.

Maria freezes. Though her eyes are open, it's as if everything in her head has come to a complete halt.

Her expression remains completely unchanged for a few beats, then unravels slowly, as if threads are loosening behind her face. 'Is that so,' she breathes. Her words are barely audible, as if she's addressing primarily herself. 'Is that so, I see, I see . . .' she repeats under her breath.

Blanket's chest hurts as she points at the cart. 'Is this him?' she asks, pulling back the sheet. 'There's another man by the bed inside.'

'And a woman, too.'

Maria looks in the cart. 'It's not him,' she says, and then immediately rouses herself to go further into the room. She peers into the face of the corpse in the white shirt sitting against the bed.

'This doesn't look like him either,' she says finally, shrugging. She examines the woman with her face burnt off as well, as if to say, *You never know.*

'So Ladybug's not here,' says Blanket. She realizes that she's trying to reassure mostly herself.

'What's going on in this hotel? All this stuff happening, and Ladybug's here too?' Pillow seems aghast.

Maria lets out a long sigh. 'Things with him always get so complicated. I don't know why. This was supposed to be an easy job. It's so funny. Where is he? Look at this mess. And off he goes, like an errant princeling,' she says, glancing around the room. 'So, you two are here to clean all this up?'

'Yes,' says Blanket, nodding. 'Inui hired us.'

'Inui?'

'Wow, what a face! You really don't seem to like him.'

'I'll be honest, I don't. This young guy, wheeling and dealing with everyone. Kissing up to anyone in power. I hate guys like that, who seem to always be saying, *Look at me, I've got everything going for me!*'

It's amusing to watch Maria go on and on.

'Well, he's an Easy Streeter, after all.'

'A what?'

'Look, Inui's the kind of guy who's always looked good, who's always known exactly what to say, who always seems like everything's going his way. The complete opposite of people like us.

250

They spend their whole life on Easy Street. So we call them Easy Streeters.'

'When you put it that way, I get it,' says Maria, smiling. 'But you realize, Inui has no friends.'

'What do you mean?'

'You and Pillow have each other, right? But Inui has no one. No one he can really trust, no one to call a real friend.'

'Oh.' Feeling unexpectedly called out, Blanket and Pillow exchange glances. 'But those Easy Streeters, they have friends.'

'They do, they do! Millions of them.'

'Easy Streeters, as you call them, may seem to be surrounded with friends, but they're just *friends*, nothing more, if you see what I mean.'

'I kind of do and I kind of don't . . .'

'What bothers me most about Inui is that he loves making fun of the way other people do business even though he never does anything for himself. Saying things like, "No one uses explosives anymore," or saying that doing business like I do, as a handler, has no future, that it's old-fashioned.'

'Sounds like him,' says Blanket, nodding.

'But the truth is,' continues Maria, her expression darkening, 'if you're dealing with Inui, you should be careful. Whether you like him or not, there's something frightening about him, too.'

Blanket and Pillow look at each other again, not knowing how to respond at first, then they shrug their shoulders.

'You've heard the rumors, right?'

'We've distanced ourselves from him for just that reason.'

'This is really no good.'

'What is?'

'I don't see how Ladybug's going to win this,' says Maria, as if coming to some sort of conclusion. Her words provoke an unexpected emotion in Blanket, and she says, 'But what about the E2 Incident? He managed to survive that!'

'True enough,' says Maria, her voice weakening. 'What do we do now, then? Where could he be?'

'Maybe it's a silly question, but have you tried just calling him?' *If he picks up, problem solved, right?*

'He's either unable to answer the phone, or he lost it.'

It's then that Blanket's phone begins to ring. Looking at the screen, she sees it's Inui. 'Speak of the devil! This always happens when we start talking about him – it's creepy, like he's spying on us somehow.'

Figuring that it shouldn't matter that Maria can hear, too, Blanket puts her phone on speaker.

'I need you to do something else for me. A rush job.'

His carefree tone makes Pillow sigh in annoyance. 'We're still doing the last "rush job" you gave us! We're in Room 2010, cleaning up.'

'This is more important. Go to the third floor. There's a banquet room called the Maple Room. Can you take some bodies out before anyone finds them?'

Blanket can't help but complain. 'What on earth is going on? There's nothing but corpses in this hotel!'

Maria, listening in, crosses her arms and purses her lips, as if amused yet still on her guard.

'There's a bit more going on today than I thought there'd be, is all.'

'This is related to the Six, isn't it? One of them is in here, too. Dead.'

'The body in the Maple Room is one of them too. Heian told me. There's someone else in there too, but I guess he's not dead. Yet. Have you heard of Ladybug?' Inui's speaking fast now, as if in a hurry all of a sudden.

Blanket looks up at Maria, who's standing in front of her. Her gaze grows sharp, as if on the verge of an outburst. *What happened to Ladybug? Tell me!*

'I know exactly who Ladybug is. Though I never met him myself,' says Pillow, looking at Maria and shrugging.

'So, he's not dead?' asks Blanket.

'That's what Heian said. She shot him with something that's supposed to put him to sleep, but he managed to lock the room from the inside. Heian's heading up to join me and my client, so it would be great if you could clean things up down there.'

'We don't want to . . .' says Blanket.

'But we'll do it,' finishes Pillow, as if splitting their answer between them.

'Thank you, I appreciate it.'

'You'll be with your client after this, then, Inui?'

'That's right. Okay, bye!'

The phone call finished, Pillow says, 'I can't believe it! More work! This place is the worst.'

'But at least we know where Ladybug is now.'

'Yes. Taking a little nap, apparently,' says Maria, smiling. The smile doesn't reach her eyes.

KAMINO

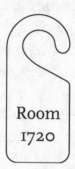

Room
1720

KAMINO, ON THE THIRD FLOOR in the Maple Room, watches Heian shoot Nanao with a dart. She sees his movements become slow and sluggish; it looks like all there's left to do is watch Heian walk over to him and deal the final blow.

I have to do something! she thinks, and then realizes she can run.

If she gets out of the Maple Room, it should draw Heian away from Nanao and toward her. And sure enough, it turns out she's right.

Heian runs after Kamino. Sprinting as hard as she can, she's closing in. As angry as if she'd been bitten by her own dog, Heian's catching up much faster than Kamino had anticipated. She grabs Kamino by the sleeve, pulling her back so hard that she falls to the ground, right on her ass.

'You don't get to do things like that! It's exhausting!' says Heian, unable to hide her rage. She pulls Kamino with her as she returns to the Maple Room. 'You shut the door?' she mutters, as if arguing with a lover. Rattling the doorknob, she gets even angrier. 'What the hell? It's locked! C'mon! This is the fuckin' worst.'

Breathing hard, Kamino is relieved. At least she managed to make things less dangerous for Nanao, however slightly.

'Okay, whatever,' says Heian. 'Let's get you up to Room 1720.' She heads for the elevators, pulling Kamino along with her.

They reach the seventeenth floor, and Heian heads straight for Room 1720. She stands in front of the door and rings the bell. 'Don't worry, we're almost done,' she says to Kamino, as if they're two part-time workers at the end of their shift. 'What on earth is going to happen to you, I wonder?' Heian laughs. 'This has all been quite a hassle, but at least I have that to look forward to.'

The door opens a few moments later, revealing a well-built man in a suit. The man casts a glance at Heian, then Kamino, then turns and disappears back into the room. Clearly displeased at the lack of greeting, Heian mutters under her breath, 'I guess he expects us to just follow him,' and pulls Kamino along with her into the room.

The room has a large marble-topped table placed in its center, with a sofa behind it that looks big enough to accommodate four people. There's a man sitting on it, facing them. He gets up, offering his hand to shake. 'Welcome, welcome. Good work, you must be tired,' he says. The moment Kamino realizes that it's Saneatsu Yomogi, the Director of the Information Bureau, is the moment she realizes that something truly out of the ordinary is happening.

'Sit, sit!' he urges, but Kamino remains standing, as if frozen in place.

Why is Director Yomogi here? Isn't it Inui who's trying to find me?

Doubts bubble up one after the other in her head. They swirl like a tornado, making them hard to grasp.

Director Yomogi. In the flesh.

The scene on the train fifteen years before replays in her head. *I was there, on that train.* She's gripped with the urge to thank him for saving her that day, but restrains herself.

Nothing about this seems real.

What kind of dream is she lost in?

She recognizes the man standing next to Yomogi as his personal assistant, Satō. He appeared in the news countless times after the incident. His name, his age, his relationship with Yomogi – everything about him is popping up from Kamino's memory bank.

'Excuse me, but where's Inui?' Heian sits on the sofa, addressing her question to the two men. There's nothing about her demeanor to indicate that she's noticed that the man she's talking to is the Director of the Information Bureau of Japan.

'Can you do something for me?' replies Yomogi. His tone is gentle, but it's clear it's an order. Kamino bridles a bit as she hears it, as does, of course, Heian. 'Yuka Kamino here is the only person we're concerned with. You're free to leave. In fact, you probably should.'

'What do you mean? I brought this woman here because Inui asked me to.'

'Oh, I see. You'd like to be thanked. Thank you. You really helped us out. I knew you all would get the job done.' Yomogi's tone is that of a superior praising his employee, but perhaps because it sounds like a performance for her benefit, Heian doesn't seem mollified in the least.

'I'm the one who recommended you to Inui in the first place. Once he knew she was here in this hotel, he didn't really want to go to the trouble of hiring a professional to get her, as it should've been simple to nab a lone woman like that. He thought it was a waste of money, I guess. But it's much more trouble if something unexpected comes up, right? So I told him he needed to hire some professionals with real skill. And I was right, wasn't I? Here you are, bringing her right to us. But where are the other five of you? Did they already go home?'

Sitting next to Kamino, Heian clucks her tongue impatiently. She jumps to her feet, and that's when Yomogi and Satō swing into action.

Yomogi reaches out and grabs Heian's left shoulder, while Satō places a hand on her right one. It looks like they're just resting their hands on her shoulders, but Heian suddenly screams. Kamino hears something drop to the floor. A blowgun rolls away from Heian's feet.

It takes so little time, it's hard for Kamino to grasp what just happened. She sneaks a glance at Heian. Her mouth is working silently, like a dog trying to bark; she's clearly in pain.

Kamino reaches over and touches her shoulder, as if to ask, *Are you okay?* and Heian howls again like an animal, then glares at her.

It takes her a moment, but she eventually realizes that Heian's shoulders have been dislocated. Both her arms hang limply, like a stuffed animal's. *Why? How? Are joints really so easily pulled apart?*

'I can't believe it!' Heian squeezes the words out. 'It's you! You two are the ones who've been killing professionals!'

'Not just professionals, but yes,' says Yomogi, sitting back down.

Satō brings a skinny man out from the back bedroom. Kamino doesn't recognize him, but his arms are dangling at his sides just like Heian's. His hair is blond, as if he's dyed it.

'Here's another dislocated doll like you. I hear this man was at this hotel to take me out. Another professional hired to kill the Director. Another failure.' Yomogi laughs, pointing at the blond-haired man.

Kamino is in a daze. Ever since she came to this hotel to meet up with Koko, everything that's been happening, the people she's watched lose their lives right before her eyes – it's all been much too much for her to get her head around. And now, seeing Director Yomogi of all people saying such horrifying things, it seems so hopelessly unreal.

Satō pulls the exhausted-looking man with the dyed hair forward by his arm, and though his face distorts, he doesn't cry out. With his shoulders dislocated, the pain must be intense. Is he used to it by now? Or does he simply know screaming would be futile?

'See that journalist over there? That's Ikeo-san. We showed him the trick to taking a shoulder apart.'

Only then does Kamino notice there's another man in the room. He's sitting on the floor near the bed, a towel stuffed in his mouth, completely still. Whether or not his shoulders are dislocated as well, his eyes are rolled up to their whites. He's clearly dead.

'We need to get it out of Blondie here who hired him. I bet he'll tell us once Inui gets here.'

Yomogi says this as if to say, *That's the only reason why we haven't killed him.*

Kamino wants to scream. *Get me out of here!* She doesn't know to whom she could possibly pray, but she can't help doing so anyway. She can't stop trembling.

At that point, Heian says something. Did she insult Yomogi? Curse him? Whatever the case, they were words with verve behind them.

Yomogi swings into action once again. He throws Heian to the ground, then grabs her head with both hands, twisting it like you'd twist a piece of fruit off a branch.

'If you'd just kept your mouth shut, we would have let you go home,' says Yomogi with a sigh. 'It doesn't pay to be rude. A little rule it's done us well to remember.'

Kamino sits frozen in place, both hands covering her mouth.

It's as if someone has taken a stick and stirred her already swirling thoughts. *Wait, wait, wait!* Her heart is screaming. *Wait, please! I don't understand anything that's happening!*

Maybe she can ask Inui to save her when he arrives. She clings desperately to the thought. She knows Inui was looking for her because of the passwords in her head, but he surely doesn't bear her any actual ill will. It's worth a shot. She can give him the password in exchange for her safety. She worked for him for two whole years! If only she could talk to him directly, they could surely reach some sort of agreement. The Inui she knew was no cold-blooded monster, after all.

Of course, she knows the horrifying rumors about him cleaning people like they were fish, but these are things she's only heard, not seen with her own eyes.

'Please relax. We have no wish to cause you pain. And if you're too agitated to remember what you're supposed to remember, that doesn't do anyone any good at all. Come over here, Satō. It's time to prepare. We're going to get the password now.'

Satō manhandles the blond-haired man back, pushing him to the floor next to the bed. He must have handled him pretty roughly, because the man cries out in pain.

Realizing that they aren't waiting for Inui to arrive, Kamino feels all the blood drain from her body at once.

KAMINO

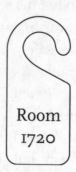

Room
1720

SATŌ SETS A TABLET ON the table. He connects a detachable keyboard to it.

'Satō, could you throw the bolt? We don't want to be interrupted by someone who might have a keycard.'

Hearing this, Kamino can't help but ask, 'But what about Inui-san? He's coming, right?' Once the bolt is thrown, all hope of rescue is lost. It also complicates things if she sees an opening and makes a run for it herself. All these impossible possibilities will become even more impossible.

'Even if Inui were here, we've always intended to ask him to leave while we do this. Once you start inputting the password, we don't need him. If he saw the data, that would be a problem.'

Kamino realizes that this is why Yomogi had to do this himself. If he asked a third party, there's always the chance they'd see the very information he's trying to hide. He has to do this with the minimum number of collaborators possible.

Is whatever you're trying to hide really that bad, Yomogi-san?

But of course she can't ask any such thing. It's not like he's going to answer, *Yes, it is,* and then everything will be all right.

Having bolted the door, Satō sits down at the tablet and starts tapping away on the keyboard.

'Inui told me that he knows where the data is, but that a password is needed to access or delete it. It doesn't seem like Inui himself has seen it. There's always the chance he's lying about that, of course, but if he is, we'll soon find out. It's meaningless to him anyway. So, he tells me you have every single one of his passwords memorized? That's unbelievable. What a memory you must have. Does your brain have a storage limit? I'd like to break your head open and take a look at what's in there!' Yomogi seems to intend this as a joke, but Kamino doesn't laugh.

'We're in,' says Satō.

Yomogi looks over at the screen and laughs. 'I'd heard it was like this, but it really is! Like a weird quiz show!'

Where were you born? The first time you tasted ice cream, what flavor was it? Question after question like this.

'There are a lot of answers to choose from.'

'Seven hundred and seventy-seven in total,' says Kamino, knowing that the moment she says something wrong, her shoulders might end up dislocated as well.

'That many?' Yomogi's eyes grow wide. 'More than I thought.'

'I was surprised too,' she answers, truthfully. When Inui handed her the list, saying, 'Memorize this,' she thought he must be joking.

'And you have all of them memorized? That's amazing. Seven hundred and seventy-seven. Three sevens. I wonder if that was on purpose. Easy to remember. But that doesn't mean we have to sit here answering seven hundred and seventy-seven questions right now, does it?'

'I believe four or five of them get selected at random to use as prompts. According to Inui, at least.'

'Four or five? But they could be any of the seven hundred and seventy-seven, so you have to know them all?'

Satō reads a prompt off the screen in front of him.

She's wondered briefly whether or not she should comply with them, but in the end, she does. After all, if she tries to keep silent or provide wrong answers, they'll figure it out and get what they want out of her anyway. By force.

'Okay, that worked. Here's the next one.' Satō goes on to ask the next question.

It's bewildering, what's happening. She's being asked to take part in a little quiz while Heian lies there right next to her, her neck broken, while another dead body sits propped up against the bed with a towel stuffed in its mouth, and while yet another man lies moaning on the ground with two dislocated shoulders.

'Speaking of seven-seven-seven, I knew a guy who told me a story about that.' Yomogi looks lost in his memories. 'You remember him, too, don't you Satō?'

'Yep, I remember that guy,' says Satō, nodding.

'He was always talking about it. "When my son was a little boy, he was playing with a toy slot machine and started crying because no sevens came up."' Yomogi does a funny voice as recounts the story, imitating the man. 'He was so serious, so sincere. It was hilarious. "My life has amounted to nothing, but I want my son to be happy!" All in tears over it.'

'Is that what he said?'

'It was so funny, I've never forgotten it. Was he serious? A man whose life amounts to nothing has kids whose lives amount to nothing, too. There's no way around it. It's really sad when you think about it.' Yomogi's voice betrays no hint of sadness.

I know that story too, Kamino almost says, but she swallows the words in time to save herself.

It's Inui. She heard that from Inui. One day, Inui came in while she was putting data into the accounting system, and he began telling stories about when he was growing up, something he hardly ever did. 'When I was a kid, my dad gave me this toy slot machine. When I played it, I could never get a seven to come up, no matter how many times I tried. I was so upset, I went and talked to my dad. I asked him, "Is this how it's going to be from now on? What's gonna happen to us, Dad?"'

'What did he answer?' asked Kamino.

'He was on the verge of tears himself. He said, "We don't need that luck right now. It'll come some other time, when we need it for something more important. Don't worry. It's gonna be okay." I remember looking at him as he said it and getting more worried than ever. I almost wanted to say, "Worry about yourself before you worry about me!"'

She recalls Inui's bashful smile so clearly.

'How did you know him?' she asks Yomogi.

Yomogi and Satō exchange looks, seemingly debating wordlessly how to respond. *Should we tell her?*

'Do you remember that stabbing incident on the express train that happened about fifteen years ago?'

Kamino nods. She doesn't say, *I was there. I was on the train.* For if she did, she'd have to thank this man for saving her.

'After Satō and I subdued the man with the knife, he ended up with a death sentence.'

'I remember that.' She remembers everything, including the sight of this middle-aged man swinging a knife wildly, stabbing everyone.

'It was him.'

'What?'

'The father who gave his kid a toy slot machine, that was him. The killer on the train.'

'Why—?'

The question escapes Kamino's lips before she realizes it, apparently striking Satō as an overly familiar way to talk to Director Yomogi, because he turns his head and glares at her.

'Why? Because we needed an incident to happen, and it wouldn't happen if there was no one to *make* it happen! If there's no killer, there's no one for me to subdue. That guy was drowning in debt. He didn't have anyone else to go to for help but us. Or, maybe I should say, we made damn sure he had nowhere else to go.'

Inui's father?

Satō reads out the third question.

Kamino's head is filled with thoughts of Inui and the incident on the train. *It was Inui's father who did that?* Consumed with her own inner turmoil, Kamino answers Satō's question mechanically, as if she were a machine made for no other purpose.

'We're all human, but some of us end up being the ones getting our strings pulled, while others end up pulling the strings. Life is cruel that way,' says Yomogi, sounding completely unbothered.

Satō, having answered the question, says, 'Next password,' and reads out the new prompt.

Inui's father's the one who was on that train that day, and Yomogi's the one who orchestrated the whole thing? How can this be?

It all comes back to her, everything that happened on the train. The blood spreading across the floor, the crying children, the fallen bodies. Screams fill her head – screams of rage, screams of terror.

Kamino opens her mouth and gives the password.

Who cares about a stupid password! She tries as hard as she can to think. About what happened fifteen years ago, about how Inui

264

must feel, about the situation she finds herself in now. She has to figure out what it all means, and fast.

'All right, it worked. We passed through all the prompts. There were four in total. We can open the files now,' Satō says. 'Shall I delete them?'

'Now that we're in, it would be a waste not to take a peek inside, don't you think?'

'Oh, there's a video. Automatic playback.'

Yomogi leans in to peer at the tablet's screen.

Looking at the two of them, Kamino wonders if she should take this moment to try to escape. They have all the passwords they needed; there's nothing else for her to do. Surely they talked so freely about the train incident in front of her because they were certain she was never going to be able to tell anyone else about it.

She knows there's a very high possibility she's about to end up like Heian.

She needs at least to put up a fight.

Kamino's heart beats faster. If no one's going to rescue her, then the only thing left to do is try to get away herself.

But her legs are trembling too much; she can't even stand up. *Why is this happening to me? What did I do to deserve this?*

'Yomogi.' It's Inui's voice. She's surprised at first, but then realizes it must be coming from the tablet. He's in the video that opened automatically just now. 'Thank you for taking the trouble to come here today. It looks like the passwords worked, too! Great.'

Yomogi snorts. 'What is this? What's he playing at?'

Inui speaks again. 'The truth is, when I told you I was going to hand over that data, well, that was a lie.'

Yomogi and Satō look at each other. This isn't what they expected, clearly. They don't seem to be fully on their guard, but they're still unsettled.

265

'I figured that since you were coming to receive information you didn't want anyone else to see, it would be just the two of you. It's not like I want a bunch of government security agents around either. So, I suggested that the deal take place here, in this hotel.'

Yomogi sighs heavily. *Why do I have to listen to this?* he seems to be thinking. *What a waste of time! Life can be a bitter thing sometimes.*

'I never expected Inui to be anything more than a useful idiot, but I never thought he'd be this annoying!'

'Are we done with her?' asks Satō, rising to his feet.

Kamino freezes, as if pinned in place.

'I guess we are. Let's go with the usual,' says Yomogi, but then he claps, as if struck by inspiration. Kamino flinches at the sound. Her heart is beating so hard she feels as though it's about to burst. 'Maybe we should spend a little more time on her than we usually do.'

'More time?' asks Satō.

'If this Yuka Kamino has such a great memory, that must mean she remembers pain, too. Suffering. Maybe she can't forget it.'

'Ahh, I see. It might be fun to see how painful it can be to not be able to forget.'

Yomogi nods enthusiastically, as if to say, *You're so quick, my dear Satō!* 'This has been quite a waste of time so far. I need to blow off some steam.'

Satō reaches over to put a hand on Kamino's shoulder. Overcome by terror of it being dislocated, she can't seem to make herself move. Her entire body seems to have surrendered at one touch.

'Which kind of pain should we start with?' Satō addresses the question to Yomogi. His face is hard to read, but somewhere deep in his eyes, something sparks, a faint flicker of glee.

Why is this happening to me? Kamino wonders again. To think

266

that she must meet such a fate just because she has a good memory. *Why me?* Distress and terror swirl together in her head, becoming something resembling spite. *I'm so jealous – of everyone!*

As soon as she has the thought, another voice pipes up within her. *What good does it do to compare yourself to others? Does an apple really need to bloom like a rose?*

And that's when she hears it. Inui's voice again, speaking from within the video.

'Kamino-chan, it's an acrostic.'

She has no idea what he's talking about. Her mind is completely blank, but somewhere in her head, gears begin to move. Her paralyzed brain is starting to shudder back to life.

'Think about the passwords. There's four of them, right? Put it together.'

Inui, in the video, is still talking to her.

Kamino recalls the four passwords she just gave out. Of course, it takes so little effort for her that one can hardly even call it 'recollection' – in an instant, the four words are lined up in front of her eyes as if someone wrote them there.

It's then that she notices the blond man near the bed start to revive. He's moving again, this professional they say was sent to kill Yomogi. His shoulders dislocated and his arms useless, his body like that of an insect with its wings ripped off, he now stands tall, as if his spine were suddenly replaced with steel.

His knee bends, and his leg pushes up. As she watches, she realizes that he's slowly starting to take a step.

She pictures the four passwords in her head, lining them up so their first letters can form a word. An acrostic. *S, U, E, E.* That doesn't spell anything.

But what about the first *two* letters of each word?

Sh, Ut, Ey, Es.

Shut.

Eyes.

Kamino closes her eyes as hard as she can. She even presses her palms to her eyelids for good measure.

As soon as she does, she senses a bright flash light up the room. She hears Yomogi and Satō cry out. The sound is like nothing she'd imagine from a human – it's like that of an animal, of some creature howling in pain. She also thinks she hears a sound like roaring, though it's possible that's not actually a sound at all.

'What's happening to me?'

'My eyes!'

She hears Yomogi and Satō shout at each other. Then she hears a sound like someone running into a wall.

'Poor Yomogi. Poor Satō. You can't see a thing, can you?'

That voice again. Inui's. It sounds somehow like it's getting closer.

She hears Yomogi and Satō struggle to get to their feet. 'Inui?' says Yomogi. But this is followed almost immediately by the sound of the Director falling back down. She can hear Satō moaning somewhere nearby as well.

'I was fourteen when my father died. It doesn't do a boy that age any good to see his father so miserable. It can really screw him up. But is that why you did it? Why you made sure to hurt him where I could see it? That's not very nice, you know.'

Inui's voice is no longer a voice in a video – it's live and in the room. He sounds calm and collected as always, but with a certain tension at the edges. Is he nervous? Excited?

'My father told me everything before he died, you know. About what you did, Yomogi. That he had no choice but to do what you wanted, saying that if he didn't, I'd end up mixed up in it too. What a funny thing to say. If a father does something like that, his child can't help but end up mixed up in it, one way or another.'

'What have you done to us, Inui?' She can hear Yomogi writhing around.

268

'Yomogi, you said something really good just now. Do you remember what it was?'

'What?'

'About those getting their strings pulled, and those who pull them. Which do you think you are now?'

Kamino hears a sound like Yomogi clucking his tongue, then the sound of flesh and bone being twisted. Then screaming.

Breathing hard, Kamino remains completely still until she hears Inui's voice again. 'Kamino-chan? Sorry about all this. I forced you to play a big part in my plan.'

What? she thinks, reflexively opening her eyes before slamming them shut again.

'It's okay, don't worry. The flash only lasted a second.'

She reopens her eyes and sees that the source of these words is the man with blond hair, whose face she doesn't recognize at all.

'It's like a bomb made of light. You set it off by stepping on it. People like to say explosives are old-fashioned, but most of the time they don't mean it. I do, though. I think it's better to avoid mass destruction if you can. It's better for the environment too.'

Kamino stares blankly at the man. What on earth is he talking about?

'If your eyes are open when it goes off, it blinds you temporarily – you won't be able to see anything for at least an hour.'

She sees that Yomogi and Satō are lying on the floor on the other side of the table. Both have blood streaming from their necks. Their eyes are open wide, staring into space, as are their mouths, their tongues lolling out.

'Um . . .'

The man standing there explaining things so casually to her, she realizes, is none other than Inui himself. Everything about him is exactly as she remembers. Except his face.

269

'I got the idea for the light bomb while I was taking some cute cat pictures.'

Inui's voice sounds as carefree as always, but looking at him, she can see he's shaking.

'I owe you a huge thank you, Kamino. And an apology.'

'For making me memorize those passwords?'

'Among other things. The fact is, this was all supposed to go a lot more smoothly. I called Yomogi, pretending there was an assassin. And then, before I could carry out the rest of my plan, you disappeared. That's when things got messy.'

Kamino can't think of what to say in response. Her mouth works silently instead.

'When I found out you'd ended up here, I figured I'd get Yomogi here, too, and then I could take care of everything in one place. But then he told me to hire the Six! That really put me in a bind. Those guys are crazy. But if I didn't hire them, Yomogi might start to suspect me. I didn't know what else to do.'

'I—' No more words come out.

'When I heard you hired Koko, I figured I could leave it to her to get you out of this.'

'You knew about that?'

'Well, I couldn't get ahold of her to make sure. Though I guess she was trying to get you away from me, so it's not like she wanted to talk. Anyway, at least I managed to get the message across to Edo and the rest not to kill you!'

Kamino thinks about Koko. Much more than any terror Kamino experienced, the worst thing to come out of this was surely Koko's death.

'You know, you said something once that really stuck with me, Kamino-chan.'

I did? Something that really stuck with him? Kamino cocks her head, puzzled.

'You said, "Forget? How?"'

'Ahhh.'

'The fact is, there's no way to forget. My father always worried how he could make sure I was happy.' Inui spreads his hands before him.

Kamino finds herself at a loss once more.

'Man, it really does hurt to get your shoulders dislocated, though, huh?' Inui raises his left hand to massage his right shoulder. 'I'm glad I got to know you, Kamino-chan. At the most crucial moment, you brought me luck.'

'What do you mean?' asks Kamino.

In lieu of answering her, Inui grows serious and asks a question of his own.

'Did I eat lunch today? Do you remember?'

BLANKET

The Maple Room, on the third floor

AS SOON AS THEY REACH the third floor, Blanket and Pillow head for the banquet rooms. Maria, accompanying them, seems to find using the staff elevator a refreshing change of pace, saying, 'I feel like I'm getting a peek backstage! How fun!' However much she might be worried about Ladybug on the inside, on the outside she doesn't appear to be taking things all that seriously.

The banquet room Inui mentioned is called the Maple Room. They stride down the hallway, searching for it.

The banquet room floor isn't the sort of place you usually see staff pushing cleaning carts around, and on top of that, Maria isn't dressed up as anything in particular at all, so there's a possibility they could get made. At the same time, as long as you act like you're supposed to be where you are, doing what you're doing, most people will come up with their own reasons for why you're there and go about their day thinking everything's fine. Or at least, that's been Blanket's experience up till now.

The huge room before them has a crowd in front of it; perhaps

272

some sort of event is about to start. They slip past and move down the hall. The Maple Room is the furthest down, but they see there's a man in a staff uniform standing at the door.

'What's this about?' says Maria, taking the initiative to walk up and approach the man first.

'Oh, it's just—' stutters the man, clearly wondering who Maria might be, but also clearly unable to just say, *And who, exactly, are you?* '—the door's locked from the inside, ma'am, so we can't get inside. I just happened upon the situation by chance.'

'Great! We were sent to take care of this, so you're free to go. We'll take it from here.'

The man may well be thinking, *Just who does this woman think she is, ordering me around?*, but if so, he keeps his thoughts to himself. 'Thank you,' he says instead, then walks away.

Pillow walks up to the door and tries it.

'Can you open it up, do you think?'

'I can pretty much break into any door a hotel might have. There are all sorts of universal keycards to swipe, of course, but you can always pick the lock, too. Even if someone throws a bolt from the inside, you can use a string to unhook it.'

'Amazing! I've been meaning to ask – would you ever consider coming to work for me?'

Not really believing Maria's serious, Blanket responds with a noncommittal little laugh.

Pillow crouches down, then starts rattling some sort of tool in the lock.

'Am I taking you away from your work, having you tag along with me like this?' wonders Maria aloud.

'You heard what Inui said on the phone just now. This is our job, too. He told us to come down here and clean things up.'

'Inui's rather presumptuous, isn't he? He should be more considerate of those on the ground getting their hands dirty.'

'Don't you think you might be a little like that too, Maria, when you ask Ladybug to do a job?' replied Blanket. People are insensitive to how they come across sometimes, she's found. One man's fault is another's lesson, they say. If only more people took that to heart, the world would be a much nicer place to live.

'Inui surprised me, though. He seems to be really putting his back into it this time!' says Pillow as she works at picking the lock.

'Putting whose back into it? Doing what? It sounded like he's relying on everyone else just like always!'

'Well, right now he's up to something in Room 1720.'

'In this hotel?'

'Yeah. With his hair blond; it looks like shit.'

'And he's messed his face up.'

'What are you talking about?'

'We were surprised when he told us what he wanted us to do. Who would have thought that Yomo-pi would have that side to him!'

'Yomo-pi?' asks Maria, bewildered.

'Inui said he hired a professional once to take out Yomo-pi, but Yomo-pi turned the tables and ended up killing him! Remember those stories about professionals getting killed by someone who dislocated their shoulders before he did the job? To think it was Yomo-pi all this time!!'

'You heard about the assassin-killer, right, Maria? Who liked to dislocate his target's shoulders?'

'Of course I did. Pretty scary at the time. Whatever happened with that? And who on earth is "Yomo-pi"?'

'I don't know how much I'm allowed to tell you, actually,' says Blanket truthfully.

'Then why are you acting so smug about it? Why bring it up at all?'

'You're right,' says Pillow, laughing. 'Let's get in the time machine and have a do-over.'

*

274

Inui, when he hired Blanket and Pillow for the job, explained it like this.

'I want to get my revenge on Director Yomogi and his personal assistant, Satō. But it's hard to get close to them without arousing suspicion. If I can get them both in the same room, as long it's not too big and there's just the two of them, I think I might have a chance. So here's the idea: I'm going to pretend to be an assassin hired to kill Yomogi, and I want you two to take me into the room and leave me there. And don't forget to tie me up!'

'A job's a job, we'll do it. But is this really going to work? Once he sees your face, he'll know it's you right away!'

'Faces can be changed. These days, even teenagers are getting plastic surgery. Who cares about a face?'

'Huh.' She always thought of Inui as someone who used his good looks as a weapon, so when he said this so lightly, she found herself unexpectedly moved.

'I'll spread some rumors that there's a professional out there hired to take out the Director. The fact is, I did hire some people to do that exact thing, they just screwed it up! So there's some truth to the lie. Then, you two will "grab" me in the hotel and deposit me in the room where the deal's supposed to take place.'

'All right.'

'So, when you say you're going to pretend to be an assassin, you mean you're going to pretend to be a *failed* assassin, is that it?'

'Well . . .'

'Do you really have to go to all that trouble, though? Even changing your face? Why don't you just shoot him while he's eating dinner, like you would anyone else?'

'He's usually surrounded by a security detail, so it gets tricky. More than that, though, Yomogi and Satō are no joke. If you don't think it through all the way, they'll see through your plan and that'll be it for you. All the professionals I hired tried it your way, looking for an opening to strike, and they all ended up killed.'

'Is he really so scary?'

'Well, he didn't earn the name "assassin-killer" for nothing.'

'I can't believe it,' said Pillow, her voice full of wonder. 'To think, it was Yomo-pi all along!'

'Okay, say he doesn't suspect you. What then? If he thinks you're really a killer, he's probably going to hurt you. At the very least, you're going to end up with your shoulders dislocated.'

'Oh, I'm planning on it!' Inui said, as if talking about going to a party. 'I can take a sore shoulder or two. Maybe it'll be fun! Frees me up to use my legs!'

'Your legs? Have you been practicing kicks?' And even if he had been, if Yomogi and Satō really were former killers themselves, it was unlikely that Inui would be able to get to their level in time.

'What I'm practicing is how to *relocate* my shoulders.'

'What?'

'If you ram them into the wall, you can pop them back in place. Never underestimate the importance of research, you two.'

'Inui, face reality. You can't un-dislocate your shoulder.'

'Yes, you can! That's what they do at the osteopath, after all. Did I never tell you? I'm a certified judo teacher!'

'You never told us.' It was impossible to tell whether he was joking with them at this point.

'Say you can use the wall to fix your shoulders. What's he gonna do while you're doing that? Sit around watching you?'

At that, Inui said, 'I'm going to steal their sight. And then I can do whatever I want.' He laughed. 'Even if my arms are useless, I can still use my feet!'

In the end, they did as he told them. They wrapped him up in a sheet, bound him hand and foot, brought him to Room 1720, and then placed the 'light bomb,' as he called it, beneath the bed.

It was a small, thin disc, like a shrunken-down CD. His plan was to take the first opportunity that came to kick it out from under the bed, then set it off by stomping on it.

'Do you really think this will work?'

To which he replied, as if talking about someone else's situation entirely, 'We'll just have to wait and see!'

After agreeing to do the job, Pillow said, 'You really trust us, don't you? If Yomo-pi caught wind of any of this beforehand, it would ruin everything. In other words, if we leaked this info, it would be the end of you, Inui.' Blanket had to agree.

'I entered the trade at twenty, and I've been searching ever since. It's taken a long time.'

'Searching for what?'

'For people I can trust. Blanket, Pillow, I trust you. I think.'

Pillow and Blanket looked at each other, then burst out laughing. 'You do know how to pick 'em!'

'Speaking of trust, though,' Blanket added, 'we've heard some unsettling rumors about you.'

'Rumors?'

It took some courage to say it aloud, but they'd vowed they would. 'Rumors that you like to dissect people for fun.'

Hearing this, Inui's face lit up with self-satisfaction, grinning from ear to ear as if to say, *Just as I thought, women love to talk!* 'I'm the one who started that rumor. So people in the trade would treat me with respect. As I just said, I've been studying anatomy to learn how to pop my joints back in place after they've been dislocated. So I thought up a more interesting reason for why I might be so fascinated by bones and muscles.'

'Really? You started such a gross rumor about yourself?'

'Isn't it perfect, though? So creepy!'

'Perfect's not the word I'd use,' said Blanket.

'Well anyway, knock yourself out, I guess,' added Pillow.

*

277

So, did Inui succeed? Blanket finds herself trying to imagine what might be happening up there on the seventeenth floor.

'I can't stand him, though. He's so unserious, and so full of himself. Making everyone do everything for him . . .' Hearing Maria continuing to go on and on about Inui, Blanket has to laugh.

Pillow stands up. 'It's unlocked.'

'Thank you.' Blanket and Maria's voices overlap as they thank her simultaneously.

They cautiously ease open the door, half-expecting that some-one might jump out at them at any moment. Keeping an eye on each other's backs, Blanket and Pillow push the cleaning cart ahead of them as they slowly enter the room.

The space is filled with long tables and chairs. Several are upended and scattered about in front of them, clear evidence of a battle.

They see Ladybug right away – he's right by the door, lying face-down on the floor.

Maria runs to his side. In a well-practiced movement, she puts her hand to his neck, presumably to check his pulse. They can't see her face, but her sigh of relief is obvious even from the back.

'Taking a little nap are we? Wakey-wakey time! It's morning!' She turns him over so he's face-up, then shakes him gently. Then she slaps his face. As much as she seems to be saying, *Mommy's here!* she's also saying, *Wake up, Daddy's home!*

'There are supposed to be some real corpses here, too,' says Pillow, pushing the cart before her, as if only remembering then that they're there to do a job. Blanket nods. They start making their way between the tables, looking for bodies.

It's then that a man appears as if from nowhere, rising up from the sea of tables. Tables and chairs fly in all directions, as if he were a human explosive hidden beneath the furniture.

278

The man's hair is standing up all over, and his face is missing some of its flesh. Blood streams from his various wounds.

'Blanket!' says Pillow, throwing her one end of a sheet.

But the man's too far away from the girls, and he's heading straight for where Maria's attending to Ladybug. He looks neither left nor right, charging across the room like a beast smelling blood.

Blanket shouts, 'Maria!'

It's at this point that Ladybug finally rouses himself from his slumber.

How awkward, thinks Blanket.

Ladybug sits up and looks around, trying to get his bearings.

The man gains speed, preparing to launch into a self-annihilating flying tackle like a dive-bomber. Maria finally notices him.

All Blanket can do is watch.

Maria forcefully pushes Ladybug, who's just staggered to his feet, back down to the floor. Blanket can see that she's pushed him so that she'll become the man's target.

Maria crouches down to pick something up off the ground. Without missing a beat or even standing back up, she throws it straight at the man's face.

The man stops in his tracks. Blanket can only see him from behind, but it looks like someone flipped a switch, turning him off mid-step.

A few moments pass, and then the man topples forward to the floor. It's not quite an earthquake, but the floor shakes slightly from the impact.

As Blanket and Pillow run over to join them, Ladybug manages to stand up again, muttering, 'Why'd you push me like that?'

'I saved you. You can say thank you now.'

'I don't know what the hell is going on.'

'I know you're pretty unlucky. So I figured that if someone

279

knocked you to the ground, I had a good chance of finding something sharp lying next to you.'

'What do you mean?' Pillow asks, looking on.

'If you fall down, Ladybug, chances are the floor will have an old nail or a picture hook or something on it that'll poke you when you land. You're the unluckiest man in the world, after all. Every bad situation you end up in just gets worse. So if you fall down, there's bound to be a nail there to fall on. It's your destiny. Knowing this, I looked around, and voila! There it was.'

'There what was?'

'A long needle. Or I guess, a dart?'

'Ahh,' says Ladybug. 'He came at me from above with that thing.'

Blanket looks back at the fallen man and sees a long, thin piece of metal – somewhere between a needle and a nail – sticking out of his forehead.

'Right down the middle, Maria! You rolled a strike!' says Pillow, looking down at the man. 'He could really move, though, huh? He really gave his all.'

It was hard to believe he could move like that with his face in that condition.

Blanket and Pillow confer for a moment, then lift the man into the cart. They begin putting tables and chairs back in place and wiping up bloodstains. They work quickly; after all, someone might come in and interrupt them at any time.

Blanket hears Maria say to Ladybug, 'I told you. Easy job.'

'Shockingly so,' he replies.

NANAO

The restaurant on the second floor

IT'S BEEN SO LONG SINCE he's eaten in a proper restaurant that Nanao can't relax. The waiters come out to present every course, explaining each one in depth, and this throws him off as well. When he says as much to Maria, who's sitting across from him, she replies, 'It's too much to eat like this every day, but you should make time to do it at least once a year. That's the charm of the *table d'hôte* experience.'

'How many times do you actually treat yourself, though, in a year? It's way less than once for me.'

'Think of it like the World Cup, then. An opportunity to go wild.'

Nanao sighs, seeing that there's no point in resisting any further. Instead, he says, 'So, this is the restaurant where Yomogi ate last year?'

'Yeah, with that journalist. They had the *prix fixe* too. The waiter remembers them.'

'Aren't there cameras in here?' Nanao glances around, checking the ceiling and walls.

'There's one at the entrance, but none inside.' It's Koko who says this, from where she's seated beside Nanao. 'They should have cameras watching every table, though, to catch people stealing things or putting drugs in people's drinks.'

'Are you the reason why there's no camera footage left from that day, Koko-san?' asks Maria.

A year has passed since everything went down at the Winton Palace Hotel. It was quite a body count in the end: not only all six of the Six, but Soda and Cola, Director Yomogi and his personal assistant Satō, and a journalist from a prominent news site. But despite their magnitude, the events of that day hardly made the news at all.

One reason for this was the impeccable clean-up. It was professional and thorough, disposing of not only the bodies in Room 525, Room 2010, Room 1720, and the Maple Room, but even the corpses stashed in the third- and ground-floor bathrooms. Maria made her offer again, saying, 'Blanket, Pillow, you do excellent work. I want to have you on my team.' But they didn't seem to see the value in joining up.

As for Saneatsu Yomogi and his faithful assistant Satō, their bodies were discovered in a burnt-out bungalow at an exclusive resort in northeast Japan, shocking the nation. 'It'll arouse less suspicion if their bodies are discovered than if they just disappear,' Maria said, making the arrangements.

Another reason the Winton Palace incident remained under the radar was the lack of security camera footage. Even if you knew the Director had entered the restaurant that day, for example, evidence of anything else he might have done in the hotel was irrecoverable.

'It wasn't me who did that,' says Koko. 'As you know, I was swimming around in the River Styx at that point.'

'The River Styx is something you *swim* in?'

Koko moves her arms like she's pawing the air. *Is she doing the crawl?*

'I bet it was one of them who did that. The Six. They had access to the camera feeds, after all. They must have deleted the data right before they caught Kamino-chan. They stopped the cameras from recording anything after that, too.'

Nanao cuts a piece off the scallop on his plate, then dips it in the sauce before bringing it to his mouth.

'How is it? Good?'

Maria's questioning irritates him.

'Of course it's good!'

'I invited you today, Koko-san,' says Maria, dabbing the corner of her mouth with her napkin, 'because I wanted you to tell us what really happened that day.'

'Now? A year later?'

'You were in the hospital for quite a while. Even if we'd wanted to ask you about it earlier, we couldn't.'

'It's true, I was only released recently.'

'I'm so glad you're okay.'

'Even the doctors were surprised. But you know, my son has games coming up. I can't miss them!'

'Koko-san, I have to ask. Is that true? I'd hear people talk about it, but . . .'

'Of course it's true! He's a star southpaw!'

What are they talking about? thinks Nanao, but then realizes he doesn't care to know. He concentrates on enjoying the food in front of him.

The events that transpired at the Winton Palace Hotel a year ago are nothing he wishes to remember anyway. They were more of a nightmare than anything.

'I worked so hard, and not a word of thanks,' mutters Nanao.

'You don't need my thanks, Ladybug. After all, I'm the one who saved you!'

'I guess. But if we're keeping count, I was the one who told you there was someone out to get you that night!'

The day after the incident, Maria easily found out who was so angry at her. She asked him to explain his grievance and, finding out it was a simple misunderstanding, they ended up smoothing things over. While it was still a good thing she didn't go to the theater that night, Maria herself seemed more preoccupied with having missed out on seeing the show.

'If we're *really* keeping count, it was Kamino-chan, not you, who told me.'

'But I was the one who asked her to!'

The truth is, when Maria invited Nanao to dinner, saying, 'I've finally gotten ahold of Koko! Let's sit down and ask her about everything over a nice meal,' he didn't want to go. It was a year later, and his memories had grown thin. The main reason why he finally said, 'Fine, I'll come,' was because he thought that maybe Koko, at least, would offer him some long-awaited thanks.

After all, helping Kamino get away was *her* job, yet he was forced into doing half of it! A little reward money would be nice, of course, but even just hearing her say, 'Thank you, you really saved the day,' would be enough.

But as the courses arrive one after the other, the chances that Koko will turn to him and say, 'I want to thank you for what you did that day,' seem ever slimmer. At the same time, it's not like he can really turn to her and say, 'I really think I deserve some gratitude.'

I guess I'm not going to get any closure on this, he thinks, resigning himself. Besides, the food set before him is all so good, it's hard to keep sulking. Indeed, the magnitude of the joy spreading from his mouth to the rest of his body makes him want to dismiss his earlier petulance entirely. *Why worry yourself over something so minor?*

The glass in front of Koko is filled with soda water, while the one before Nanao is filled with cola. When she took her seat beside him earlier, Koko said, 'We really did wrong by Cola and Soda, didn't we? I feel terrible about it. It's the first anniversary of their death, after all.' And then they ordered their drinks, though it was hard to say how fitting it was as a tribute. 'What's going on with you two?' Maria said, finding herself the only one accompanying her meal properly with wine.

'Koko-san, do you know what happened to Kamino and Inui? They disappeared after everything was over,' asks Maria after finishing the meat course. 'Did you help with that?'

'I was in the hospital!'

'You're not one to let that stop you,' says Maria, raising both hands to mime typing.

Koko simply smiles, neither confirming nor denying anything. 'I'm really not at liberty to say. But they make a nice couple, don't they? Serious, thoughtful Kamino-chan and lighthearted, resourceful Inui.'

'Did they run off together? I don't really know them that well, but did they really have that kind of relationship?'

'I wouldn't know either,' says Nanao.

'They didn't have that kind of relationship then, but I think perhaps they do now.'

'What a mystery.' All sorts of things remain mysteries to Nanao. What did Director Yomogi have to do with any of this? And what exactly did Inui and Kamino do to him? 'I remember there were guys hired to guard the exits that day. How did Kamino manage to get out?'

'Smuggled out with Inui, apparently. Blanket and Pillow told me there were already some delivery guys ready to do the honors,' Maria tells him, not seeming to care much about the matter.

'Inui and Kamino apparently want to go overseas, somewhere truly far away, but first they need to make some money. Even Inui's doing legitimate work.'

'He's working? Himself? Isn't that like telling a cat, "Don't sleep"?' *There's no way*, Maria seems to be saying. 'Besides, if their whereabouts are ever leaked, they could be in real trouble.'

'Well, let's say I really did help them get away. It would be a total reset on their lives.'

'Okay.'

'No one would ever find them. That's what I'm good at, after all. So they'd be able to start a new life together freely. They wouldn't need to hide – they could be sitting at the next table right now.'

Nanao turns his head to look at the table beside them. It's empty. 'Humph.'

'Don't be like that,' says Maria, pointing at Nanao. 'You owe Kamino your life, after all.'

'Is that so?'

'You're the one who told me: she saved you by running out of that banquet room when she did.'

'True enough. But thinking about it more, I realized that if she'd never mixed me up in her whole deal in the first place, I'd never have been in that situation at all.'

He almost adds, *If anything, she should be thanking me!* But then, dessert arrives.

In the very center of the enormous plate set before him sits a piece of cheesecake decorated with a drizzle of chocolate sauce and a dainty scoop of ice cream. Compared to what preceded it, it strikes him as conspicuously conventional.

Nanao picks up his fork and cuts himself a piece of the cheesecake. The moment it hits his tongue, he exclaims, 'Ah!' There's some sort of citrus mixed into the taste of the cream cheese; it fills his nose as he chews. This is followed by a sharp note of spice, pricking his taste buds with something that resembles – but isn't – bitterness.

286

'What is it?' asks Maria, her mouth filled with her own piece of cheesecake.

'Yuzu pepper! Works better than I imagined.'

Maria furrows her brow. 'I don't taste anything like that.'

Startled, Nanao looks at the piece of cheesecake on Maria's plate, then looks again at his own. He sees that the color of his is slightly different, and looking closer, he can make out tiny specks of pepper.

Seeing Nanao crane his neck to examine the cheesecake on her plate, too, Koko smiles, enveloping him in her warm gaze.

Nanao looks around again, searching for the kitchen, but right at that moment, a waiter passes by, carrying another table's drinks. The waiter suddenly slips, spilling the wine on his tray all over Nanao. 'Oh no!' cries another waiter, rushing over to help with the mess, but he ends up slipping and falling as well. As the situation spins out of control beside them, Nanao and Maria look at each other.

'Happens all the time.'

'Honestly, it doesn't even bother me anymore.'

Koko looks surprised for an instant, then bursts out laughing. *It's one thing after another, just like always*, thinks Nanao with a sigh.

'Oh right, I meant to ask. Blanket and Pillow mentioned something back then,' says Maria, going back to her cheesecake.

'What was it?'

'You were apparently muttering something while they were helping get you out of there. About how you shouldn't compare yourself to others? Then something about apples?'

He indeed remembers saying that as he was leaving the Maple Room. Even as he lamented his life consisting of one unfortunate event after another, his head filled with fog and confusion, he remembers repeating those sentences to himself like a mantra.

'We have to admit, it made sense to us,' Blanket and Pillow had said, laughing. 'It would have been nice if someone had told us that back in high school.' There was something lonely about them even as they laughed together, thought Maria.

'Kamino-chan won't ever forget, you know,' says Koko a bit later. She says it as if talking to herself, without raising her head to look at Nanao.

'Forget what?'

'What you did for her.'

'Aah.'

'Right?'

'I guess she couldn't even if she wanted to.'

Lost in his thoughts, Nanao uses his fork to sweep his last morsel of cheesecake through the chocolate. *Wait, is there a message written there?* he thinks, but it's too late; whatever the chocolate might have spelled out is now obliterated. He puts the chocolate-covered cheesecake in his mouth, but all he tastes – that clumsy waiter! – is wine.

AUTHOR'S NOTE

AS HAS BEEN THE CASE in all my books, the world depicted in *Hotel Lucky Seven* is entirely fictional, a pure product of my imagination. It may be set in a Tokyo hotel, but I used no particular district or real hotel as a model; I consulted people in the hotel business for their expertise, but I modified many aspects of how elevators and hotel rooms work to fit my own purposes. Furthermore, the yuzu-pepper-flavored cheesecake that appears in these pages is something I've never tried myself, and so I cannot vouch for its taste.

In this sense, I urge you to think of this book as one taking place in a fictional building in a fictional country filled with fictional characters (eating fictional cheesecake), with no relation to any actually existing people, buildings, or events.

In addition, there are a few scenes in which characters voice their opinions on capitalism, observations that are the product of a series of remote conversations I had with the author Keiya Mizuno. I want to take this opportunity to thank him for the wonderfully wide-ranging, laughter-filled discussions we shared as I wrote this novel.

Kotaro Isaka

ABOUT THE AUTHOR

Kotaro Isaka is a bestselling and multi-award-winning writer who is published around the world. He has won the Shincho Mystery Club Award, Mystery Writers of Japan Award, Japan Booksellers' Award and the Yamamoto Shugoro Prize and fourteen of his books have been adapted for film or TV. He is the author of the international bestseller *Bullet Train*, which was made into a major film starring Brad Pitt and Sandra Bullock.

ABOUT THE TRANSLATOR

Brian Bergstrom is a Montréal-based lecturer and translator. His translations have appeared in publications including *Granta*, *Aperture*, *Lit Hub*, *Mechademia*, *The Penguin Book of Japanese Short Stories* and *Elemental: Earth Stories*. His translation of *Trinity, Trinity, Trinity* by Erika Kobayashi won the 2022 Japan–U.S. Friendship Commission Prize for the Translation of Japanese Literature. His most recent translation is *Slow Down: How Degrowth Communism Can Save the Earth* by Marxist philosopher Kohei Saito.